"Okay, Stacy, you ~~~ ~~~~~ round," Chris said.

"Is that what we're having, Chris—rounds? Why must we be opponents?"

"Don't you know?" he asked, his voice rough.

"Know what?" she cried as she felt herself being drawn irrevocably closer.

"This." His lips touched hers gently, very gently, yet never had a kiss felt quite so compelling. Stacy felt herself sagging against him, her bones dissolving and her muscles melting like hot wax.

Abruptly Chris drew back, putting her away from him, and Stacy could only stare at him, her lips parted in surprised yearning.

"Now you know the reason," Chris said, his voice thick and low with suppressed passion. "I want you, Stacy. God help me, I never could leave you alone— and thirteen years later, not a thing has changed. I guess I'll always want you . . . even when it's no good for me and no good for you."

Dear Reader,

Sophisticated but sensitive, savvy yet unabashedly sentimental—that's today's woman, today's romance reader—you! And Silhouette Special Editions are written expressly to reward your quest for substantial, emotionally involving love stories.

So take a leisurely stroll under the cover's lavender arch into a garden of romantic delights. Pick and choose among titles if you must—we hope you'll soon equate all six Special Editions each month with consistently gratifying romantic reading.

Watch for sparkling new stories from your Silhouette favorites—Nora Roberts, Tracy Sinclair, Ginna Gray, Lindsay McKenna, Curtiss Ann Matlock, among others—along with some exciting newcomers to Silhouette, such as Karen Keast and Patricia Coughlin. Be on the lookout, too, for the new Silhouette Classics, a distinctive collection of bestselling Special Editions and Silhouette Intimate Moments now brought back to the stands—two each month—by popular demand.

On behalf of all the authors and editors of Special Editions,
Warmest wishes,

Leslie Kazanjian
Senior Editor

ANNE LACEY
Rapture Deep

Silhouette Special Edition

Published by Silhouette Books New York

America's Publisher of Contemporary Romance

SILHOUETTE BOOKS
300 East 42nd St., New York, N.Y. 10017

Copyright © 1988 by Anne Lacey

ISBN: 0-373-09449-3

First Silhouette Books printing April 1988

America's Publisher of Contemporary Romance

Printed in the U.S.A.

Books by Anne Lacey

Silhouette Special Edition

Love Feud #93
Softly at Sunset #155
A Song in the Night #188
Magic Season #317
Golden Firestorm #365
Treasures of the Heart #395
Intrepid Heart #422
Rapture Deep #449

ANNE LACEY

hails from Baton Rouge, Louisiana, an ideal jumping-off point for her ardent explorations of antebellum homes up and down the Mississippi River and her frequent visits to her two favorite cities, Natchez and New Orleans. Having lived in Arkansas, Oklahoma, Arizona, Mississippi and several places in Texas, and having traveled extensively in the United States, Europe and Canada, she is admittedly a rolling stone. Even when she's busy writing, Anne keeps a bag packed at all times; after all, she never knows when a chance to travel might pop up.

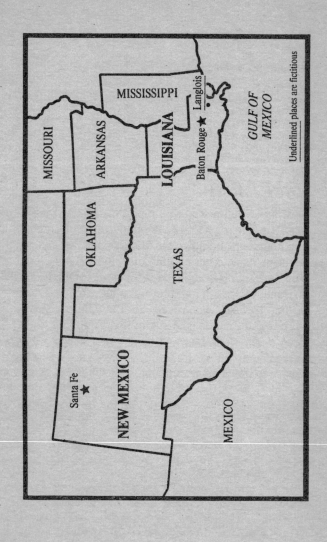

Underlined places are fictitious

Chapter One

The shining luxury sedan glided up the long, curving driveway. Stacy Thomasson, watching from an upstairs window, drew an audible breath.

In just a moment I'll see Chris again, she thought. Trying to ignore the trembling of her hands holding back the lace curtain, she drew another breath deep into her suddenly labored lungs.

Rapidly Stacy's eyes swept over the appealing scene below. The driveway was bordered by thick hedges and flower beds where flamboyant roses, hibiscus and lilies were in bloom. From the lush manicured lawn sprang sturdy oaks with streamers of Spanish moss as well as tall magnolia trees heavy with huge, waxy white blooms. June in Langlois, Louisiana was just as deliciously green and gorgeous as Stacy had remembered.

But now, moving closer by the second, came the gleaming automobile. Stacy knew Chris Lorio would be driving—Chris Lorio, the man who topped Stacy's personal list of People I Hope I Never See on Earth Again.

She hadn't sought this meeting, and she would never have agreed to it if she'd been summoned back by anyone else... anyone but Lynn.

Stacy was trembling all over now, and she stared down at herself in dismay. The uncontrolled emotional reaction was so wholly unlike her that she felt bewildered, even disconcerted. *Unfinished business?* she wondered, the psychological term leaping out of nowhere and into the forefront of her mind.

Absolutely not! She and Chris Lorio had been finished with each other for many years. They weren't even the same people they'd once been—they couldn't be—for too many events had swept through *both* their lives since that long-ago summer.

The sedan eased to a stop before the front door, parking right behind Stacy's aged Monte Carlo.

There's no reason to be afraid, Stacy assured herself wryly as she rubbed her hands down her sides, drying the palms that nervousness had turned slick. You're not eighteen anymore, a girl from a hick desert town whose greatest claim to fame is being Gary Thomasson's girlfriend. You're a grown woman. A mature adult. And you've handled clients a lot tougher than this small-town lawyer is going to be!

The brief self-lecture had a steadying effect on her as she peered down at the expensive car below. When the man seated behind the wheel did not immediately emerge, Stacy knew Chris must be sitting there, thinking.

By now he would have read New Mexico on the license plate of the unfamiliar car in his drive. He would know that Stacy was here. And just what would Christopher Lorio be thinking and feeling after thirteen years?

"Chris was so angry, Stacy! Why, I've never seen him in such a state! He kept threatening to find you and wring your neck! It was just a summer fling, of course—he's said as much. But it really hurt his pride when you ran off and married Gary."

Across the distance of all the years, Stacy could still hear Lynn's clear voice ringing in her ears. *"That is all it was, wasn't it, Stacy? Just a . . . a summer thing?"*

Lynn Ashley had been understandably devastated. Lynn, Stacy's third cousin and best friend, had always expected to marry Chris Lorio. She couldn't understand how two people she'd loved and trusted could have had "a summer thing"—if, indeed, that was all it really was. And what could the newly married Stacy, within earshot of her husband, reply except, "It wasn't important, Lynn, and it's all over now."

Just a summer thing . . .

Oh sure, Chris's pride might have been dented. He'd been as arrogant as a young prince back then—a prince who'd misplaced his crown temporarily but still expected the peasants to bow. He wouldn't have appreciated being dumped, and in his mind, no doubt, that was what Stacy had done to him. He wouldn't consider that he had abandoned her first.

Apparently where Stacy was concerned Chris had never mellowed, and he could certainly be a formidable enemy. Only Lynn had known how to get around him, as she had when he'd tried to halt the correspondence between the cousins. "I certainly told Mr. Lorio just what he could do with that idea," Lynn had written to Stacy. "Why, you and I have been pen pals ever since we learned to write! Of course, I'm sure you remember how Chris is. He thinks he was destined to rule the roost, *any* roost, so sometimes I have to be quite firm."

Oh, yes, Stacy certainly remembered how Chris was . . . or, rather, how he used to be. *Hungry* described it best. Even Lynn, who had known him far longer and could manage him much better than Stacy, still hadn't quite understood his constant, gnawing hunger for everything he'd ever missed. But Stacy, who'd recognized Chris's volatile mixture of arrogance and insecurity, had always suspected he would run roughshod over anyone who stood in his way. Maybe you had to have suffered deprivations of your own to really understand that kind of hunger. But understanding it didn't mean Stacy had liked the trait.

Well, he had it all now. Of course, he'd lost a few skirmishes along the way. He hadn't been able to prevent his wife and her cousin from staying in close touch through the years. And there had been one major loss, too. He hadn't been able to hold back death, try though he had to prolong Lynn's life.

As Stacy watched from above, the well-waxed door of Chris's sedan opened at last. His long legs came out first, followed by the rest of his body, dressed in a perfectly tailored summer suit of light gray and a soft white shirt. A bold scarlet tie broke the blandness with a blaze of color. Contrasts. Conflicts. They were always present in Chris, even in his choice of attire, Stacy thought. Nor did he fit her rather jaded picture of a small-town Southern lawyer. No, this man looked very uptown indeed.

Stacy's heart started to pound again as she stared down into his thick, midnight-black hair.

Abruptly Chris stopped beside the car, but before Stacy had caught more than a glimpse of his face, he bent over to study something on the driveway. One long, tanned hand reached out to brush a small black pool that Stacy noticed for the first time. He straightened, shaking his fingertips with disdain.

Stacy groaned aloud. Recently her aging car had developed a host of ailments, the latest being a voracious appetite for oil. Undoubtedly the Monte Carlo had leaked oil onto Chris's immaculate concrete drive. So much for good first impressions.

Quickly Chris turned, and his eyes flashed up to the very window where Stacy stood watching him. Guiltily she shrank back behind the curtains, her emotions in turmoil. But her breath caught in her throat at the brief glimpse of his handsome, well-controlled face. Damn it, what was the man doing to her before they'd exchanged a single word?

She couldn't tell from this distance if his features had changed, but his physique certainly had. At twenty-three

Chris had been rangy—indeed, almost thin. *Lean and hungry* had been Stacy's private description for him.

Now, at thirty-six, Chris wasn't nearly so hungry. Plenty of solid meals had finally filled out his magnificent, more-than-six-feet frame. Although he would probably never carry an extra ounce of weight, no one would ever call him "bean pole" again.

But, of course, that had been one of the *nicer* things Chris Lorio had been called.

Lordly. Opportunistic. Hard-driving and pushy. Stacy had heard them all. Especially the one acid-tinged word that, in all probability, accounted for the others: *bastard*.

Being born illegitimate in small Langlois, Louisiana, where everyone knew everyone else, must have been a painful burden. The town had never ceased to speculate on Chris's parentage: exactly which two people had farmed out their exceptionally bright and handsome child to the uncertain care of Bonnie Lorio? It was a question that had consumed the local population for years.

Well, no one in this picturesque town would ever dare to call Chris a bastard again—at least not to his face!

Money was equated with power down here in the southern Louisiana parishes, and Chris certainly had plenty of money now. He'd married it, inherited it and—most gratifying of all, Stacy suspected—he'd also made it himself.

Stacy heard the front door slam. Soon a murmur of voices reached her straining ears. Obviously Preston, the male servant who had greeted Stacy on her arrival, was filling in his employer.

Should I go out and meet Chris? Stacy wondered. It seemed like the more friendly and forthright thing to do. On the other hand, a reunion scene at the top of the stairs seemed rather too dramatic a setting, and of course there were purely practical considerations. A staircase meeting might allow audible words to drift down to curious ears below. No one who hated gossip as much as Chris Lorio always had would appreciate having that happen.

Still, Stacy longed to get this inevitable meeting over with. Delay was only increasing her case of nerves. Anxiously she paced back and forth. Finally she walked around the foot of the huge antique bed that had been Lynn's.

Hanging on the wall opposite the bed was a gallery of framed photographs. Instinctively Stacy's eyes went to the oldest picture there. It showed two adorable children, each standing with an arm draped over the other's shoulder.

They were classic opposites, even at the ripe old age of nine. Male and female. Dark and light. Ragged and neat.

Chris Lorio and Lynn Ashley.

The vital little boy with overlong hair falling across his forehead and almost into his hot defiant eyes seemed to have energy enough for two—scruffy-looking though he was. Although the little blond, blue-eyed girl wore expensive clothes and had a well-cared-for look, it failed to mask her faint air of fragility. Each an outsider in a different way, Chris and Lynn had united to present a formidable front to childhood tormentors, Stacy knew. Combined charm had gradually won over most people. Combined intelligence had successfully dealt with others.

How did I ever manage to slip between that winning two-some? she wondered, her eyes misting momentarily. And how did Lynn ever manage to forgive Chris and me, much less care for both of us again? Forgiveness was not a virtue Stacy had found easy to cultivate.

But perhaps Lynn knew that the brief aberration that had been Stacy-and-Chris should be blamed on flaming youth. It was, after all, just an unfortunate interlude. A misstep, quickly rectified. Then Lynn and Chris had been back together again "until death do us part."

In the end, that had been all that could separate them.

Now, as Stacy moved along the small gallery, other photographs traced the course of Chris and Lynn's union. A montage of high-school pictures culminated with senior prom and their graduation. Then there were shots of the happy pair during their college days . . . later, more taken in

Europe together—a trip that still brought a twinge to Stacy's heart.

Next, they were seen celebrating the opening of Chris's first law office. Following that came Lynn's engagement picture and their lavish wedding. Then a honeymoon in Bermuda, followed a couple of years later by a major surprise: a fat healthy-looking baby, drooling on his mother's shoulder. Quickly he grew into a toddler walking along a beach with his hand in his daddy's. Finally he was a potbellied three-year-old, dragging a tiny, still-flopping fish toward a wheelchair in which sat Lynn, frail and wan but laughing with obvious delight.

"How sad!" people always exclaimed upon hearing of Lynn's death. Apparently they didn't realize she had outlived even her most optimistic doctor's projection by fully fifteen years. Chris must have taken very good care of her indeed.

A brusque knock sounded on the door, and Stacy spun around. *Chris.* Suddenly once again it was hard to breathe. Think poise, she urged herself. Think peace and calm.

"Stacy?" The deep male voice was low but nonetheless authoritative.

"Come in, Chris," she managed to call out in her normal voice.

The door opened, and although Stacy had already glimpsed him on the driveway below, she hadn't been prepared for her first close-up look at Chris after so many years.

She'd never forgotten how he looked, of course. Still, she was amazed by how much she had failed to remember. Now he filled the doorway, and for a minute all she could do was absorb the images that passed rapidly before her eyes like a series of colored slides. Then she felt an unexpected inner stirring, as if something sleeping deep inside her had suddenly awakened.

Time had only enhanced Chris's good looks. Black eyes still blazed in his hard and handsome face, and although his overall appearance was blatantly masculine, even aggres-

sive, the bones and planes of his face had still been exqui-
sitely molded. New faint lines crinkled around the corners
of his piercing eyes and bracketed his sensuous lips.

Stacy took heart from those lines at Chris's eyes and
mouth. At least he looked as if he smiled more than he used
to.

He wasn't smiling now. In fact, as she watched, a small
muscle jumped in his lean brown cheek, and his first words
to her carried a sting. "Well, you certainly took your own
sweet time getting here." Even as he spoke, Chris closed the
door behind him, assuring them of privacy.

"Well, yes, I suppose I did," Stacy replied, looking up at
him. Thankfully her voice emerged crisp and controlled.

"It's been six months," Chris continued, his black eyebrows rushing together. "I thought you'd reneged on your
promise to come."

"It's more like five months, I believe," Stacy countered.

"Actually it's five months, three weeks and one day," he
challenged, raising the date of Lynn's death, specter-like,
between them.

"Yes—and when you called in January to tell me about
Lynn, I asked if I should drop everything and come," Stacy
reminded him, struggling to retain her calm facade. "In case
you've forgotten, Chris, you said there was nothing I could
do—that Lynn's death wasn't exactly unexpected and that
you had all the arrangements in hand."

To her distress, Stacy felt her breasts rising and falling
rapidly, betraying her inner agitation. *But I just didn't know
he would still be so handsome,* she thought irrelevantly, as
if in apology for herself.

What did *he* feel? Were there any emotions left at all? she
wondered.

Apparently not. Except for that one revealing twitch, his
face was smooth and bland. Stacy envied his composure as
well as his apparent indifference.

Rapidly she continued. "In fact, Chris, you specifically
told me to come when it was convenient and to be prepared
to stay at least a month. So I waited until I could arrange an

appropriate time off from work. In my business there's never a good time.''

"Okay," he allowed. "I just didn't expect such a long delay."

"I also had to arrange for Taylor's care," Stacy went on.

"Taylor?" Chris tilted his proud dark head in inquiry.

"My son," Stacy snapped, angered by his seeming ignorance.

"Oh, that's right. You have a boy, too."

Stacy felt certain that Chris, with his steel-trap mind, wasn't nearly as oblivious of her life or her child as he was pretending to be. Surely Lynn—the beloved wife whose death he still measured by days—would have mentioned Taylor's existence at least on a few occasions.

"So where did you park your son?" Chris continued casually.

"He's spending a week with Gary, then he'll go off to summer camp," Stacy replied.

"That sounds enjoyable." Although Chris's tone was coolly conversational, as he spoke his gaze raked Stacy from head to toe.

It wasn't a sexual gaze; that sort of look would have angered her, allowing her to take refuge in fury. No, this was a careful look born of sheer curiosity, much the same as the look Stacy had trained on Chris when she'd peered down at him from the window. Had she changed since he'd seen her last? Stacy wondered. Did he find her body different as the result of bearing a child?

Stacy was dismayed to feel her breasts tighten beneath the brush of his dark, inquisitive eyes. She leaned back against the bedpost and folded her arms across her chest, trying to appear as casual as he did. "Frankly, I wonder if Taylor will like camp—or visiting Gary in Santa Fe either." Stacy sighed. "Any other child would, of course, but Taylor sometimes seems to enjoy being perverse."

Unexpectedly Chris's mouth swept up, and his eyes crinkled attractively at the corners. I was right, Stacy mused. He does smile more than he used to.

"As one parent to another, this is funny?" she asked, her voice rueful.

"Taylor sounds like Robbie when he digs in his heels. But, no, I don't suppose you would find it funny. By the way, have you seen Robbie yet?"

"No—and I want to," Stacy added hastily. "Lynn's letters were always so full of him! He was certainly the light of her life."

"And mine," Chris agreed, his face brightening now as he discussed his son. "Lynn should never have had Robbie, of course. I always expected we'd adopt children. But she was determined to go through with the pregnancy, even though she never fully recovered from Robbie's birth."

"I'll bet she thought he was worth it," Stacy added, her voice softening as she thought of her gentle and generous cousin.

Chris threw Stacy a startled look, as if surprised by her insight. "Definitely," he stated firmly. "Lynn was always grateful for so many things the average person takes for granted—like waking up every day. Robbie's a lot like her, though I suppose the poor kid looks more like me. He must be taking a piano lesson this afternoon. At least I hope that's where he is."

"Piano?" Stacy couldn't help exclaiming in surprise.

"His mother was a very good pianist," Chris reminded Stacy.

"Has Robbie inherited Lynn's talent?" she asked.

"Frankly, I'm beginning to doubt it. Last year piano was something of a novelty. But Robbie's eight now, and he recently discovered baseball and diving boards." Chris's broad shoulders shrugged negligently. "Robbie informed me last week that he now hates piano, and if I keep making him take lessons he'll cut off all his fingers and run away from home forever."

Stacy burst out laughing at the extravagant statement. "Now that's a comment worthy of a young Lorio!"

"You think so? Well, I told you the kid had inherited a few unfortunate genes."

Even as he spoke, Chris's glance roamed casually around the room. Was she imagining it, or was he glad for an excuse to look away? Stacy wondered. "Do you have everything you need to be comfortable?" he asked.

"Oh, yes," she assured him. "Preston was very helpful, and his wife—Miriam, I believe?—also came up to see about me."

"Good. I think you'll find them glad to be of help. Well, I'll go now, Stacy. You'd probably like to rest a bit before dinner."

Chris's rapid strides placed him back at the door before the impact of his words had registered fully. "Wait!" Stacy cried. "I don't know where I'm supposed to start with Lynn's things or what—"

"Later," Chris interrupted, his voice firm. "I'm not such a slave driver that I expect you to start work the day you arrive."

"But I need to return home as soon as possible," Stacy protested. "I have responsibilities."

What she didn't mention was that she also had problems, quite a few of them, including her ex-husband's reluctance to take Taylor for the week, and a really bad feeling about Taylor and his costly summer camp.

"Of course," Chris agreed smoothly, "but humor me on the night of your arrival, Stacy. We can discuss everything before dinner."

A sudden wave of weariness chose that moment to strike, and Stacy swallowed further protests. "All right," she agreed, knowing it wasn't really her long trip but the strain and tension of meeting Chris again that had exhausted her so completely.

"Shall I send Robbie to see you when he gets home?"

"Yes, please!" At least Stacy could agree wholeheartedly to that suggestion.

"Okay." Halfway through the door, Chris paused to glance back at her. "You're looking very well, Stacy."

So apparently she'd won his grudging approval. Stacy savored the small victory in silence. And except for his

opening salvo, which probably had been sparked by irrita-
tion at her delay, Chris had been entirely pleasant and polite. But hardly personal. They were like chance
acquaintances being reunited at a watercooler. Or casual
friends who had bumped into one another on a busy street
corner.

"You look good, too," Stacy added softly.

They had meant so much to each other once. For a few
blissful weeks during that unforgettable summer they had
been as close as two people could ever be. Even now, whenever Stacy heard the word *honeymoon* she always thought
of the weeks she'd shared with Chris. Wouldn't it be marvelous if they could surmount all the bad memories—those
later memories, colored by anger, resentment and bitterness—and gradually grow to be the friends Lynn had always wanted them to be?

Or was that a completely impossible dream?

Stacy shed the white jumpsuit in which she'd traveled and
took a long relaxing shower. Then she debated what to wear
for dinner. Once she'd settled on a cool dark sheath with
which she could wear her clunky yet attractive Indian jewelry, she began to ponder footwear.

In New Mexico flat sandals and bare tanned legs were
perfectly suitable for casual nightlife. But here in the more
formal South, where traditions clung to the very last gasp,
Stacy wondered if she might not look too casual without
panty hose and proper shoes. Slipping the dress over her
head, she decided she'd chance going bare-legged and being
comfortable.

Dressed, Stacy peered anxiously at her face in the mirror,
trying to see if it showed the telltale lines of age.

Fortunately the skin program she used so religiously in the
desert had been doing its work. Her face still looked fresh,
smooth and lightly tanned. Stacy had not deliberately set out
to acquire her tan, made wary by articles about skin cancer
and premature aging. But even with sunscreen, her simple
yet active life-style, which kept her outdoors frequently, had

allowed a certain amount of natural color to creep over her face and limbs.

Tonight she applied a dab of blush, a bit of lip gloss and then more than a touch of eye makeup, since it enhanced what she knew were her best features—the expressive eyebrows, large green eyes and long swooping lashes.

Actually the woman who looked back at Stacy from Lynn's makeup mirror had not really changed very much. This woman might have been an older sister to the girl of eighteen who had once fallen so hard for the enigmatic Chris Lorio.

This woman, like the girl she'd once been, was tall and slender with deep auburn-brown hair, which looked deceptively brunette at night. But an intrinsic shyness left over from childhood had clung to the girl, while this woman had a more polished and sophisticated look.

Ever since that summer here in Louisiana, life had not allowed Stacy to be shy. Her abruptly changed personality had been just one more thing Gary had resented about her.

But, of course, once Taylor had been born she'd never been able to please Gary again.

A knock on the door interrupted Stacy's thoughts. This wasn't Chris's authoritative knock. It was much softer, followed by a hesitant pause. Rapidly Stacy crossed the room and swung open the door.

Robbie. He was handsome and sturdy in clean jeans and a white knit shirt. His face had a just-scrubbed look to it.

Unexpectedly Stacy's eyes brimmed with tears. Emotions even more fierce than those she'd experienced at seeing Chris again surged through her. Robbie combined traits from each of his parents, Stacy observed. His hair was medium-brown but would probably darken, and his eyes were hazel. His soft child's jaw and a certain tenderness and vulnerability about his mouth made Stacy feel immediately protective of him. He had Lynn's fair skin but Chris's build, being large and tall for his age. Thank goodness he'd obviously inherited his father's strength and vitality, too.

Even before he spoke a word, Robbie had become the world's second most important child to Stacy. And the way he looked up at her— She tried to define that look. It was not quite eager, but it was more than merely curious. *Hopeful* was the word.

"Ma'am, my daddy said you wanted to see me," Robbie announced. Stacy could see the effort the polite words to a stranger cost him. His innate shyness must come from her side of the family, she thought. Chris Lorio had never been shy about anything in his life.

"Oh, Robbie, I sure did!" Stacy exclaimed over the lump in her throat. "Why, I've been wanting to meet you for the longest time."

"Daddy says you knew my mom." Again that hopeful look flashed on his face.

Stacy battled back the tears that kept threatening to overtake her. "I sure did," she repeated. "Why, your mother and I were cousins and pen pals and best friends, too!"

A bleak awareness turned the vulnerable child's face older and sadder. "I sure miss my mom," said Robbie Lorio, and there was an eloquence in his simple words that almost undid Stacy.

"I know you do, Robbie. I miss her, too, and right now I'm feeling pretty sad about everything," Stacy added huskily. She blinked back more tears. "I—I know big guys like you don't much like to be hugged, but I'd sure appreciate one—if you'd let me, I mean."

Although she longed to haul Robbie straight into her arms, life with Taylor had taught Stacy always to ask first. *Ah, Taylor!*

Robbie looked up at her compassionately. "I guess it's okay," he said, and wrapped his arms around Stacy's waist.

Stacy buried her lips in his soft warm hair, recognizing its texture, remembering its touch. *Chris's hair.*

"Now," Stacy said when the boy had released her, "come sit down and tell me all about yourself."

Apparently Robbie recognized her own feelings for Lynn, or else he was simply starved for motherly attention. He confided that he liked to play ball, swim and ride his bicycle. He also enjoyed watching TV and playing games on his daddy's personal computer. He was going to be an ace fighter pilot when he grew up—or, at least, he thought so now.

He hated spinach, music lessons and Ted Thackery, a real nerd who lived in the house across the street. Ted was scared of practically everything, it seemed, and couldn't even swim.

"Daddy said you have a son, too," Robbie went on, growing progressively more at ease as he continued to talk with Stacy.

"Yes, he's twelve. Taylor is his name," Stacy said, and yielded to the desire to brush Robbie's dark brown hair off his forehead.

"Is he gonna come here to visit, too?" Robbie asked in excitement.

Stacy shook her head emphatically. Lord, just the thought of Taylor in this particular environment made her blood run cold.

"I sure wish . . ." Robbie's voice trailed off wistfully, and he sighed, resigned apparently to yet another summer spent mostly with adults or the timid Ted Thackery.

Stacy wondered why Chris didn't send his son to summer camp, too. He could afford it easily—unlike Stacy, who expected to live on bread and water for the next six months. Although she made a decent salary, raising a child in the modern world grew increasingly expensive. It seemed like something—insurance, taxes, car repairs or Taylor's eternal appointments with the dentist—always managed to gouge a chunk out of her paycheck.

"What time is it, Miss Stacy?" Robbie asked abruptly.

Stacy glanced at her wristwatch. "It's almost seven."

"Uh-oh!" Robbie jumped up from his chair. "Dinner's at seven-fifteen and Daddy said to have you downstairs 'fore that so you could have a drink."

"Oh, we'll still have plenty of time," Stacy soothed as she noticed the worried frown creasing the tender skin between Robbie's eyes. It was an expression no child of his age should wear, and suddenly she wondered if Robbie might be afraid of his father. Chris at his worst had sometimes frightened people much older than this little boy.

As Stacy crossed the room to turn off various lights she remembered the first time she'd ever seen Chris Lorio. The other girls with whom she'd gone to a summer dance here in Langlois had pointed him out to her, giggling and whispering over his fierce frown when he'd noticed their attention. Chris Lorio was *so* handsome—so intelligent, too. He had one more year of law school, then he would probably practice in the law firm headed by Knox Kinard and Congressman Hamilton Bainbridge. Yes, such a wonderful future! But Chris was also wild and unpredictable, a real terror with women. Some with whom he'd been briefly involved had even hinted that he was dangerous.

"But Lynn says—" the baffled Stacy had begun.

"Except with Lynn," the girls had amended hastily. Yes, Chris must definitely love Lynn, they related further, because he was always kind and protective toward her. When she spoke, he smiled. She was the nice girl he would undoubtedly marry after he'd finished sowing his wild oats with wilder ones. But don't be deceived by Lynn's endorsements, they warned. To the rest of the world Chris could certainly be a—a . . .

"A bastard?" one of the older girls suggested slyly, and then they had all collapsed in waves of mirth. It had earned them an even blacker glare from the subject of their discussion.

Chris's expression had said he knew damned well what they were talking about, and he didn't appreciate being an object of curiosity for a gaggle of giggling fools. In the furious scorn and indignation of that glare Stacy had wished that the floor would open up and swallow her alive. At least she hadn't laughed as the others did. She watched Chris take note of that fact, and it seemed to modify his frightening expression. Then something else began to flicker in the dark depths of his eyes as their gazes caught and held.

"Hurry, Miss Stacy," Robbie blurted now, interrupting Stacy's reverie.

"Don't worry," she said, seeking to reassure the child as she flicked on a small bedside lamp. "I don't particularly want a drink, though I suppose I might take a glass of wine since it's a special occasion."

"Why is it special?" Robbie asked, holding the door open for Stacy like a well-trained little gentleman. "Is it because you're back here in Louisiana?"

"No," Stacy said, then she bent down to give the boy a smile. "What makes it really special is that I've met *you*."

Chris stood waiting for them in the family room, and as she and Robbie entered, Stacy noticed Chris's eyes scan her quickly. At least she saw no disapproval of her sheath.

Chris's words confirmed as much. "I'm glad you didn't get all dressed up," he remarked. "I forgot to tell you that Robbie and I usually dress down for dinner."

"I don't blame you. Changing into comfortable clothes is always the first thing I do when I get home from work."

Stacy spoke automatically, distracted by the sight of Chris as he stepped out from behind the bar. Again she was struck by how handsome—indeed how devastatingly handsome— he looked in his casual attire. It was, of course, a purely impersonal observation, she hastily assured herself.

Chris's khaki shorts and short-sleeved gold cotton shirt were eminently suitable for the Louisiana weather where temperatures outside presently hovered close to ninety. His long, muscular brown legs were covered with thick, dark hair, and Stacy smiled faintly as she observed the old beat-up brown loafers on his feet.

Holding a tall, frosty-looking glass in one hand, Chris motioned to the well-appointed bar behind him with the other. "What would you like to drink, Stacy?"

"Wine," she said. "Or whatever you're having, Chris, if you've stirred up something special."

His black eyebrows shot up. "No, I didn't. Should I have?"

"Oh, no! It just looked like you were holding some exotic concoction, and I didn't want to disappoint you if you'd been laboring over a hot blender." Stacy stopped, wondering if he'd take offense at her flippant words.

Instead he laughed. "You've forgotten, Stacy. Impressing people has never been one of my higher priorities."

"Now how could I have forgotten a thing like that?" she gibed gently.

Chris gestured to his glass. "What I'm drinking is club soda with lime and a few crushed mint leaves. The combination tastes good and nasty, like a real drink."

"Oh," Stacy said, realizing she'd forgotten something else about Chris: he almost never drank alcohol. He'd always said he hated both the taste and the smell of it. Momentarily she'd forgotten he'd grown up with an alcoholic.

"Wine," Stacy requested, tearing her gaze away from the lithe movements of his lean body as he stepped back behind the bar. "Just half a glass, please."

"You still drink like I do," Chris nodded, then glanced down affectionately at his son who had trailed him behind the bar. "What about you, sport?"

The boy looked up at him with open adoration. No, Robbie didn't appear to fear his father, Stacy decided, but he certainly had a king-size case of hero worship. That was normal for a boy his age—although Taylor had skipped that phase utterly. His relationship to Gary had always been a mutually uneasy one.

As Stacy continued to watch Chris and Robbie's pleasant interaction she couldn't help but be surprised. Somehow she'd never imagined Chris Lorio in the role of parent—yet how naturally parenting seemed to come to him. Of course it had come easily to Stacy, too, even though Taylor could be the most obstinate, difficult and strong-willed of children—as his various baby-sitters would be happy to confirm.

"I want cherry soda—with a real cherry in it, too, Daddy," Robbie requested.

Across the child's head Chris glanced at Stacy. "Robbie always likes anything with cherries. Remind you of anyone?"

"Yes, of course," Stacy said with an awkward little laugh. Lynn had always adored gooey, chocolate-covered cherries, as well as cherry liqueur and cherries jubilee. For a moment Stacy's eyes held Chris's as they each obviously remembered.

Then Chris turned away to pour Stacy's wine. He placed a cocktail napkin beneath the stem and handed the glass to Robbie. "Try not to christen the carpet, okay?" he instructed.

"I won't," Robbie said, laughing. Carefully he bore the half-glass of white wine to Stacy, who had just taken refuge in a large leather chair.

She sipped and found the wine's cool, delicate taste exactly right for a hot summer night. "Speaking of spills, Chris," she began, determined to introduce the thorny subject herself, "I'm sorry that my car is leaking oil. I noticed it had made a mess of your driveway."

"Oh, I've already hosed it all off. But a car that leaks oil may have serious engine trouble," he warned her, handing Robbie the requested cherry-flavored drink.

"Don't remind me," Stacy replied with a shudder. "Every time I turn around that car needs a new something-or-other, and it never seems to cost less than a couple hundred bucks."

"I have an excellent mechanic who knows better than to cheat me," Chris remarked conversationally as he came out from behind the bar again. "Shall I have him take a look at your car tomorrow, Stacy?"

"I'd appreciate it," she said and took another sip of wine. She drank so rarely that she could already feel the effects beginning to move through her veins. At least the rush of warmth made her feel more relaxed, and she found herself appreciating Chris's steadfast courtesy, too.

Actually, she'd had a lot of late-night fears as she'd anticipated her return to Langlois, Louisiana. Several times she'd awakened to find her heart racing and a sheen of perspiration covering her body. But so far her anxiety had proved mercifully unfounded.

Marriage and fatherhood had definitely softened Chris, as his new smile lines had suggested. Undoubtedly he'd needed the warmth and solid devotion of a good woman like Lynn and the love and hero worship of a child like Robbie. What immense, overpowering strength the truly gentle often wielded, Stacy found herself thinking. *I* would never have been so good an influence on Chris, she admitted ruefully.

Or was she kidding herself about the peaceful atmosphere? Stacy wondered. Although she didn't like to think the worst of anyone, life had taught her wariness. What if this pleasant Chris was merely a role assumed for Robbie's benefit?

Suddenly his sweet forbearance seemed suspect. Forgiveness had never been one of Chris's strong suits, either, she thought, a part of her becoming more wary and alert, waiting for the other shoe to drop.

Chris took a seat on the sofa where Robbie was perched, across from Stacy. As he sank back into the cushions, one long bronzed leg rested across the other in a studiedly casual gesture. Too casual? Stacy considered.

"Tell us about your job, Stacy. Exactly what do you do in Albuquerque?" Chris asked. He spoke in a conversational tone and his face looked open and friendly, but his dark eyes watched her closely.

"I write advertising copy, TV spots and various other promos," she replied. "We handle several clients who sell swimming pools, hot tubs and Jacuzzis. Business was better for all of us a few years ago when hot tubs were new and exciting."

"So you work for an advertising agency?" Chris probed.

"Yes. It's small and, I'm afraid, a little too specialized. I've been there almost seven years," Stacy added.

"I believe Lynn mentioned once that you went to college and worked toward a degree," Chris commented.

At least his recall was getting better, Stacy noticed. But, goodness, was Lynn going to be mentioned in every other sentence they spoke? Of course, these two guys had loved her, and with good reason. Lynn had been a woman of great warmth and character. But she was gone now, and the frequent interjections of her name into conversation were beginning to make Stacy uneasy.

"Yes, after Taylor was born I attended the University of New Mexico," she said guardedly. "It was difficult with my family responsibilities, but I felt a need to complete my education."

"Frankly, I was surprised," Chris remarked. "I hadn't remembered you as being particularly ambitious."

Stacy looked up sharply, stung by his casual reference to their shared past. No, he had probably remembered her only as a wildly in love, do-absolutely-anything-for-you girl. And maybe I was that way once, Stacy thought, looking back down into her drink. But motherhood and the realization that she had a marriage probably destined to sink had definitely matured her.

Gary's numerous affairs had provided yet another motivation.

When Stacy failed to respond to Chris's barbed comment, he moved on to a new topic. "Let me explain exactly what Lynn wanted you to do, Stacy, since you're so eager to get started on this project. Robbie, you'd better listen to this, too."

"All right, Daddy," Robbie said curiously.

"Stacy, Lynn wanted you—and only you—to sort through her personal possessions. She also preferred that you be the one to sift through the contents of the attic. That's where things belonging to her mother and grandmother, and probably even her great-grandmother, are stored. The attic was always a chore Lynn intended to undertake herself just as soon as she felt stronger. There are some quite nice antiques up there."

Chris spoke crisply, his attorney's mind evidently having catalogued the facts. "Now, Stacy, everything from Lynn's own clothes to her grandmother's old churn is yours, if you wish. And anything you don't want to retain for your personal use may either be sold for your profit or donated to charity."

Stacy nodded. Chris had already hinted at this in a stiff, dictated-to-a-secretary letter she'd received soon after Lynn's death.

"If you need any assistance—and no doubt you will in moving the boxes and barrels in the attic—Preston will be glad to help you." Chris's incisive gaze swept over Stacy's face. "Is that clear?"

"Of course," Stacy said with another nod, wondering exactly what was going on here.

The mystery came clear when Chris turned back to his son, a concerned look filling his black eyes. Robbie kept staring down at the tips of his tennis shoes as though he didn't want to look up at the two adults. "How about you, sport?" Chris asked the boy gently. "Do you understand that Stacy will take your mother's clothes and all her other things and dispose of them?"

"Yes, sir," mumbled Robbie.

"This was what your mother wanted Stacy to do. She wrote it all in her will. So now we must help Stacy to do what Mommy wanted. Okay?"

"Okay, Daddy," the child said, his voice barely more than a whisper.

"Robbie has been going into Lynn's room quite a lot lately," Chris remarked conversationally to Stacy. "It's because he misses her, of course, and feels so lonely. But it's really best now for both of us to start letting her go."

So Chris had realized the necessity for that, too, Stacy thought with relief. She was also aware that he'd been the one most constantly invoking Lynn's memory. It was an obvious contradiction, of course, but then Chris Lorio had always been full of those.

Still, over the long haul he had usually proved to be realistic and levelheaded. Otherwise he could never have achieved the professional success he had.

But tonight as Chris watched his bereaved child, Stacy saw an expression almost like bewilderment playing over his mobile face. He really didn't understand Robbie very well, Stacy realized. The son, with his innate sensitivity and that revealing edge of shyness, was far more vulnerable than his father had ever been. Chris Lorio had always worn a coat of armor that few barbs could pierce. As a result—and probably for the first time in his life—he wasn't exactly sure what to do for Robbie.

Stacy wasn't completely sure, either, but at least she knew how to begin. She rose and crossed over to the sofa where she sat down on Robbie's free side. There she slipped an arm around the little boy and silently drew him close to her. For a moment his body felt stiff and unyielding and she thought he might rebel. Then gradually he began to relax against her.

A minute later Miriam stood at the door, announcing that dinner was served.

Chapter Two

The moon was round and yellow, the heavy night air fragrant with the exotic essence of roses, magnolias and cape jasmine. Katydids sang into the hushed, torpid darkness while tree frogs croaked back a hoarse response. An occasional restless bird in the great live oak trees fluttered its wings disapprovingly as Stacy passed on the garden path below.

Soft southern nights...they were still just as she'd remembered. The warm humidity left Stacy's lips feeling soft, her skin dewy. Unconsciously her back arched, and she stretched sinuously, more aware of her body than she'd been in months.

She refused to admit her awakened senses might have anything to do with Chris's intense black-eyed gaze. She'd felt his eyes watching her off and on throughout the simple but satisfying meal of chicken casserole, steamed broccoli, fresh fruit salad and large puffy dinner rolls. Dinner conversation had proved surprisingly easy. Stacy had simply relied on the time-tested technique of inquiring about their mutual acquaintances, all of whom seemed to be married and have children. But even as Chris had talked with her in a seemingly natural and easy way, Stacy had felt that unfathomable gaze of his watching her carefully, as if trying to probe beneath her skin.

"No dessert?" Robbie had cried at the meal's conclusion.

"You and those desserts." Chris had pretended to heave an exasperated sigh, but his eyes rested fondly on the boy. "We don't have to have dessert at every meal, you know."

"Yes, sir," Robbie had agreed, ducking his head.

"Stacy, does your son always expect a reward for eating his dinner?" Chris had inquired.

"I'm afraid you won't get much help from me, Chris," Stacy had admitted ruefully. "Taylor has always been partial to sweets."

"See!" Robbie had crowed triumphantly to his father.

"Well, I just happened to see a big lemon chiffon pie lurking way back in the refrigerator. I told Miriam we'd have dessert in my study in about twenty minutes. Is that okay?" Chris had inquired of his son.

"Oh, yes, sir!" Robbie's vast relief that he would not be deprived of dessert after all had caused both Stacy and Chris to suppress smiles.

Immediately after they arose from the table Stacy had excused herself, pleading weariness and a willingness to forgo the lemon chiffon pie. But once upstairs in the room that had always been Lynn's she had found herself strangely restless. She wasn't really tired enough to sleep, although her shoulder muscles felt so stiff they ached. Undoubtedly it was nervousness from being here and seeing Chris again, but the long hours behind a steering wheel hadn't helped, either. Soon Stacy slipped down the staircase and out into the night.

Why hadn't the cicadas started their nightly chorus? Stacy wondered, strolling around the large house. She could still remember the insects' shrill soprano song from that long-ago summer.

"Why do they make such a racket?" she'd asked Chris one evening, just at dusk.

"The cicadas?" he'd said, twining a strand of Stacy's long, straight hair around his index finger. Lights from the pool lit his face as he studied her thoughtfully. "Oh, they have quite a story to tell us."

"What sort of story?" she said, pleased by his unexpected whimsy.

"It's all about their lives, their loves, their adventures. Why else would they carry on so?" Chris had turned to kiss Stacy then, one of those long, hot, passionate kisses that had wiped everything from her mind but him. And for that night, at least, Stacy had forgotten all about the clattering cicadas and their tuneful story.

She remembered them now, noting their silence. Perhaps it was simply not late enough in the season for the cicadas to sing.

Stacy made her way slowly across the New Orleans style courtyard with its spacious patio, its orange and banana trees, and into the gardens that had been Lynn's joy and delight. She stopped there, turning to look back at the house, from which bright lights glistened like jewels.

It was a large, proud, characteristically Southern home of white-painted brick. Lofty Corinthian columns supported a second-story balcony, which overhung the wide veranda encircling the house. The architecture almost screamed Greek Revival, but rather than being a genuine antebellum mansion from the 1840s, the "Ashley house," as it was still known, was a copy built a hundred years later. By now the house looked time-weathered enough to fool all but experts or history buffs.

Lynn Ashley had grown up in that house, because her parents had owned it. But as renowned archaeologists they had spent much of their time away and, in consequence, were less attached to their home than other people their age. When Lynn and Chris had married, the two Dr. Ashleys had deeded the house to the young Lorios. They had already found a smaller place they preferred in Mexico, not far from a dig on which they'd worked for years.

Now, of course, the large white house belonged to Chris—and what a change it must have been for him after so many years in Bonnie Lorio's ramshackle hut on the edge of town. But Chris had adapted easily, as if to the manor born—the displaced prince assuming his rightful position at last.

Stacy turned away from the house, but hesitated where two garden paths converged. The pool area would be rife with memories—memories that had been trying to steal over her since she'd arrived in Langlois. Memories that represented a Pandora's box Stacy frankly feared to open. She'd put the trauma of the past behind her; why relive it now?

A garden bench beneath a large oak tree shone in the moonlight. After a moment's uncertainty, Stacy walked over and sat down.

God, how sorry he was she'd ever come back!

From the balcony beyond his study Chris saw Stacy strolling down the garden path. Although the bright full moon kept scuttling in and out of clouds, it was beaming its very brightest when Chris stepped through the French doors and out into the honeyed night.

Behind him he'd left a happy little boy. Robbie was crazy about both lemon pie and computer games. Tonight he'd eaten two pieces of pie and had played four such games with his father. Chris had allowed Robbie to win the last two, having thrashed him thoroughly on the first couple.

Chris tried to walk a fine line with Robbie, teaching him he couldn't expect to win in life all the time but still permitting him victory often enough that he didn't grow up fearing competition, either, or feeling hopelessly outclassed.

And sometimes Chris just plain indulged his son, like letting Robbie have two pieces of pie when the boy had continued to plead hunger. Chris still remembered all too well just what it was like to go to bed hungry.

He was trying to be, to Robbie, the sort of father he'd always wanted for himself, and on balance, Chris thought he succeeded most of the time. Lynn had always praised him as a good father. And overall Robbie's childhood had been as Chris had intended—completely unlike his own.

With painful clarity Chris remembered what a hostile, snapping little animal he'd been when he was Robbie's age. Remembered how he'd waded into a fight with two older, bigger boys who'd taunted him in the school yard, calling him a "woods colt." Chris hadn't even known what the colloquial rural term meant until they'd spelled out "bastard."

Chris still thought that separately he could have punched either guy's lights out. Like most bullies, they were essentially craven at heart. But together they'd finally overpowered him, and the beating they'd given Chris had been vicious. They'd swaggered off, leaving him crumpled in the corner of the playground trying to gather strength just to crawl to his knees. He was vowing he'd rather croak than cry when the frail little fair-haired girl drew his battered head into her lap. She was sobbing as she tried to wipe blood from his lips with a dainty lawn handkerchief she'd pulled from a pocket of her dress.

Chris turned to snarl at her. "I don't need your damn stinkin' pity!" he'd planned to say. At seven he cussed quite fluently, as all of his teachers had learned to their dismay.

But the words died away as his bruised eyes looked up into Lynn Ashley's pale face. When he saw her bluish-tinged lips Chris had felt his anger simply evaporate. Perhaps it was the genuine grief in her stricken blue eyes, or the worshipful adoration that he read there. Perhaps it was the perception, unusual for one of his age and background, that Lynn was simply too gentle and delicate a creature to wither with sarcasm or blast with oaths.

"Aw, hell, they didn't hurt me much," he'd muttered and used Lynn's dainty handkerchief to wipe the dirt and blood away, even spitting a tooth into it. Fortunately the tooth had been hanging loose anyway. And, ever after, Chris Lorio knew he had one friend, at least, and he'd always been one for Lynn.

Now, looking down on his proud gardens below, Chris muttered to the spirit of the woman who'd shared so much of his life. "Lynn, you were wrong. You should never have invited Stacy back here."

God knows he'd done his best to rid both his life and his marriage of Stacy. But vulnerable, gentle Lynn—who very rarely dug in her heels over anything but could be an absolute bulldog when she did—had fought him tooth and nail about Stacy.

She would not cease corresponding with her cousin as Chris had suggested early in the first year of their marriage, and the disagreement had turned into such a long and vehement struggle between them, as each withdrew in wounded silence, that Chris at last had feared for Lynn's health. Grudgingly he'd given in, but in so doing, he'd extracted one concession from Lynn.

She was never to mention Stacy's name in his presence or relay any of her news, since Chris didn't care if Stacy, her husband and their kid lived or died. Matter of fact, he'd definitely prefer the latter.

Lynn had kept her promise, but being the clever woman she was, she'd also left Stacy's letters scattered around. Ultimately when Lynn was out of the house, puttering in the gardens or sunning by the pool, Chris would pick up Stacy's letters and scan them, even though he usually ground his teeth with impotent rage.

Lynn hadn't mentioned Stacy to Chris again until the very last, when imminent death was certainly sufficient reason to forgo a ridiculous vow.

"Daddy?"

Chris gave a start of surprise at being abruptly returned to the present. Then he turned around to face his son. "Yeah, Robbie?" he said casually, walking back into his study.

"I finished reading that chapter on the Wright brothers. It was neat, them flying that plane and all! Now can we play another game?"

"No way," said Chris firmly. "It's your bedtime."

"But it's summer vacation!" Robbie protested.

"I'm well aware of that," Chris said with an unwilling grin. "That's why you get to spend your days climbing trees with Ted Thackery or swimming in the pool, which keeps Preston tied up watching you. It's why we played four computer games tonight and you got two pieces of pie. So off to bed with you, you poor kid!"

His son flashed him an unwilling grin in return. "Okay, Daddy."

"Want me to come tuck you in, sport?"

Robbie shot Chris an incredulous look. "You gotta be kidding!"

"All right, I won't. But come give me a hug. There's no one to see us, I promise you."

Another reluctant grin flashed on Robbie's face, then he bounded into Chris's arms. *God, I love him so much!* Chris thought. *If anything ever happened to Robbie—*

He forced himself to stop such a thought, although he supposed such superstitious fears flashed through every parent's mind sooner or later. You couldn't help thinking about accidents and diseases, murderers, kidnappers or rapists. Fortunately, faced with a healthy and reasonably careful kid, such thoughts were fleeting.

After Robbie had left, Chris returned to the darkened balcony. Stacy was no longer on the garden bench below, but Chris thought he would have heard her if she'd come into the house. His ears seemed to be automatically attuned toward the new person in residence here.

He wished that were *all* that felt attuned to her presence.

No, Chris definitely hadn't wanted Stacy back here, and he had good and sufficient reason for feeling as he did. He could still recall the sinking sensation in the pit of his stomach when Lynn had uttered the verboten name during her final illness.

"Chris, I want to leave all my personal things to Stacy. And everything that's stored in the attic, too. She's been more than a cousin to me. I think of her almost as if we were sisters."

It was no time to argue with a gravely sick wife. "All right, Lynn," Chris had said in a low voice.

"You'll remember to put that in when you redo my will?" Lynn went on insistently.

"Yes, of course," Chris agreed, trying not to let his complete dismay show.

Soon after their marriage Chris and Lynn had each made a will leaving all their possessions to each other. But Robbie had been born since then, and Lynn had wanted to make a special bequest to him, as well as to Miriam and Preston, who had served the family so long and faithfully.

So Chris had drawn up Lynn's new will as she'd wished; she'd signed it with a flourish and a special smile of thanks to him.

Now, as a result, Stacy was back.

Now, too, Chris knew part of the reason he'd so dreaded her return.

Over the years it had been easier for him to cast Stacy in the role of tease and temptress. To think of her as a fiery, sexy little wench who'd been glad enough to fool around with Chris for a few summer weeks but who had soon dashed straight back to her old boyfriend, probably before Chris's ship to England had cleared New York harbor.

But with Stacy's return to Louisiana, Chris was forced to realize that it really hadn't been that way at all. Stacy had been an inexperienced girl of eighteen with a fresh, vibrant beauty and a vitality and excitement about life to match Chris's own.

Perhaps that was why he'd made the consummate mistake of getting so hung up on her.

Her physical adult presence in his home was a painful reminder that she was really no wanton hellcat but a basically nice and likable person. Although he still couldn't understand why she'd done what she'd done, dumping him so suddenly, the low, slow sigh that suddenly escaped him was an admission—for the first time ever—that she might have had reason.

After all, not everyone was as tolerant of the foibles of Chris Lorio as Lynn had been.

Maybe he'd pushed Stacy too fast and too far. Been too interested in her body instead of her mind. Used her too often to slack the passion she built in him with just a flash from those gorgeous green eyes. Hell, who knew? She'd come along when his youthful hormones were raging. Still, Chris thought she should have granted him the courtesy of an explanation.

And Stacy was still too damned attractive for Chris's peace of mind. That lithe, youthful figure of hers, particularly her long graceful legs, were bringing back thoughts he'd be wise to suppress. Old memories he'd thought successfully buried had suddenly taken on new life, springing up, unchanged by their long tenure in the underground of his mind.

During dinner Chris had tried not to look at Stacy often or long. He'd tried to keep his glance light and casual when he did look. But that had just given him the opportunity to notice other things about her. The low pleasant tones of her faintly Western-flavored speech. Her sharp memory and keen intelligence as names of old acquaintances rolled off her tongue. And her rare but rippling laugh still seemed to yank a cord deep within him.

Most of all, Chris had been struck by the natural, instinctively mothering manner she'd displayed toward Robbie.

That the sexiest woman he'd ever known should also turn out to have such a strong maternal streak was the greatest surprise of all, Chris admitted to himself. It should have cooled him like a dash of icy water, but instead it perversely heightened her charms, even increased her erotic attraction for him.

At last he was getting down to brass tacks, Chris thought frankly. Stacy still raised his temperature. But, damn it, he refused to let himself be drawn toward her again! Once had been quite enough.

"It's just this unnatural life I've been living," Chris grumbled under his breath.

Even before Lynn had died she'd had several years of serious illness. During that time the passion in their marriage had been mostly transmuted into tenderness and affection, although there had been occasional golden moments that shone all the brighter because they were rare.

Chris knew he would carry those wonderful, golden memories for the rest of his life.

Since Lynn's death Chris's mind had stayed focused on Robbie. His and Lynn's child came foremost as Chris tried to help Robbie work through the shock, pain, anger and grief of losing the mother he'd adored. So Chris hadn't had time for a casual fling, even if he had wanted one. And he hadn't. He didn't want to sully Lynn's memory with a meaningless episode or become notorious as a man-about-town. He'd worked too hard to win this town's respect and approval. Also, in another couple of years Chris thought he might run for Congress, since he'd always had political ambitions. Still, the way he'd been living since Lynn died was neither natural nor normal, especially not for a healthy, hot-blooded guy.

But what on earth was Stacy Thomasson's abiding and apparently eternal attraction for him? Chris wondered in exasperation.

Was she still down there, walking in the gardens? Or would she—dare she?—wander over by the pool and cabana where once, so long ago, they used to meet? Did she even remember that epic summer when Lynn had been in Europe with her parents, leaving Chris as acting caretaker for the house and grounds?

What did it matter whether she remembered or not, whether she was presently indoors or out? Stacy was a big girl, Chris thought impatiently, striding back into his study. He paused to lock the French doors, then crossed the room swiftly.

He intended to check on Robbie, as he always did, to be sure the child was sleeping, then he would go to bed himself. He was certainly not going to roam around outside, intruding where he probably wasn't wanted, anyway.

Yeah, you never meant to read her letters, either, a small voice deep inside of Chris gibed.

Stacy sat for several minutes on the garden bench, as if gathering strength to confront what was to come. Then she rose and walked slowly in the direction of the swimming pool. Just why she felt so drawn, even driven, to return here she still didn't understand. It was a place haunted by youthful memories. Memories of being so much in love with Chris that nothing else in the world had mattered—not Gary, who was eager to marry her. Not Lynn, who was away for several months, enjoying a lengthy European tour. And certainly not Stacy's stern, religious grandmother, with whom she'd lived in Langlois that summer.

No, there had been only the long hot summer, the torrid, sultry nights . . . and Chris Lorio.

A small sigh escaped her. She had tried to put a lot of years and a lot of miles between herself and those memories. It was galling to have them threaten to rise up now, phoenixlike, as fresh in her mind as though they'd happened yesterday. She could still remember her mouth burning beneath Chris's and the sure, steady glide of his confident hands. Could remember her senses swimming in surrender and her heart pounding in frenzied excitement with the implicit promise of the deep rapture to come.

Now that she was older and wiser, Stacy knew how dangerous it was to ever love someone like that—so wildly and intensely, so utterly without inhibitions. Because once you'd loved in that particular way you were ruined for any other kind of romantic relationship. Ordinary, garden-variety love didn't suffice—as Stacy had unhappily discovered when she'd married Gary. She'd longed for the blaze of passion, followed by deep, complete fulfillment that Gary couldn't provide.

Did Chris still remember how it had been with them once? Stacy found herself wondering. Or did he, the widower still apparently so devoted to his late wife's memory, ever let himself remember?

As she reached the end of the path at the back of the estate Stacy felt obscurely disappointed to find the pool area dark and deserted. But then why should it be lit when both Chris and Robbie were in the house? Stacy's mind drifted back to that long-ago summer, when Chris had kept the pool lights blazing invitingly at night.

Was the pool filled with water? Stacy wondered as she drew closer. The moon was skulking behind a cloud again; still, from the glow cast by a distant streetlight just beyond the high back wall, she could discern the pool's dark depths. She heard a wind-stirred ripple.

Four white wrought-iron chairs, lacy as a girl's petticoat, sat clustered around a matching table, topped with an oversize pool umbrella. A couple of long lounge chairs looked even more comfortably inviting on the wide concrete apron beside the pool. Slowing, gazing around through suddenly misty eyes, Stacy made her way toward one of the lounge chairs. Just as she sat down, the full moon slid out from behind its cloud, and the soft deep darkness lightened. It illuminated the outline of a tall man.

There was plenty of light for the startled Stacy to see Chris as he stepped off a path that ended by the side of the cabana. For a moment time seemed suspended as present appeared to melt into past, and to Stacy, the sight of him now was practically heart-stopping.

She remembered the cabana as a cheerful place decorated in white and lime green with lots of squishy, waterproof cushions covering most of the furniture. Fully a hundred times Stacy had dreamed of being back in that cabana with Chris, not to mention all the nights when she'd tried desperately to forget, to get on with her life without him.

Now her heart, which had stalled at the sight of him, began to thump irregularly as she looked across the pool toward Chris. She almost expected to see him wearing his black skin-tight trunks, the ones that had hugged his lean hips and concealed little of his impressive male endowments. But of course he'd discarded those years ago. Still, it was something of a shock to see him still attired in the khaki shorts and gold shirt he'd worn at dinner.

So he did remember, too! He must—or surely he wouldn't have come here.

Or... was that really why Chris had come—as if to keep an unspoken rendezvous between the two of them? Suddenly Stacy doubted it, for as Chris drew closer, she could see that cold anger marked his face. Anger and a steely resolve.

Her heart gave an involuntary protest, banging against her rib cage. She knew now that the other shoe had dropped.

For the first time since Stacy's arrival, his face lay unmasked. Harsh anger and an elusive something else flickered over the hard, handsome features as he stared at Stacy.

He crossed the pool's apron and stopped a scant foot away from her chair. "You know, I really hoped you wouldn't come out here tonight," he said roughly. His voice held a biting-cold edge.

That makes two of us! Stacy thought fervently, gripping the arms of the lounge chair as she felt her body tense. Lord, how she hated scenes—she'd always gone out of her way to avoid them. But aloud she tried to sound indifferent. "Oh?" she inquired with manufactured calm.

"If you hadn't remembered, Stacy, and hadn't bothered to come, then we could have kept on playing our nice, polite game of we're-practically-strangers. But now I'm going to ask you all those questions I've wondered about through the years—even though I know I'll kick myself when I wake up tomorrow."

Stacy began to tremble. She really didn't feel up to questions or to having the past dragged up again. Still, if there were questions burning Chris alive, she knew she should try to answer them. She would have to anyway, sooner or later. Other men might repress their feelings and restrain their tongues, but Chris always erupted sooner or later. In fact, his candid honesty and strong emotions were two of the things Stacy had always found most appealing about him.

But they weren't appealing right now.

Awkwardly she cleared her throat, then regretted the nervous sound. The key was to stay cool, to act casual and sophisticated. For that matter, why couldn't she *feel* that way, as well? "Frankly, Chris, I'm not sure why I did come here tonight," she stalled.

"Then let me suggest a reason." He had never looked bigger and taller than he did now, looming over her, his icy voice almost expressionless. "This was a fork in the road for you...for both of us, actually. You had a choice to make—Gary or me. Well, Stacy, we both know who you chose...and how well the decision turned out." His lips twisted cynically. "I wondered if you might not be feeling just a trifle nostalgic tonight."

Stacy shrank back in the chair, but her voice was spirited when she replied, "Obviously you're not feeling nostalgic. I'm not particularly, either."

"No?" His expression in the bright white moonlight grew skeptical. "What, then?"

"Well, if you must know," Stacy said tightly, "I was simply daydreaming about how it was to—to be..."

"To be what?" he demanded, his voice curt.

"Young and in love," she finished.

"Oh, surely you're not going to try that old tired line?" Chris gave a sigh of exasperation. "Come on, Stacy, we're both old enough to take the truth. And enough years have passed now that it doesn't matter anymore. So satisfy my curiosity. If you and Gary were such a hot item, why did you ever get mixed up with me in the first place?"

"You fascinated me, Chris," Stacy said honestly. "You looked just as sleek and dangerous as a mountain lion."

"Really? Well, you were certainly the little lion tamer, weren't you. But it was all over so fast I hardly knew what had hit me. I'd no sooner gotten back to the States, just a few weeks after I'd left, and my girl—who had vowed and sworn she would love me forever—had run off and married somebody else.''

"Is that the version of How It All Ended that you've chosen to believe?" Stacy flared back, meeting Chris's cool and faintly contemptuous gaze with one of her own. "*My* story is considerably different. I asked you not to leave me. I pleaded with you to skip the trip or take me along. I think I must have had a premonition—"

"Of what?" he interrupted. "That you couldn't even stay true to a man for a mere two months?"

Chris and his damnable pride! That pride had always driven him, dominated him. Apparently, it dominated him still.

"You know that wasn't all there was to it," Stacy went on defiantly. "You were bound and determined to go tearing off to Europe on the spur of the moment and hang whatever I might want! You couldn't resist showboating with an important man like Congressman Hamilton Bainbridge. Then you were going to link up with golden princess Lynn and her very prominent parents—"

"Not many people would turn down an all-expense-paid trip to Europe," Chris snapped right back. "After all the years I'd been through, scrambling for bucks and trying to make something of myself, I thought I was finally entitled to have a little fun."

"Well, I hope you enjoyed yourself, Chris, because I sure got left behind holding the bag!" Abruptly Stacy stopped, biting her lip. She was suddenly, desperately afraid that she had said too much.

With her words his expression changed to puzzlement. "What are you talking about?" Chris demanded. "Are you telling me you were jealous of Lynn?"

"Is that idea so impossible to entertain?" Stacy cried, seizing on the excuse he'd offered. "Oh, sure, I loved Lynn, but she'd always had lots of advantages over me, like wealthy parents who'd sent her to an Ivy League college. She could afford to be sweet and generous—certainly she had the advantage where you were concerned. Why, she'd known you forever. I'm not saying my feelings were very mature, but for heaven's sake, Chris; I was barely eighteen!''

"You may have been young, but you always knew exactly what you were doing, Stacy. We both did,'' Chris insisted angrily.

"Maybe,'' she muttered, but he was already off on another tangent.

"Actually, Stacy, I don't think it was love or jealousy or even Europe that mattered most to you. I think, in the end, it came down to the fact that I was the notorious town bastard—which sure bothered the hell out of your pious old grandmother. I could read it in her stiff face every time I came up the steps of her house.''

"Well, it certainly didn't bother me!'' Stacy protested, appalled that he could think her such a snob.

"I'm afraid I don't believe you,'' Chris said coldly. "There was only one person it never really bothered: Lynn.''

Lynn, always Lynn! During that long-ago summer she'd been an almost tangible presence between them—and she was certainly a presence standing between them now.

Stacy wasn't aware of drawing a slow deep breath until she exhaled in a sigh. "Look, Chris, I'm delighted you always had Lynn on your side. I'm glad the two of you made such a good marriage and that you had Robbie. And you're at least partially right, because something about you always did bother me. But it wasn't the circumstances of your birth. No, it was your ferocious, hell-bent determination to get everything you'd ever missed.''

"Baby, when you're born a bastard in Langlois, Louisiana in the fifties, you missed out on a hell of a lot. Who wants to celebrate your birthday? Or how about Christmas? Well, forget those Currier and Ives scenes. I spent holidays watching Bonnie Lorio drink herself into a stupor while I sat wondering who my real parents were and just how they were celebrating. And what about the man who'd fathered me—that nebulous figure in the background who sent money to Bonnie each month? Oh, not that he did *her* any favors. To an alcoholic like Bonnie, money was a green light straight into d.t.'s, cirrhosis of the liver and premature death.''

As Chris spoke, his voice growing fiercer with each sentence, he bent closer to Stacy until she could feel the warmth of his breath. And as he talked it was as if something inside him kept pushing, driving—yes, maybe even hurting. But surely she hadn't provoked such pain, Stacy thought, appalled. Not for a moment could she let herself believe that.

Still, she discovered that her hands held the arms of the lounge chair in an absolute death grip. "Look, Chris, I'm desperately sorry you had to live through all that," Stacy blurted. "I know it must have been very painful—"

"You're right—it was. And I sure didn't need to get shafted by a beautiful, fickle *bitch* in the bargain!"

Hurt pride. Enormous touchy ego. Obviously that was all this really amounted to, Stacy reassured herself. She heard their echoes in his cold, angry voice and felt goaded. "Well, at least you survived," she said, speaking with equal frostiness. "We both did—and I found your leaving every bit as painful as you found mine. Maybe someday I'll tell you just how it feels to be a girl who's been dumped, deserted and left in one hell of a—"

"What really went wrong?" he interrupted, his voice slicing through her own. "That's all I want to know. It's what I've waited thirteen years to ask you, and so far, Stacy, I don't like any of the answers I've heard. Lynn, Gary, Europe... It's like you're offering me a smorgasbord of—of excuses and saying, 'You need a reason? Okay, take your pick.' So why don't I believe you?"

Stacy welcomed his interruption. Hotheaded herself, she knew she'd been about to utter words she would bitterly regret. "I'm sorry you're disappointed, Chris, but I simply don't know what else to say. You left me that summer to go where you wanted and do what pleased you. Six weeks later you still hadn't even written me a decent letter and—and just about that time Gary drove over from Albuquerque to ask me to marry him. I figured you and Lynn were practically engaged by then."

His eyes narrowing in cool appraisal, Chris took a step back from Stacy and then another one, allowing her breathing space once again. "All right," he said heavily, and to her surprise, she realized he was apparently buying this explanation. He didn't like it—but at least he believed it, and that was the important thing. Grimly he turned away, his shoulders rigid.

Stacy gulped with relief. She'd always heard that if you had to tell a lie, you should keep it as close to the truth as possible. She'd just successfully tested the theory. Now all she had to do was get out of this chair and go back to the house. But with the pool inches away on her left and Chris standing at her right she would have to pass perilously close to him, risking the brush of his body against hers, to effect an escape.

"Do you need a hand up?"

To Stacy's surprise Chris had turned back. Somehow he had sensed her dilemma. She nodded, and his large masculine hand, a smooth one now with well-tended nails, reached down to her. "Thanks," she muttered. As he helped her up, Stacy felt her smaller hand swallowed by the heat and strength of his. The familiar touch triggered electric memories of all the ways he'd once touched her.

They stood scant inches apart, but still Chris didn't release Stacy's hand. Instead he used his grip to slowly draw her closer.

He wasn't—he couldn't be— But suddenly Stacy knew he was intent on kissing her. Shocked, she started to pull out of his grasp, but his other arm came around her, pinning her to him and crushing her breasts against the wide wall of his chest. Shakily Stacy turned her head away. But that just prompted Chris to force her chin up in his determined effort to reach her mouth.

"Please, Chris," Stacy gasped, her heart pounding so she could hear only a dull roar in her ears. Her mind was clouding, and she wondered dimly why it was she'd felt so sure she must resist.

But then Stacy knew why she'd struggled, as the still-familiar smell and feel of him crept back into her awareness. She inhaled Chris's clean, natural scent mingled with the light woodsy after-shave he'd always favored. And once again, after so very, very long, she felt the sinewy warmth of his length and hardness pressed to her and the hot velvet mouth gliding across her cheek. Abruptly Stacy descended from indignation and protest, into painful, fervent longing.

She felt Chris's lips moving remorselessly along her jaw until, with a sudden sound between a moan and a sob, Stacy turned her head, allowing their lips to meet.

As her mouth yielded to his, their combined heat ignited, glowing ever brighter, hotter, hungrier.

Why was she so surprised? one part of Stacy's mind inquired. With Chris there was always this intense sexual heat, as though a rapacious fire burned inside him, seeking to devour anything in its path. No wonder he'd frightened a few of the town's women so that they'd whispered later that he was dark and dangerous, desirable and sexy, all in the same breath. No wonder the serene Lynn Ashley had been taken aback by Chris at times, even though she'd adored him.

But Stacy had always been able to answer Chris's need with a matching fire of her own—so maybe she had been a lion tamer of sorts. She could always make Chris gasp and moan and utter soft inaudible sounds of longing and need. And she suspected he'd never quite forgiven her for possessing that power.

Well, right now, Stacy knew she would never forgive *him* for still making her respond in this old, unbridled way.

Flames ignited by his lips seared through her until her skin prickled deliciously. Automatically her arms slid up, circling and tightening on his neck. Oh, yes, her traitorous body remembered him well—too well.

Their lips clung, unwilling to part, as though time had been scrolled back—all the way back to their first deep, intimate kiss. For one more moment their lips rubbed, caressed, teased and tantalized in eager reacquaintance.

Then Chris stepped back and the spell was broken.

Stacy might have enjoyed the sound of his ragged breathing, except that her own wasn't any steadier. The rapid-fire rise and fall of her breasts testified to her own inner agitation—and her own arousal as well. Now was surely the time for sophistication—no, make that pseudo-sophistication, which was the best she could possibly manage with her senses still reeling and her heart pounding madly.

"What was that all about?" she asked as Chris turned away from her. Her voice sounded suitably light and amused although Stacy had never felt less like laughing.

"Just checking out old vibes."

His voice had swung back to its earlier coolness. At least the icy anger was gone, but Stacy wasn't sure that his faint air of triumph was any improvement.

She drew another breath, trying to halt the spinning feelings that continued to assail her, still trying to wish away desires that should never have been rekindled. "I don't appreciate your attempt to resurrect old vibes, Chris." Below the sophistication she heard a gratifying clink of steel. "I didn't come back to Louisiana for a few cheap thrills."

"Are you sure, Stacy? Then I guess you came to scoop up all the goodies Lynn left you." Chris swung back around to face her, his expression as inscrutable as a Buddha's.

Fury welled up in her, but Stacy sensed that Chris was still struggling to control his heated desires and turbulent emotions.

"Yes, I'm sure. And I don't deserve your dirty crack. If I were so eager for a few trinkets and antiques I wouldn't have waited almost six months to come!" she flared.

"You might have a point," he conceded with a reluctant ring of respect.

Despite his admission Stacy wasn't about to drop the matter. Give Chris Lorio an inch and he would always try to take the proverbial mile. "I want an apology," she demanded, thrusting her chin toward him belligerently.

"All right. You have my apologies," Chris replied promptly, but his voice sounded more distant with each word he uttered. As far as *he* was concerned the scene was over.

Not hardly, Stacy thought with determination. "I also want your assurance that this won't happen again. I don't want to worry about locking my bedroom door," she added firmly.

Chris flashed her a swift, surprised look that seemed to acknowledge that Stacy was much better at sparring with him than she used to be. Of course, Chris didn't know all the practice she'd had with the headstrong Taylor. Oh, yes, she thought grimly, little Stacy's had to learn to look out for herself.

"Well, Chris, I'm waiting," she snapped, "or else I'm leaving Louisiana tonight, oil leak or not."

"All right. You have my promise, Stacy," Chris replied.

She didn't dare delude herself and think she'd won. For some reason it suited Chris to yield to her . . . temporarily. "Thank you," she hissed between her teeth.

"Actually, I'm rather used to avoiding that particular bedroom door," Chris went on, speaking as casually as if he and Stacy hadn't just had words. "As you've probably gathered, Lynn and I had separate bedrooms during the last few years of our marriage."

"Oh, Chris, surely you're not trying to tell me that you, of all people, have been living without sex?" Stacy cried impetuously, the words uttered unthinkingly from genuine disbelief.

"That's exactly what I'm saying, if it's any of your business," Chris said tightly, his hands balled into fists at his sides. "There was no skirt chasing on my part. I wouldn't have had any cruel gossip get back to Lynn for anything on earth!" He paused, making an obvious and visible effort to hang onto his temper. "You don't need to worry that I'll batter down your bedroom door, Stacy. Brute force was never my style."

No, she thought, but artful seduction certainly was. Could she really arm herself against him, should Chris choose to exercise his considerable charm?

At least for the moment there seemed little danger that he would try, Stacy thought. Right now he was angry with her all over again, resenting the inference she'd made about his sexual nature. But, good Lord, she of all people should know how deep and hot his basic sensuality ran. How was she to know that, loving Lynn, he'd become a willing celibate?

She glanced up to find him still glowering at her, in foul temper indeed. She hadn't forgotten how Chris could run hot one moment, cool the next. It was all part of his elusive, enigmatic appeal.

But that appeal had been to a young, immature and inexperienced girl, Stacy assured herself desperately. She wasn't vulnerable to Chris Lorio any longer—or so she silently repeated to herself as she walked rapidly back to the house through the softly fragrant night.

Chapter Three

Good morning, Miss Stacy!"

"Good morning, Robbie." Stacy forced a smile to her lips even as she glanced warily around the large clean kitchen. Then she relaxed a little; apparently she and Robbie were alone.

"I'll bet you'd like a cup of coffee," Robbie said, jumping up from his chair at the breakfast table.

"Yes, that would be nice," Stacy agreed. She'd slept poorly and now had a wisp of a headache to show for her restlessness.

"I knew you would 'cause Daddy always wants coffee first thing, too. And he never likes to talk much in the morning." As Robbie spoke he led Stacy across the kitchen to the utility area. There, on the counter by the sink, stood an automatic drip assembly with a pot half full of fresh-smelling coffee. Its aroma wafted deliciously toward Stacy.

"Where are the—?" she began.

"Cups? Right here." Robbie went up on tiptoes to open a cabinet, then reached even higher to extract a mug for Stacy. "Do you want cream or sugar?"

She shook her head. "Just black."

Robbie poured the coffee for her, and Stacy took it gratefully. After a couple of sips she began to feel a little more human.

"You want breakfast, Miss Stacy? I can fix it," Robbie offered.

Hunger was the last thing Stacy was feeling right now. She shook her head emphatically, adding, "Thanks, though, Robbie."

He led the way back to the table where Stacy took a chair opposite his. Only then did she notice a crumpled paper napkin at that place, as well as an empty coffee mug, twin to her own.

"Oh, I seem to be in your father's seat," she said, awakening to the scene around her.

"He's gone." Robbie reached over and dropped the used napkin into the empty mug, then moved both items out of Stacy's way.

"Chris has left already?" Stacy asked, seeking verification.

"Yes, ma'am. Daddy likes to get to work before everybody else. He says he gets more done the first hour than the whole rest of the day. See, at nine the phones start ringing and clients come in and his secretary starts asking him questions."

"Yes, I see," Stacy said, studying Robbie over the rim of her mug. His clothes were almost identical to the ones he'd worn yesterday except that his jeans were noticeably faded and his knit shirt was blue and had a small hole on the shoulder. These clearly were play clothes.

Robbie is going to be a good-looking young man one day, Stacy found herself thinking. He's such a handsome child now.

Yesterday she'd seen his insecurities, his vulnerabilities—and had been struck by his resemblance to his mother.

But today he seemed more Chris's child, knowledgeable and independent. Or was she just making those comparisons because she still had Chris on her mind?

The moonlight scene with Chris had been hard to forget, she admitted, although she'd certainly tried. She'd had trouble falling asleep, and even after that she had started awake frequently, troubled by each unfamiliar creak or strange night noise, of which Louisiana supplied plenty to bedevil her desert-oriented ears.

Mostly she had been troubled by the undeniably strong physical response Chris had aroused in her, in spite of the fact that she found him something less than likable. Although his concern for Robbie was reassuring, his lingering bitterness and anger toward Stacy masked any clear picture of the man he'd become.

But beyond last night's overt hostility, by demanding that she believe he had been Lynn's faithful husband Chris had unwittingly revealed something else: that it had been a long time since he'd had a woman, and like it or not, he was hungry for one. Stacy found that knowledge more troubling than she liked to admit. And she knew part of her problem was that it had been a long time for her, too, since she'd shared her bed. Chris's kiss had reminded her of that quite painfully last night.

Suddenly Robbie laughed. "Miss Stacy, you look like you're miles away."

"I'm sorry, Robbie." Instantly she was contrite. "Tell me what you plan to do today. And, by the way, why don't you call me just plain Stacy?"

"Thanks," Robbie said, looking relieved at being able to drop the Southern courtesy. "I guess I'll just do what I always do. Ted'll come over and we'll probably play up in our tree house until it gets real hot. Then I'll swim—Ted just splashes in the shallow water. Preston tells us when it's time to get out. What're you going to do today, Stacy?"

"I suppose I'll get started with my work," she said gently and saw Robbie duck his head back down to his cereal bowl. "I hope you don't mind, Robbie."

"No. I understand . . . now that Daddy 'splained it," the child assured her quietly.

Good, Stacy thought and reflected that if she'd gone to bed last night with Chris on her mind she had certainly awakened this morning thinking of Lynn.

Part of it was simply sleeping in Lynn's room, of course, being surrounded by her possessions as well as the faint lingering fragrance of gardenias, Lynn's favorite perfume. When Stacy had first awakened this morning, to the chatter of birds in the trees outside her windows, she had seen a grayish mist filling the room. Immediately she had jerked bolt upright in bed while frightening thoughts of ghosts had superstitiously flooded her mind. Then she'd realized that by turning off her room air-conditioner and leaving her windows wide open to the night air and nocturnal sounds, she had invited the early morning haze, natural to humid South Louisiana, to drift inside.

Cousin Lynn is not back to haunt me or anyone else, Stacy had thought as she'd stumbled out of bed to close the windows and turn on the refrigerated air. When she awoke next, an hour later, the sun was up over the horizon and the eerie mist had cleared from the room.

Now, as Stacy looked across the table at Robbie, her thoughts took a different direction. "Where are Miriam and Preston today?" she asked.

"Oh, they'll be here soon," the child replied casually. "They tend to things in their own apartment first. It's here at the back of the house, y'know. Anyway, Daddy and I are used to getting our own breakfast. Can I fix you some now, Stacy?" Robbie ended on a coaxing note.

"I don't—" Stacy stopped, seeing the disappointment forming in Robbie's eyes. "All right—but something light."

"Toast," Robbie decided, "and juice."

He wouldn't let Stacy help him, moving confidently from the refrigerator to the table with butter, marmalade and a pitcher of cranberry juice. He refilled her coffee cup, then dropped two pieces of bread into the toaster.

"You like toast light or dark?" he asked.

"About medium, I guess," Stacy replied, watching Robbie in amazement. Taylor might be four years older than Robbie, but he was used to his mother setting all meals before him. Of course, a kitchen was scarcely Taylor's milieu.

"How long have you been fixing your own breakfast, Robbie?" Stacy asked curiously.

"Long as I can remember," he said matter-of-factly. He reached for the toast as it popped up and began to butter it. "My mom never felt good, you know. So Daddy and I always fixed her juice and tea and toast and took her up a tray. Then we'd get our own breakfast. On weekends Daddy fixes omelets or waffles, but he doesn't have time other days."

"I see." Stacy nodded as the picture of the household's workings gradually began to take shape in her mind.

"When I was real little I couldn't help," Robbie went on, seemingly enjoying the chance to confide in Stacy. "So Daddy would tell me to go pick a flower for Mommy. We *always* put a flower on her tray."

"How lovely," Stacy said softly and wondered how it would feel to be loved like that. She didn't know. She'd had no such experience at being a cherished wife—her honeymoon with Gary had scarcely ended before his resentment of her swelling stomach had begun.

Of course, Taylor loved her. But he'd always been such an independent kid that Stacy sometimes felt almost like any mother would have suited him just fine.

Now Robbie rose and carried his dishes to the sink. There he rinsed them and stacked them neatly in the empty dishwasher. Stacy watched him in absolute fascination. She always went through pure almighty hell just getting Taylor not to wreck the place!

"You need anything else, Stacy?" Robbie asked her, turning from the dishwasher.

"No, dear, I'm fine," she smiled. "The toast is delicious. Thanks again."

He smiled with pleasure. "I'll be in my room. I'm reading a neat book Daddy gave me. It's all about the first men who learned to fly airplanes. They were the Wright brothers."

"Sounds interesting," Stacy said, smiling back at the boy.

"Yeah. But I get tired of reading books pretty fast. It's too much like school. Anyway, Ted oughta be over soon." Robbie's smile became a sigh. "What a nerd!"

After Robbie left, Stacy got herself a final cup of coffee. She sipped it slowly as she considered how to begin removing and sorting Lynn's possessions. Empty the drawers first, Stacy concluded, then she'd have space to put any items she decided to keep. Tackle the closets next— A timid knock on the back door interrupted Stacy's reverie. She arose from the table, casting a wry look at the casual peppermint-striped duster she'd thrown on earlier. Of course, she'd intended just to grab a cup of coffee and flee right back to her room. She hadn't known she and Robbie would get into a conversation or that he'd practically insist on her eating breakfast. Now Stacy had to confront whoever it was with a face bare of makeup and hair that had received only a cursory brushing.

Fortunately it was only eight-year-old Ted.

After Robbie's description, Stacy was primed to recognize the neighboring boy immediately. Ted was slight, with nondescript hair and coloring. In addition to being cursed with a timid manner, his ears and front teeth appeared too large for the rest of his features.

In a shy, reedy voice he asked for Robbie.

Stacy introduced herself and told Ted that Robbie was upstairs in his room. "He's expecting you, Ted," she added, trying to make her manner friendly and welcoming. Robbie was right, Ted did seem to be afraid of everything, Stacy thought as the boy allowed her only a tiny half-smile before scurrying past her and dashing for the staircase.

Stacy then followed Robbie's example by carrying her dishes over to the sink, where she rinsed them and tucked them out of sight in the dishwasher before heading upstairs to shower, shampoo and dress. Her first full day back in Langlois, Louisiana had begun.

* * *

She hadn't realized it would be quite so painful, Stacy thought, working steadily to ignore the lump in her throat. She looked up at Miriam with relief, welcoming the older woman's luncheon summons after several hours of diligently sorting clothes.

"It's hard, isn't it, Miz Thomasson," Miriam said sympathetically. Her broad, plain, middle-aged face reflected her own still-lingering sorrow.

"Yes," Stacy said, rising from the carpet and an ever-growing pile of lacy lingerie.

"You keeping those?" Miriam asked curiously, pointing to the heap.

"No. I couldn't—not someone else's intimate attire," Stacy said.

"But a lot of those things haven't even been worn," Miriam said economically.

"Yes, I'd noticed," Stacy agreed. Then, since an explanation stronger than tender sensibilities was apparently called for, at least in Miriam's practical opinion, she added, "I checked the sizes. They're too small for me."

"Hmm...that's probably true," Miriam said after a moment's reflection. "Miss Lynn was mighty thin along toward the last."

Stacy pushed her hair back from her face. She didn't want to hear about the last. In fact, she wanted a break from everything associated with death and dying. "What's for lunch?" she asked, guessing from Miriam's ample proportions that the housekeeper liked not only to cook, but to eat as well.

"I figured you'd like something cool," Miriam replied, "so it's chicken salad stuffed in a big ol' tomato with melba toast and iced tea."

"Sounds wonderful," Stacy said, then she frowned slightly. "But will Robbie eat that sort of thing?"

"Sakes alive, how'd you know that?" Miriam exclaimed in surprise. "No, for Master Robbie I've fixed just plain sandwiches and potato chips."

"Well, I know a bit about growing boys." Stacy smiled, following Miriam out of the room.

"Guess you would, for a fact," the housekeeper nodded.

"Will Ted Thackery be staying for lunch?" Stacy asked as they started down the stairs.

"No, that little pest goes home at noon every day. His mama insists on it. After lunch she makes Ted lie down and rest for a while." Miriam shrugged her broad shoulders. "At least it gives us a break from him, though most afternoons Ted comes wandering right back. Robbie got tired of Ted the first week school was out. But he's a lonely little boy with his mama gone, bless her sweet soul."

Stacy frowned. "Robbie shouldn't be spending all of his time with Ted. He needs other playmates." Then she glanced anxiously at the housekeeper, hoping her critical comment wouldn't be carried straight back to Chris. To Stacy's relief Miriam nodded fervently.

"Yes, he does," the older woman agreed. "I've tried to tell Mr. Lorio, but he just kind of brushes me off. Oh, not that he's uninterested or anything," Miriam added hastily, as if fearing that she was being too critical now. "Mr. Lorio thinks the sun rises and sets on that child! But . . . well, I don't think Mr. Lorio's ever been too sociable himself. I'm not sure he even knows what it's like to be young and lonely. But Robbie's different."

Yes, he is, Stacy silently agreed as Miriam led her out onto the shady patio. What a shame Taylor and Robbie can't trade places for the summer, she thought. Robbie would dearly love camp and the companionship of other boys, and my own little lone wolf would adore unlimited access to a pool and a tree house!

"Robbie, you c'mon and eat lunch with your cousin Stacy," Miriam called. She motioned for Stacy to sit at an outdoor table where two places were set with brightly colored stoneware and large fabric napkins.

What a charming oasis of peace and quiet this was, Stacy thought, glancing around the patio. Squirrels scampered up and down trees, watched over by a fat, lazy orange cat who sat swishing his tail.

There were numerous large flowerpots set around the patio containing various plants in bloom—white caladiums, lavender chrysanthemums, daisies, sweet peas, tulips, peonies and geraniums. Curiously Stacy studied the attractive pottery, which looked Mexican. Lynn and Chris had spent a lot of time in Mexico, usually visiting Lynn's parents; Stacy wondered if they'd brought the pottery from their various trips.

After a moment Robbie appeared barefoot, his swimsuit dripping and his brown hair slicked against his skull. He snatched up a towel and dried himself hastily before sliding into the chair opposite Stacy's.

"Are you gonna eat that big tomato?" he asked, his nose crinkling with disdain as he regarded Stacy's salad plate.

"I sure am," Stacy said. "Why, this tomato is vine ripe and very tasty."

"Yeah, I know. Preston grows 'em. He's always watering and tying up his tomato plants while he watches me swim. But I don't like tomatoes."

Once again Stacy spoke before she thought. "Neither does Taylor," she said absently.

"That ought to do it, Janice," Chris told his long-time secretary. "Just retype those first couple of pages and then Barney can take that petition over to the courthouse to be filed."

"I don't retype anymore. I simply key in the corrections and hit Print," said Janice Clayton with a grin. "I sure do love that word-processing system you bought me, boss!"

"Glad you're pleased," Chris said, leaning back in his executive swivel chair and watching as Janice scooped up the contents of his Out basket.

Now was not the time to remind her of how vehemently she'd fought the installation of the system four short months ago. Since Janice had always resisted anything involving computers, Chris had simply had the machine and software delivered while Janice was away on vacation. Although there'd been a brief stormy scene upon her return, when faced with an accomplished fact Janice had adjusted and learned to use the equipment she'd initially despised. For a young person she often displayed an older person's resistance to change, Chris mused.

On the other hand, Janice at twenty-six had certain ideas that were entirely modern and up-to-date. After Lynn had died Janice had expressed her sympathy in a matter-of-fact manner.

"Chris, I know how difficult it must be. If there's anything I can do for you—"

At the time he'd been hearing those same trite words so often that he'd cut tiredly through the flow. "Thank you, Janice."

"I mean *anything* at all." At her emphasis his head jerked up, and for a moment, their eyes met—hers communicating an unmistakable message, and Chris's receiving and digesting it.

He had deliberately pretended to misunderstand. "Thank you, Janice. Everyone has been very kind. I knew Lynn had a world of friends, but I didn't know quite how many."

He'd left the choice to back down, shut up and continue to work as his secretary up to Janice. If she'd persisted with overtures, Chris would have terminated her without regret. Only a damn fool mixed a professional relationship with a personal one, in his opinion.

Janice had understood. Probably she knew, too, that nowhere else in a town the size of Langlois was she likely to earn the salary that Chris paid her, and she had Barney, her mildly retarded brother, to help support. To Chris's relief any resulting tension between Janice and him had soon been buried in the mundane details of everyday office life, and their squabble over Chris's determination to upgrade to modern word processing had provided a welcome diversion.

Now, as Chris watched Janice move around his office, picking up two files he'd left atop a bookcase and straightening a picture frame hanging on the wall, he was suddenly struck for the first time by a subtle resemblance she bore to Stacy.

Janice wasn't as pretty as Stacy, but her features were pleasant. She had thick, straight red-brown hair and the same slender, leggy type of figure. Both women moved with a quick grace.

Well, well, Chris thought in something like surprise. Twice in the past two days he'd gotten a new and unexpected insight into himself.

Last night, by the swimming pool, he had discovered that he was still very bitterly angry with Stacy for jilting him thirteen years ago. His anger might be outdated and completely inappropriate, given the circumstances, but there it was. He still hadn't gotten over his rage at her. Perhaps he never would.

Equally ridiculous was the deep, unexpected attraction to her he'd felt last night. And whenever he thought about that kiss— For the first time Chris could understand people who felt so stricken with embarrassment that they dropped their head into their hands and groaned with regret. Today he was that same self-reproachful figure. What in the world had prompted him to kiss Stacy as he had?

And what in the world was he going to say when he went home from work and saw her tonight? Should he pretend the scene had never happened? Apologize for it more sincerely? Or try to take his cues from her?

Chris scowled. The two latter ideas, groveling in remorse or taking his cues from someone else, had never held much appeal for him.

"Whoops, boss, if you're going to glower like that I think I'd better go to lunch." Janice spoke lightly as she turned toward the door.

"Sure, go on," Chris said agreeably. "Oh, say, I don't suppose I've had any clients cancel their appointments?"

"No such luck. Mrs. Ethan should be here any minute."

"Okay." Chris sighed. "Have Barney bring me something to eat when he gets time."

"Sure thing. Oh—I was about to forget. While you were conferring with Mr. Turner and his daughter, Floyd at the body shop called. That repair bill on your relative's car is going to be a humdinger. Floyd wants to talk to you about it."

"I'll give him a call. Thanks," Chris added as the door closed behind her.

He'd hired Janice when she was just eighteen and straight out of business school. It was an obvious mistake, Knox Kinard and other older attorneys in the law firm had thought, since a man like Chris—already burdened with a sick wife and a small child—clearly needed an efficient, mature and experienced legal secretary.

But Chris had elected to stick with Janice. She was particularly motivated to succeed because of Barney's needs as well as her own. Chris admired her loyalty and had utilized Barney's ability to run simple errands, for which Chris had generously overpaid him. It had taken Chris a while to train Janice, true, but then he'd had exactly the sort of secretary he'd wanted. By the time Chris had been ready to leave Bainbridge and Kinard to establish his own firm, Janice was ready for the big leap, too.

Now, for the first time, Chris admitted that maybe there had been another reason he'd hired her eight years ago.... Because, in a few small ways at least, Janice had reminded him of Stacy.

"Did you know my mother for a long time, Stacy?"

Luncheon was over. Stacy and Robbie were in Lynn's room, seated on the carpet, where Stacy continued to work, under the child's steady scrutiny.

At least Robbie's questions provoked gentler memories she didn't resist recalling. Stacy could deal with these less complicated images of Lynn. "Well, let's see, Robbie. I must have known your mother for thirty years," she said, shaking out a nightgown and matching peignoir. She dropped the frilly nightclothes into her steadily growing pile of things to be donated to either Goodwill or the Salvation Army.

"Thirty years!" Robbie exclaimed, as if it was at least a century.

"Well, I don't remember much about our first few years," Stacy explained with a smile. "I was too young. But Lynn and I were both born here in Langlois, though my folks moved to New Mexico when I was just two."

"Who was oldest?"

"Your mother was older by four years," Stacy explained, reaching for another peignoir, another matching nightgown. "She'd been wanting a baby sister, but her parents just wouldn't oblige so she sort of adopted me, everyone says."

"And y'all were cousins?" Robbie asked curiously.

"Yes. Lynn's mother and mine were first cousins and had been friends before us. But Aunt Ruth—she wasn't really my aunt but that's what I always called her—was super smart and really liked books and studies. My mother said that everyone was afraid Aunt Ruth would be an old maid. Instead she met William Ashley at college and married him. Mother always said Ruth sure had the last laugh since Bill had plenty of money and a whole string of college degrees."

"That's my grandparents, right?"

"Right," Stacy confirmed. "My own folks weren't nearly as prosperous or well-educated. They married straight out of high school and had a whole passel of kids they could barely feed. That's why they moved west. In New Mexico Dad got a better job as a mechanic on an Army base—at least till the base shut down. After that my family was in hot water all over again."

"If Mom lived here and you were way out in New Mexico, how did you stay friends?" Robbie asked curiously. One of his small brown hands trailed idly through the lace on a peignoir of his mother's.

"Well, Lynn used to come and visit us in New Mexico. That's because her parents were archaeologists and often off on digs, especially during the summer when they could get students to help them. Aunt Ruth and Uncle Bill thought the dry climate in New Mexico was better for Lynn anyway. So she'd spend most of the summer with us, and she and I always shared the same bedroom. My little sister would move out so Lynn could have the other twin bed," Stacy related.

"Uh-huh," said Robbie, his hand now stroking a silken gown.

"I think Lynn always liked being just one of the kids," Stacy finished.

"I would!" Robbie said fervently. "I sure would like a brother."

"What's wrong with a sister?" Stacy asked, finding stockings to add to her pile.

"Ted has a baby sister, and he hates her," Robbie informed Stacy. "But I think I'd rather have even a sister than nobody at all."

"Well, there are disadvantages as well as advantages to being one of a big family," Stacy pointed out. "Since I had two older sisters all my clothes were hand-me-downs. I used to dream of having a brand-new dress that no one else had ever worn before. Oh—and a room to myself. That seemed like the height of luxury. Or living in a house that had more than one bathroom. When I was growing up someone was always banging on the bathroom door, wanting to get in."

"Well, I guess that's still better'n what Daddy had. He said he and Bonnie Lorio used a privy. You know what that is, Stacy?" Robbie asked.

"Yes, I know," said Stacy, smothering a smile.

"An' they didn't have any running water at all. They caught water in a rain barrel. And Daddy says there were always bugs and mosquitoes in the water. That's why he moved out soon's he got to be sixteen and had a job at a gas station. He moved to a boarding house, he said. But you know what? He tried to make ol' Bonnie move, too, but she wouldn't! She stayed right there in her shack without any good water or anything until Daddy says she drank herself to death."

Robbie related Bonnie Lorio's sad demise without senti-
mentality, although Stacy was quietly appalled. She'd
known, of course, that Chris's early life had been filled with
deprivations, but he'd never revealed to her that they were
quite so extreme. And why had he told such sordid details
to his child?

Of course, every kid always asked, "What was it like
when you were growing up, Daddy?" followed by an endless set of questions.

Unbidden, Chris's words from the previous night drifted
back to Stacy: *I didn't need to get shafted by a beautiful,
fickle bitch.*

Remembering them made Stacy wince now, just as she
had last night. If Chris had been truthful with Robbie—and
she'd never known him not to be truthful—she was now
better able to appreciate why he'd uttered such scathing
words, however untrue and inappropriately timed they'd
been.

"Master Robbie!"

Miriam's indignant voice from the doorway swung both
Stacy and Robbie around. "Yes?" Robbie said.

"Go get out of those wet swim trunks right now!" Miriam commanded. "You take a shower and wash your hair
and put on clean proper clothes, do you hear?"

"Okay," Robbie said agreeably, hopping up from the soft
beige carpet. "But I'm not really wet anymore, Miriam. I
got dry when Stacy and I were eating lunch on the patio."

"I don't care! You know your daddy would have a fit if
he came home and saw you—"

"All right, I'm going," Robbie said. "Bye, Stacy."

"See you later, Robbie," Stacy called after him.

"That child!" exclaimed Miriam, her hands on her ample hips as she stared after him. Then she turned back to
Stacy with a rueful smile. "I guess he's just a typical boy."

"He seems like it to me," Stacy said diplomatically. She
wanted to be careful not to take sides on anything since she
would be in the heart of the Lorio family for so short a time.

"Well, I don't know about boys," Miriam went on. "I had a couple of girls myself. And Master Robbie pulls stuff that girls never even thought of doing!"

Miriam spelled out an aggrieved tale of finding garter snakes in the pockets of discarded jeans, a dead frog preserved in the freezer for show and tell, a pail of water in which minnows swam left on the porch for *anybody* to flounder into. Robbie's further sins included scarred and scuffed floors, mud tracked over a just-waxed kitchen floor and pebbles and seashells washed in the dishwasher. As for his bedroom—

"I finally told Mr. Lorio I wouldn't go in there anymore. No ma'am, I'm scared to. No telling what's going to come wiggling out to bite me!"

"Yes, he's a typical boy," Stacy said wryly. "I've had two brothers as well as a son. Believe me, they all feel called on to capture wildlife. There are some horrible critters in the West, too. Rattlesnakes and Gila monsters and scorpions, not to mention a hundred or more varieties of cactus."

"That's why I'll take girls any time! Oh, I wanted to give you a couple of phone messages, Miss Stacy."

"I've had phone calls?" Stacy asked, jumping up quickly. "Is my son—" Her earlier bad feeling about Taylor came surging back.

"Oh, no, ma'am, nothing long distance to worry about. First, Mrs. Thackery—that's Ted's mother—called to welcome you, she said. Also said she'd drop over this afternoon about four. That means she'll bring along something to eat," Miriam added wisely. "Usually it's cookies or cake. She's a pretty fair cake maker."

"Thanks for telling me." Stacy gestured to the shorts and halter top she wore. "I'll want to change into nicer clothes."

"Just wear slacks," Miriam advised.

"And the other call?" Stacy inquired.

"Oh, that was Mr. Lorio. He didn't want me to interrupt you. It's something about fixing a bunch of things on your car. He'll have all the details when he comes home this afternoon."

Stacy gave a soft moan. What would fixing "a bunch of things" entail? she wondered. More to the point, what would it cost?

All at once she felt drained and unbelievably weary. When Miriam left, Stacy stretched out on Lynn's double bed, intending only to rest for a moment. Instead, the next thing she knew she'd slept for almost an hour and she had to fly to be ready by the time Mrs. Thackery arrived.

"Just call me Betty," Mrs. Thackery insisted after Miriam had shown her into the formal living room where Stacy, dressed casually yet neatly, stood waiting.

"It's nice to meet you, Betty," Stacy said and offered up her own first name as well. "Won't you have a seat?"

"Well, I really can't stay but a minute. I just wanted to bring you a cake and say hello."

"The cake looks wonderful," Stacy said politely. Actually a Dutch chocolate cake with thick fudge icing seemed too heavy a dessert in such hot and humid weather. More truthfully Stacy added, "I'm sure the men will enjoy it."

Betty Thackery gave her a conspiratorial wink. "I've never met a man yet who didn't like chocolate, have you?" Without waiting for an answer she hurried on. "My, but I was surprised when Ted told me that a pretty lady with dark red hair had moved in at Mr. Lorio's."

Stacy frowned, not knowing if Betty was being deliberately snide or if she'd just made a careless choice of words. Stacy darted a wary look in the woman's direction but was unable to read anything from Betty's face with its all-too-ordinary features.

There was certainly a resemblance between Ted and his mother, Stacy thought privately. Betty had the same nondescript coloring usually described as a "dishwater blonde," and a similar round-shouldered figure.

"I am the late *Mrs.* Lorio's cousin," Stacy emphasized stiffly and then explained her mission in Langlois.

"Oh—so Lynn wanted you to come here," Betty Thackery mused.

"Yes, she did," Stacy said, her voice still tight. She had Betty pegged now. She was the neighborhood gossip—maybe the town crier as well. Betty was the type who reveled in bad news and especially relished anything of a faintly scandalous nature.

While Miriam served them soft drinks over ice, Stacy talked on, relating her whole long association with Lynn.

"I swear that dear woman was a saint." Betty sighed. "I used to visit her often, and I always came away inspired. Such a lovely, lovely soul."

"Yes, Lynn was wonderful," Stacy agreed. But a saint? That, she thought, was a bit much. Her lips twisted as she tried to control her sudden impulse to smile. Lynn, who'd always had a good sense of humor, would probably have roared at hearing herself proclaimed divine.

"I used to wonder how that sweet little thing could put up with Chris." Betty sighed.

"Chris?" said Stacy, startled. "What do you mean?"

"Oh, just that he's such a cynic, my dear. I'm afraid his strange early life left him very callous and uncaring."

"In exactly what way?" Stacy probed, and enjoyed seeing the woman trying to justify her put-down.

"Well, for instance, I don't think he's sent that poor little Robbie to church one single time since Lynn died. And I know for a fact that she wanted Robbie to attend. He's always enjoyed Sunday school, too. But Chris is no more interested in his son's religious instruction than a pagan. I also know that the parson's wife—Mrs. Glover, her name is—has been very disturbed over the situation."

Betty Thackery paused, looking at Stacy expectantly.

Clearly she was being enlisted in a cause. "I'll speak to Chris about it," Stacy said coolly, making certain that her words promised absolutely nothing.

"I hope he'll listen to you, dear." Betty Thackery flashed Stacy another sly smile and rose, glancing around for a place to set down her glass. "I really must go now. My baby will be waking up from her nap, and I don't like to leave her with

the hired help for very long. The only people you can get
nowadays are so dreadfully undependable.''

Stacy would have liked to think that the kindly and efficient Miriam, who was out in the hallway dusting, had not
overheard those derisive words. But she doubted it.

No sooner had Betty made her welcome departure when
Robbie came bounding down the stairs.

"Daddy oughta be home soon," he crowed happily to
Stacy, and she realized with a sudden pang that Chris's arrival was the highlight of the child's day.

Then at the thought of seeing Chris again, the sinking
sensation returned to Stacy's stomach to war with her
equally intense sense of anticipation—quixotic feelings
warning Stacy that Chris was still capable of casting his
contradictory spell.

Chapter Four

Chris was tugging at his paisley tie, trying to loosen its knot, as he entered the house. With his wheat-colored suit coat slung over his arm and his thick black hair in tousled disarray, he looked treacherously handsome, Stacy noted.

"My God, what a day," he said by way of greeting to Stacy, Robbie and Miriam, gradually unknotting the stubborn tie.

"Are you tired, Daddy?" Robbie asked him solicitously.

"Tired doesn't begin to hack it, sport. Wiped out is more like it. I had wall-to-wall clients." One large hand touched Robbie's head as Chris rumpled his son's hair into an amusing replica of his own. "It's been a hectic day, an unbelievable week and a hell of a month. Right now I need a long swim, something cold and wet to drink and then a hot shower."

The collar of Chris's pale blue shirt was the next clothing casualty as he tore open the top two buttons. "Miriam, could you serve dinner twenty minutes later than usual?" he asked. Stacy heard the pleasantly delivered order behind the seemingly polite request.

Miriam nodded resignedly. At last, Chris's eyes swung to Stacy.

She felt as if her whole body flushed beneath his probing, black-eyed gaze. Not that it was insolent in any way—on the contrary, Chris's expression as he gazed down at her was so controlled and courteous that Stacy wondered at her reaction. Maybe it was her own awareness that her clothes concealed nothing from him—he'd seen years earlier what decorum now kept her hiding so modestly. Or perhaps it was her memory of the time spent in his arms last night . . . of their surprisingly passionate kiss . . .

"Good afternoon, Stacy," Chris said quietly. "Have you had a good day?"

She shrugged. "It went well enough, I suppose. Miriam said you'd had some word on my car?"

"Yes. Let's discuss it a little later, if you don't mind," Chris suggested, and Stacy had no option but to agree. She was no more in control here than Miriam. Both of them had to obey Chris's courteously phrased but very definite orders.

"Is it . . . bad?" she asked Chris nervously.

"Well, it's not exactly good—but it could be worse."

Spoken like a true lawyer, Stacy thought, since the comment told her exactly nothing.

"I'll go swimming with you, Daddy!" Robbie offered eagerly.

Chris hesitated, and for a moment Stacy felt as if she could peer inside his mind. Right now he needed peace and quiet, a few minutes alone to rewind and regroup. But as Stacy watched Chris made himself smile at Robbie.

"Great, sport. Go find my bathing trunks, will you? And climb back in your own."

"Okay," Robbie said excitedly, starting up the stairs. Then he paused to glance back at Stacy. "You come swim, too, Stacy!" he urged.

"Thank you, Robbie," she began, "but I don't think—"

"Yes, do," Chris cut in smoothly. "We'll enjoy having you."

Stacy knew immediately what he really meant. Her presence might deflect some of Robbie's attention from his world-weary father. Actually a swim did sound appealing. "Thank you, I will," she agreed.

Stacy had started to follow Robbie up the wide curving staircase when she overheard Miriam telling Chris that Mrs. Thackery had dropped by with a chocolate cake.

"Came to case the situation, I suppose," Chris said tiredly. Then to Stacy he added, "So you've met Betty. Odious woman, isn't she?"

Despite herself Stacy couldn't help smiling, and she and Chris fell into step together as they went up the stairs. "Yes, she is," Stacy agreed.

"I guess Betty grilled you like a detective?" he inquired.

"No. I gave up before she could start the third degree and told her my whole life's story in lengthy, boring detail," Stacy volunteered.

Chris suddenly shot her a swift amused look. "Not all of it, I hope!"

Flabbergasted, Stacy stopped and stared at him. But as Chris walked on without further comment she concluded that he'd meant nothing serious by the remark. It was just the sort of light, humorous thing adults said to each other all the time. He wasn't really alluding to their own long-ago relationship, was he?

She couldn't read him on this as she had when she'd understood his bone-deep weariness. Once again Chris defied her best guess. Shrugging, Stacy went into her bedroom where she drew out her least-favorite bathing suit.

In a season of skimpy suits Stacy's was practically matronly—dark, one-piece and flatteringly cut to emphasize her waist, which was still quite slender, but deemphasize her feminine hips and thighs, which had always been a little too rounded to suit her.

Even in the modest suit, though, Stacy felt almost naked when she thought of the sweeping scrutiny of Chris's knowing eyes. Once upon a time his gaze had swept her boldly, smolderingly, undressing her inch by inch as if it were his absolute right. Even though he didn't look at her like that now, Stacy felt sure she would remember and be self-conscious.

She snatched up a thick beach towel, which she draped saronglike around her waist, then stepped into sandals. Last she scooped her thick hair into a ponytail, secured it with a rubber band and dashed back downstairs before she could lose her nerve.

The pool...and Chris... But she wouldn't let herself think about that or about those two young lovers left far back in time. Not now. Anyway, it would all be quite different in full daylight with Robbie popping up between them, she thought.

Ever since she'd been back here a part of her kept wanting to remember, Stacy realized, even as another, stronger part tried desperately to forget. That's how badly she'd been hurt once by things that no teenager had ever expected to cause pain: summer, moon glow and, most of all, love.

Chris finished his laps and drew himself up, dripping and panting, onto the sun-warmed apron of the pool. For a minute or two he concentrated on steadying his breathing, then he glanced down to mid-pool where Stacy had earlier demonstrated a surface dive to Robbie; the boy was now practicing with all his might to duplicate her feat.

Momentarily Chris felt grateful to Stacy for keeping his son entertained. She'd been a swimming instructor years ago so she definitely knew her business. And this instruction had brought Chris a little time to relax.

Chris still marveled at how damned tired and tense a man could get just sitting in his office handling other people's problems all day. Mental activity wore him out in a way that physical activity never had. He grinned involuntarily at the sudden thought of what the town would say if he abandoned the practice of law to run a service station again.

That's how he'd put himself through college and law school, pumping gas, hand washing cars, changing and fixing flat tires. That sort of work had never tired him like this. On the other hand, Chris knew it had also nearly killed him with boredom and that he would miss the challenge of law if he ever gave it up. Fortunately there really weren't too many days like today.

His energy returning in a slow, gradual wave, Chris rose and walked over to the poolside table, where he dropped into one of the shady chairs beneath the umbrella. He reached into an ice bucket and a second later ripped the tab off a can of light beer, took a long gulp and shuddered. He couldn't imagine how anyone could make a career out of drinking this stuff.

But Bonnie Lorio had certainly given it her best shot. Her face rose up before him—not the wrinkled parchment of her later years, but Bonnie as Chris had known her when he'd been young. Blowzy and plump, Bonnie had dark hair, always mussed, and her fire-engine red lipstick was usually smudged. She'd had some Indian blood, reflected in her high cheekbones and the slightly bronze cast of her skin. Her brown eyes, bloodshot and glazed when she was drinking, had always been kindly on those rare occasions when she was sober.

Bonnie had never really been able to give Chris much care since she hadn't even managed to look after herself properly. Still, in her way, Bonnie had loved the child, and Chris had loved her, too, even as the town wailed that he was growing up wild, undisciplined and probably even undernourished. But when a kid knew he really mattered to somebody he could survive and even thrive on a diet of Cokes, potato chips and canned beans.

When Chris had heard for the first time that Bonnie was not his "real" mother, he had totally disbelieved the story. Even Bonnie's own confirmation hadn't convinced Chris, especially since she'd had so few other details to provide. She'd always said that she'd answered a knock at her door late one night and a man's deep voice had asked her to step

outside but not turn around. He'd said he had twenty dollars to give her just for listening.

"So I did what he said," Bonnie had always related. "I
heard him out. Heard that there was a lady who'd had a
baby she didn't want her family and friends to know about.
But she did care about the baby and wanted to be able to
keep an eye on him as he grew up. So she'd asked this man
to help her find someone close by to keep the kid. And the
only one they could think of was me.

"Well, he told me he'd mail me two hundred dollars every
month just to keep the baby, and I thought I'd gotten rich
for sure! I said yes, I'd do it, so the man told me I'd have to
knock off the drinking for a while and keep my nose pretty
clean till the baby got bigger 'cause he was awful little now.
Then the man told me to go back inside the house and not
come out until I'd heard his car drive off. So I did just like
that gentleman said—and, my, he was a fancy fellow with a
real famous-sounding voice. When I came out again, there
you were, lying in a basket on the porch, sound asleep."

Even at the age of seven, when he'd first heard this story,
Chris had been cynical enough to doubt it. Still, that baby-
in-a-basket story really did happen occasionally, with
abandoned babies left at churches or hospitals.

Later Chris had learned that Bonnie was sterile. As a
young woman she'd contracted a pelvic disease, neglected
it and wound up having an emergency hysterectomy. A
doctor had told Chris all of this while reviewing Bonnie's
medical history the first time she'd been hospitalized with
d.t.'s. So Bonnie couldn't have been Chris's natural mother,
even if there hadn't already been plenty of witnesses in
Langlois who could verify she'd never been pregnant.

Bonnie had always claimed she didn't know who Chris's
parents were any more than anyone else in town did. Either
she'd been a more skillful liar than Chris believed or she was
too fearful of jeopardizing that precious two hundred dollars a month to name names or indulge in speculations.
Eventually Chris had had to solve the mystery himself.

As he'd grown older Chris had realized that he really shouldn't have been ragged, dirty or hungry. Someone was paying Bonnie well to keep him, but she drank up most of the money or, worse, sometimes gave it to a man. By the time Chris was ten he was old enough to be ashamed of Bonnie. Ashamed of her drinking and the shack where they lived and the men with whom she cavorted, who came around late at night and were frequently still there, snoring, when Chris woke up the next morning.

He'd first learned about sex listening to the noises Bonnie and the various men had made. Once, when Bonnie had made the mistake of getting involved with a particularly violent one, Chris had even had to come to her rescue—biting, clawing and scratching until her would-be attacker had fled.

Of course, his childhood hadn't been all bad. Living close to the deep woods with an ambling bayou nearby had given Chris trees to climb, plants and animals to study and a place of peace to be alone with his thoughts and dreams. His ambitions had been fueled while he lay on his back, soft moss beneath him and the leaves of a huge oak overhead, making intricate patterns against the sky.

Still Chris was fervently glad that Robbie was growing up with an entirely different sort of life. He'd always wanted any child of his to live as comfortably and normally as possible.

Of course, with Lynn's illness and death, a truly "normal" life had escaped Robbie just as surely as it had escaped Chris himself. And Robbie was a boy who had really needed his mother. Just look at the way he'd attached himself almost immediately to Stacy.

Stacy... Chris tried not to think about her, but he couldn't keep her image out of his mind for long. Now he glanced back at the pool to see her demonstrating the surface dive for Robbie once again. The sight of her rounded feminine derriere and long shapely legs immediately ignited a fire in his loins. Shifting uneasily in his chair and determined to ignore Stacy's physical appeal, Chris found himself won-

dering with amusement just where she'd found such a Grim
Granny swimsuit.

Abruptly his amusement faded. Had Stacy bought the suit
specifically as a means of discouraging him? Chris wondered. Had she anticipated trouble with Chris Lorio before
she'd even left New Mexico? Or was he being paranoid?

Well, she'd sent him signals of disinterest—the trouble
was he didn't believe them. Not when he remembered how
she used to wrap her arms and legs around him and almost
burn him up with that sweet hot mouth of hers and the in-
cendiary pressure of her body against his.

He remembered her response to him last night. Thought
again of how her initial resistance to his kiss had dissolved
into fire and renewed desire. She could wear Mother Hub-
bards to her chin and she wouldn't fool him—no, not at all.

But there was one sure reason he and Stacy weren't going
to get physically involved again, Chris assured himself, and
that was his definite decision not to, no matter how sexy she
was.

Chris took another swig of his beer, finding the taste more
refreshing. Since he'd never had any trouble handling alcohol, he occasionally allowed himself a beer after a really
god-awful day. But, always, at the back of his mind any time
he elected to drink, came disturbing thoughts and memories of Bonnie.

And always, when he thought of involvement with a
woman, any woman, there were inner warnings that caused
him to move slowly and carefully, prompted by thoughts of
Stacy. Chris had long ago promised himself that he would
never again live through anything like *that* brand of torture.

Robbie was a quick learner. Already he was getting the
knack of a surface dive and executing it flawlessly. Stacy
praised him, then glanced at Chris to see if he wanted to add
his congratulations to hers. Instead she saw that his attention was focused on her. Intercepting his smoldering gaze
was like being licked with tongues of fire, and suddenly her

whole body felt heated, her breasts grew heavy and a delicious tingling ran along her spine and the backs of her legs.

Earlier she'd tried not to notice how dynamic Chris looked in a bathing suit, had tried not to visibly admire his physique...but she hadn't been able to avoid seeing it, either, as he went in and out of the pool, then strolled around nonchalantly.

He had a symmetrical back, his muscular shoulders tapering to a narrow waist and straight spine. His buttocks were taut, his thighs lean and his calves hard-muscled. His body hair followed the usual male pattern, fanning over his chest and then arrowing down to dive below the waistband of his white trunks. Chris was a beautifully built man, even more beautiful than he'd been at twenty-three, Stacy thought. Now she saw the promise of the very young man completely fulfilled.

For a moment Stacy's eyes locked with Chris's. Then, before either could wrench their gaze away, Robbie came bubbling to the surface in triumph. "Daddy, did you see me dive just then? Stacy says I've got it near-most perfect."

"Yeah, sport, you looked great!" Chris applauded. To Stacy he added, "Robbie's a natural when it comes to swimming, isn't he?"

"He sure is," Stacy agreed. "I've never seen a kid any better."

"How about your son?" Robbie asked a trifle anxiously. "Does Taylor swim good?"

"Like he'd been born with gills." Stacy smiled. "He passed lifesaving in the spring."

"But you think I'll be as good as *he* is?"

The insecurity of a young motherless male touched Stacy's heart. Robbie might have all the material possessions a child could desire, but the need for self-confidence and adult approval was something quite independent of money. She reached out and caught him close, giving him a half splash, half hug. "You'll be just as good—maybe even better!" she promised.

He hurled himself happily into her arms, but when Stacy glanced up again Chris was studying them with a frown on his face. Did he want her to resist being affectionate with Robbie? she worried. If so, he was expecting too much.

The hard lines of his face gave her no clue, and soon he stood up to leave.

"Stacy, I'll be in my study in fifteen minutes. Why don't we discuss your car then?" he called.

Her heart gave a little skip of apprehension. Playing with Robbie, instructing him and demonstrating the dive had provided a welcome break and distracted her for a few minutes. Now it was time to deal with real life again. Now it was time to really worry.

"Six hundred dollars!"

The blood drained from Stacy's face until she looked like she might faint from shock. Despite Chris's overall disinterest in Stacy's car or her cash-flow problems, her white, distressed expression aroused the unwanted pull of concern. He wondered if he should offer her—what? Water? A stiff drink? Medical attention?

Then he realized that he had something even better to offer her: an alternative.

Consulting the slip of paper on which he'd jotted down figures, Chris continued, "According to Floyd, six hundred dollars is what it would cost to get your car in good shape again. He can do a patch-up job for three hundred—but he won't guarantee it will get you all the way home to New Mexico."

Apparently three hundred dollars also blew Stacy's modest budget, Chris saw. She continued to be pale with a pinched look around her mouth.

Silently Chris swore a whole string of expletives. He didn't want to get mixed up in any way in Stacy's problems or Stacy's life. Nor did he want to sympathize with her. Three hundred dollars was no more than pocket change to Chris now, although he could still remember being so damned poor that he'd parted reluctantly with every dollar.

"Look, Stacy, don't worry," Chris heard himself saying roughly. "We can work something out."

"There's no way," she choked, and glancing up at her again, Chris saw that she was teetering on the brink of tears. *My God, was she ready to cry over a lousy three hundred dollars?*

Despite himself, his lawyer's curiosity was aroused. "Doesn't that advertising agency where you've worked seven years pay you a living wage?" he asked.

She was fumbling for a tissue now, he saw, groping for the box on his desk. He pushed it closer so she could help herself. "Salaries in New Mexico are pretty low," she said shakily. "I make what's considered good money, but with all of the expenses for Taylor..." While Chris listened, Stacy started to enumerate them.

"What about your ex-husband?" Chris interrupted, his eyes narrowing. "Doesn't he help support Taylor?"

"No." Her expression still watery, Stacy gave a quick shake of her head.

"He doesn't support his own child? Well, why don't you have him thrown in jail?" Chris snapped, his exasperation increasing.

"I . . . just couldn't do that," Stacy stammered.

For God's sake, why? Chris wondered irritably. Why was Stacy letting Gary Thomasson off the hook? Did she still love her ex-husband? She must. What other explanation was there?

And yet, as he saw her drying her eyes with the tissue, a slow kindling rage began to build in Chris. Damn, he would never understand certain women or the men they picked! For that matter he couldn't understand any father so utterly disinterested in the welfare of his own flesh and blood that he'd let a kid go without the essentials.

Chris's own father had made a thousand mistakes, many of them grave and irreparable. But at least he had tried to do the right thing by his illegitimate son. His intentions had been good, even if Bonnie Lorio's thirst had been greater.

Stacy ran out on me so she could marry a guy who won't even support his own kid, Chris thought with renewed resentment and felt his rage flare higher. Somehow he was going to have to come up with coherent words, he realized, because Stacy was looking at him now, waiting expectantly to see how they could "work something out." In spite of her reservations she obviously hoped Chris was a magician with a rabbit or two up his sleeve.

And, as a matter of fact, he did have one.

Rather than let her suffer any longer Chris went brusquely to the heart of the matter. "Look, Stace—" unconsciously he used the nickname he'd bestowed on her long ago "—what Floyd says is that your car really isn't worth fixing up."

What Floyd, who had an imaginative—and probably criminal—mind, had actually said was more emphatic: "Mr. Lorio, you know what I'd do with that rusty tin can? If it was mine, I'd drive it straight into a bayou and collect the insurance!"

"Oh, great," Stacy muttered now.

"You probably ought to think in terms of buying a new car instead of fixing up the old one."

"That's impossible," she blurted.

"No, it isn't," Chris said, exercising, for him, inordinate patience. "Didn't you hear anything I said yesterday? Lynn left you all her personal possessions. You're practically an heiress."

"You said clothes—and antique churns stored up in the attic." Her smooth, pretty face looked up at him in confusion. "I thought you were talking about items that would bring a few hundred dollars, at most."

"Well, I guess I was," Chris conceded. "But there's also Lynn's jewelry." He arose and walked rapidly over to the wall where he began unlocking the safe he'd had installed there some years ago. He dialed the combination, the tumblers whirled and the door opened slowly.

He came back carrying a square mahogany box, which he set on the desk before Stacy. "Take a look in there," he directed.

Her green eyes, wide with shock, flew to his. Then she opened the box, gasping at the sight of its contents glittering up from the cream satin liner.

"That's Lynn's grandmother's engagement ring," Chris pointed out when Stacy timidly withdrew one of the smaller items. "See the old-fashioned setting? But the stone is more than a carat, and it's considered a perfect diamond." His face twisted deprecatingly. "Lynn's own engagement ring was only half that large, but then I was a still-struggling young attorney. Later I wanted to replace it, but she wouldn't let me. It's down there on the second tier.

"Now, I was doing a bit better when I bought her the diamond pendant and earrings," Chris went on. "But the set of sapphires celebrates the first really big case I won. I see you like the emeralds—they belonged originally to Lynn's mother, but she gave them to Lynn long ago. I guess you remember how Ruth is. The only valuables that interest her are shards of ancient pottery that people like you and me wouldn't glance at twice."

Stacy's eyes kept widening, but her hands dropped from his desk and fell emptily into her lap. "Chris, I can't take these things," she whispered.

"Of course you can," he protested.

"Jewelry that *you* bought for Lynn? No. Absolutely not." Her voice was quiet but also emphatic and resolute.

"Well, I'm afraid you'll have to," Chris drawled. "You're the only person, Stace, with any legal right to the jewels. You must decide whether to keep or dispose of them." He leaned back, preparing to enjoy the spectacle of need-and-greed versus scruples.

Stacy drew an uneven breath. "All right. I can do that right now. I return to you Lynn's diamonds and sapphires for your second wife. The emeralds go straight back to Aunt Ruth. Anything that's left over, the pearls and heirloom gold and that rather nice jade piece, are for Robbie to give his bride one day. There!"

Despite Stacy's wanness, satisfaction was in her voice as she, too, leaned back in her chair. But Chris felt totally confounded. Stacy had just disposed of the most valuable items of Lynn's personal property in the fairest way that he could think of. He was ashamed to think that he'd ever even toyed with the idea of concealing the jewelry from her—in his heart, he, too, had felt that gifts he'd given Lynn should not be Stacy's. Still, it hadn't been Chris's legal right to decide—evidently, Floyd wasn't the only one with an occasionally larcenous streak in his soul.

But apparently it was not an affliction from which Stacy suffered.

Why was he so surprised? Chris wondered. As she'd pointed out to him last night, a woman truly bent on grabbing everything she could would have hotfooted it to Louisiana in no time flat.

"That's a lovely gesture, Stacy, but are you sure you can afford it?" Chris asked quietly. "There is still the problem of your car."

As he talked he had risen unconsciously. Now he perched on a corner of his desk, not far from her.

"I know," Stacy said. Then abruptly she dropped her face into her hands and began to cry in earnest.

"Oh, for—" Instinctively Chris made a move toward her, then stopped himself. Weeping women had always disarmed him. Even Bonnie, shedding her crocodile tears of drunken remorse, had managed to tug at his heartstrings.

Stacy sobbed quietly until Chris began to grow exasperated, although whether with himself or with her he really didn't know. "Look, Stacy, a few hundred dollars... that's chicken feed!"

She gave a strangled sound. "For you, maybe."

"And you, too. Look, you've got to think big to ever get anywhere," Chris argued.

"I attended that motivational seminar, too," she choked out.

"Well, you must not have been paying attention," he retorted. "So since you're not in the new-car market for a while, I'll pick one of the other alternatives. And don't worry about how you'll pay for it, either. And, damn it, don't look at me like I know you're about to look at me! There are no strings. If you don't want Chris Lorio doing you a favor then consider this a favor from Lynn. She loved you and wanted you to come back here. She certainly wouldn't have wanted you inconvenienced and made unhappy because you had.''

"Thank you," Stacy said, and Chris heard the quiet sincerity warring with a husky desperation in her low voice.

He looked over at her thoughtfully. She had been tense and uptight ever since she'd arrived yesterday, and Chris didn't think he alone had inspired such emotion. Of course being in Lynn's house without Lynn had probably been a wrench to her. "Cash flow isn't the only problem you've got, is it, Stace?" he asked her on a hunch.

The instincts that had made Chris a good lawyer weren't off-base now. Stacy's wet emerald-green eyes widened in surprise. "How on earth did you know?"

"All my clients say I'm telepathic," he countered lightly. "So what's wrong? Your job? Your boy?"

"Both. Taylor's twelve and already he's too much for me to handle. He's so willful and headstrong and—reckless! According to his teachers he's a holy terror in school and he's started swearing fluently. He's very bright but his grades this past year have bottomed out. And now I just keep having this bad feeling about his being away at camp," Stacy concluded.

Chris couldn't imagine why Stacy was telling all this as if it concerned him as well. But if she found some solace in the retelling then he guessed he could sit and listen, tired though he was from the endless recital of woes he'd already listened to today.

"What about Gary? Doesn't he have any influence with the boy at all?" Chris inquired.

"Gary is...indifferent." Stacy stopped, swallowing hard. "Taylor knows it, too. While I can't say that fact has caused Taylor's behavior, it certainly hasn't helped it."

"No, it wouldn't," Chris said, then he frowned thoughtfully. Stacy's Taylor reminded him of someone, but offhand he couldn't remember just who. Then he drew a breath. "Look, if Gary is indifferent to his son then that's all the more reason you ought to at least threaten to throw him in jail for nonsupport.''

"No, I—I just can't bring myself to do that," Stacy said again.

"Do you still love Gary that much?" Chris asked steadily. Something in him was determined to know.

She stared at him, aghast. "I don't love Gary at all! I never—I mean, I stopped caring about him long ago."

For some reason Chris couldn't define her reply filled him with relief. Probably it was relief that she wasn't a total fool, he rationalized. "Well, for the moment let's leave the problem of your son, Stacy, since I don't have any answers to direct toward that situation. At least he's safely tucked away for now."

"At least we hope he is!" Stacy said, a small semblance of humor returning. "With Taylor you always have to be on guard."

"So what's with your job?" Routinely Chris moved on to the next problem.

"It's shaky, very shaky. Everyone in the agency has been sitting around quaking for the last couple of months. Early sales are way down, and of course the particular products we plug are things you usually sell to a customer just once. Repeat business isn't high." She sighed.

"Swimming pools, hot tubs and Jacuzzis, I believe you said."

"Yes—and with the current economic climate and housing starts down..."

Patiently Chris listened to what he considered fearful thoughts, wild projections and office gossip.

"I think you've been listening to the wrong economic forecasts, Stacy," Chris said as soon as he was able to get a word in edgewise. "All the reports I've been reading say the southwestern desert is one of the fastest-growing regions in the U.S. With more people moving there more new houses will be constructed, and those new people in the new houses will want the accoutrements of the good life, don't tell me they won't!"

"It's true that the desert population is increasing," Stacy mused, a little color beginning to brighten her face again.

"See? You've been letting the fear prophets get to you. You have to tune out pessimistic people or they'll drag you right down with them. Anyway, even if you lost your job, so what? By the time I was twenty I'd lost a half dozen, usually because I shot off my smart mouth. But you know something really interesting, Stacy? I always found a better job," Chris assured her. "Always."

She drew a deep breath and then, as Chris watched, her shoulders straightened and her chin came up. She'd always had plenty of spirit and spunk, that's why her tears had surprised him so much. *She's just been tired and overloaded,* he thought, *and that kid of hers sounds difficult.* Chris diagnosed Stacy's malady impersonally, as he might any client's.

"Thank you, Chris," she said quietly, and rose from her chair.

When she stood, he did, too, sliding off the desk. Carefully, he stepped back to allow her to pass. But, at the last moment, Stacy glanced up at him again and hesitated, as though something about him had surprised her. Well, he was surprised, too, by the depth and extent of various matters plaguing Stacy, as well as by her conscientious concern about her child and her job. In Chris's opinion, too many people were irresponsible.

"Hey," he said softly. "I do apologize for last night—and I really mean it this time. I know I acted like a nut. Frankly, Stace, I don't know what got into me."

She didn't turn, but her hand touched his arm spontaneously. Suddenly simply wrapping his arms around her seemed like the easiest thing in the world for Chris to do.

"This isn't a pass, it's a hug," he said roughly. "Lynn used to say there were times in all our lives when we just needed to be hugged."

"Yes," Stacy breathed, and for a moment she allowed Chris to hug her.

Last night she'd been an exciting presence in his arms. Today, in his gentler frame of mind, Stacy just felt *natural* somehow. Her still-damp hair smelled clean and sweet. The brush of her skin felt unbelievably smooth. Looking down Chris could see her incredibly long, thick eyelashes.

In his arms she seemed small, almost fragile, which surprised him. Fragility wasn't a characteristic of Stacy's he'd ever recalled. But of course she'd stayed the same size, while he'd filled out to become a considerably larger man.

Suddenly Chris wondered if childbirth had changed the shape or size of Stacy's breasts—if it had left stretch marks on her stomach or broken delicate veins on those thighs he'd scarcely glimpsed. Then Chris wondered at his own curiosity.

Having a baby had left all those marks on Lynn, and they were the only thing about Robbie's arrival that she'd bewailed. But Chris hadn't been bothered by the changes at all. Rather, he'd seen them as badges of honor for carrying his husky son.

Perhaps now he kept concentrating on Stacy as someone's mother so he wouldn't think of her as soft, smooth and desirable. Those were the kind of thoughts that got him into trouble.

The moment Chris felt her arms drop he released her. Stacy turned toward the door, leaving him with the feeling that they had both acted in a surprisingly generous and accepting way toward each other.

There was a discreet knock on the closed study door. "Dinner," Miriam announced.

"Good. I'm ready to eat," Stacy said casually, throwing the words over her shoulder to Chris. "Do you have an appetite, too?"

"Always." He grinned and followed her down to the dining room where an exasperated, famished youngster awaited them.

Chapter Five

Stacy's next couple of days were quiet. She continued to sort through Lynn's numerous possessions and tried to fit herself smoothly into a new and quite different household.

She hadn't seen much of Chris since that astonishing early evening meeting when she'd found him kind, friendly and helpful. The hard brief hug of reassurance that he'd given her had been even more surprising. Compassion and sympathy were the last things she'd expected from Chris after his scathing denunciations by the pool the night of her arrival.

As usual, the contradictory Chris Lorio had managed to confuse and confound her. Stacy only wished that confusion was all there was to it. Reluctantly she'd had to admit to herself that she still found the man attractive—but then almost any normal woman would. She didn't intend to dwell on the fact or let herself be influenced by it in any way. But she remained grateful for Chris's help in the matter of her car.

The Monte Carlo was back now, and running so smoothly that she wondered if Chris had ordered the minimum-priced job, after all. At first she'd thought of asking him. But a little reflection on the matter advised her to simply accept what had been given and to repay when she could.

Gradually Stacy's days fell into a pattern. She allowed herself the luxury of an extra hour of sleep, then she arose to eat breakfast with Robbie. After he and Ted went off to the tree house or the pool, the latter always under Preston's watchful gaze, Stacy resumed her work. Persistence paid off. Within a few days she'd almost finished sorting through Lynn's possessions, extensive though they had been.

Most of the things would be donated to charity, since it made no sense to Stacy to keep garments that wouldn't fit her. But from the mounds of clothes she'd scrutinized, Stacy had chosen a few items as investment contributions to her own slender wardrobe.

An alligator belt and matching handbag were two. Then there was a small white satin evening bag, delicately trimmed with pearls and infinitesimal seashells. An irresistible short-sleeved shirt of emerald green silk had also been set aside, as well as some basic black leather pumps, carrying the label of an enormously expensive designer, that fit Stacy's feet as if molded precisely for her.

She'd kept a few nonwearable items, too: a slender volume of poetry that she knew Lynn had cherished and a romantic novel they had both adored when they were in their teens. Additionally there was a painting of the desert that Stacy had selected for Lynn. The artist, an unknown at the time, had garnered considerable renown in the following years.

These were the only personal possessions Stacy intended to take back to New Mexico with her. For the small amount of space they would consume she might as well have flown here. But of course she still didn't know what lay in the attic that she might want to transport home with her.

Frequently, following lunch, Robbie sidled into the room to sit by her side. Occasionally he liked to explain various items to Stacy, too. "See that paperweight? Mom bought that when we went to the crystal cavern way up in Kentucky."

"If you remember it, then you should keep it," Stacy had said, gently folding Robbie's small brown hand around the paperweight.

On another occasion he'd looked wistfully at his mother's radio, which, as Stacy had discovered, had an excellent tone. "Daddy got that for Mom 'cause she liked to listen to operas. But he sure doesn't! He says opera always sounds to him like two cats with their tails tied together. But he wanted Mom to enjoy it."

"I'll leave the radio for you, Robbie," Stacy promised, but she didn't immediately offer up this item since Robbie already had a radio in his room and Stacy enjoyed listening to music while she worked.

Around four-thirty each afternoon the household began to stir in preparation for Chris's return. Without question he dominated the scene. He usually swam with Robbie before dinner, Stacy learned, and although they had extended her a blanket invitation to join them at any time, she usually chose to decline. She just didn't feel comfortable wearing a bathing suit around Chris. She felt those black eyes of his watching her much too often, anyway.

Dinner with him was a necessary fact that she must endure. Then Chris and Robbie went off to watch television or play video games while Stacy retired to her room either to write to Taylor or to read. She had been pleasantly surprised by the amount of time that Chris spent with his son, and although Robbie usually asked Stacy to join them if she wished, she suspected that politeness prompted his invitations. But there was no reason she and Chris should have to rub elbows any more than absolutely necessary. Personally Stacy thought they'd do better to stay out of each other's way.

So why did she find herself sitting alone in her room thinking of the man? Every time Stacy caught herself doing it, she set down her book and went back to work. The sooner all her sorting and sifting was accomplished, the quicker she could go home, she thought longingly.

But the day Stacy finally did a careful survey of the attic she received quite a shock. There was much more stored up there than she'd ever imagined.

The next day brought another shock, in the form of a scrawled postcard from her twelve-year-old son. Like Taylor himself, the message was brief, direct and unnerving.

Dear Mom, This place stinks. Taylor

"Stacy? Can I bother you for a minute?"

"Sure, Robbie. Say, what gave you the idea you were bothering me, anyway?" she asked the child curiously.

"Daddy said I was probably driving you nuts by now."

Stacy started to retort to that, then thought better of it. But privately she vowed to correct Chris's erroneous impression the next time she saw him. She enjoyed spending time with Robbie. Paying close attention to him and answering his questions were an important part of building his self-esteem and a very small return indeed for the generosity Lynn had always shown her. And that aside, Stacy just plain *liked* Robbie, thinking him a very dear little boy.

But probably Chris was anxious for Stacy to finish her work as soon as possible and clear out of his house.

"Daddy asked me why I wasn't calling you Miss Stacy anymore, like he said I should," Robbie volunteered, sharing more of what was on Daddy's mind.

"I'll tell Chris I gave you permission to quit doing that," Stacy replied, and saw relief cross Robbie's face. After a moment he launched a new topic.

"Stacy, today's Saturday, y'know?"

How could she *not* know? Chris had obviously gotten up on the wrong side of the bed. He'd been carping and criticizing all day, finding fault with everything and everyone. Although he'd cooked a large omelet and Robbie and Stacy had praised both its taste and its fluffy texture, Chris had been immensely dissatisfied with his creation. He had scribbled a scathing note asking Miriam where in the hell she'd been buying eggs.

Later, Chris had been outraged when the pool-cleaning service had shown up on a Saturday. What in God's name was wrong with coming on a weekday? he stormed. On Saturdays people were trying to relax from their week's labor. It was infuriating to come out all ready for a swim and find men just starting work at the pool—

Stacy hadn't been on the scene to see what transpired. But she'd certainly heard it all through the balcony windows she'd left open to catch the fresh morning breeze.

A short time later, she'd heard Chris ordering Robbie to clean up his room, which, in the opinion of his father, "looked like a den for pit vipers."

This exchange had been the worst of all. Apparently Robbie had either dawdled or else Chris had found the work he'd performed inept. Chris had stormed some more, calling his son lazy and careless and adding, "I grew up in a hovel but you didn't. By God, I don't think you appreciate half of what you've got!" until poor little Robbie was reduced to tears.

Stacy could certainly understand how exasperating kids could be. Wasn't she dealing with Taylor's resistance to summer camp right now? And boys typically hated anything that smacked of housework.

As soon as Stacy had heard Chris march off she'd sped down the hall to Robbie's room. Once there, she honestly had to agree with Chris—it was a wreck. Even Taylor's had rarely looked worse. Still, Robbie was very young with a lot to learn about proper vacuuming, dusting and bed making. Stacy demonstrated a few techniques, being careful to let Robbie do the actual work.

At some point she'd glanced up to see Chris standing in the doorway, obviously back to check on his son's progress. Although he still wore the scowl he'd had all day, it no longer looked quite so fierce. Stacy threw him a harried look, trying to say without words that she really wasn't intent on interfering. It was her personal opinion, however, that Chris was being an absolute boor.

Chris, in turn, glanced over to see Robbie dusting with a real semblance of industry. So, with a brusque nod to Stacy, he'd turned and walked silently away.

Now, late in the afternoon, when Robbie asked Stacy if she was aware today was Saturday, she was certainly very aware indeed. And she couldn't help wondering just what in the devil was wrong with Chris.

"I was just thinkin', Stacy, that—well...maybe you'd want to go to church tomorrow and could take me," Robbie hedged.

Church suddenly seemed like a very appealing idea to Stacy—a lot better than spending a Sunday with Chris snarling and snapping. Besides, she had promised Betty Thackery to discuss with Chris the topic of his son's religious training. True, Stacy didn't really like Betty, but still, having given her word, she should have followed through.

First, though, came a question of utmost importance to her. "Do you really enjoy going to church, Robbie?"

"I like Sunday school better," he confided. "I get to see the other kids and my teacher tells lots of neat stories, even though ol' Mrs. Glover who plays piano for us always drools over me. Church—" Robbie shrugged. "That's boring, 'cept I like to hear the music. Man, that pipe organ can make some wild sounds!"

Stacy tried not to smile at his descriptions. "Well, I'll tell you what, Robbie. I'll be glad to take you if your Daddy agrees. I'll talk to him about it tonight." Hopefully Stacy added, "Maybe he'll be in a better mood."

"That's a good idea, Stacy. He might feel better then. Right now he's got a headache and he's lying down in his room," Robbie said with a sigh.

"Oh, did he tell you that?" Stacy said in surprise.

"No. He never ever talks about 'em. But Mom and I always knew when his head hurt," Robbie explained. "See, Daddy only gets mad and yells when his head hurts awful bad."

* * *

This particular migraine was a real bitch, Chris thought resentfully. There were fully a dozen other ways he'd prefer spending Saturday to lying in a darkened room with an ice bag on his relentlessly pounding head.

The headache had started around noon yesterday when lights began to hurt his eyes and auras started appearing around the heads of people. Immediately he'd swallowed the first dose of a strong prescription drug, but the medicine had been of little use, as usual.

Thank God he only had two or three of these miserable suckers a year.

"Consider it a price you pay for superior intelligence," his family physician, George Hutton, had told Chris. "Idiots never get migraines."

Right now Chris thought he'd settle for a little less I.Q. and a lot less pain. Remorse gnawed at him, too. He'd been a real bear all day, even making Robbie cry—and Robbie didn't need any more reasons to cry. Chris sighed and hoped his son would forgive him.

Worse, he'd been all primed to pounce on Stacy, too. The moment he'd heard her clear, soft voice coming from Robbie's room he'd turned about as civilized as a wounded savage. His first thought was that she'd by God come rushing to Robbie's rescue, and since Chris was determined to instill a sense of responsibility and self-discipline in his son, he wasn't about to let the boy get off scot-free. So Chris had gone lurching down the hall, ready to shout at Stacy, too, for pampering the boy and doing his work for him.

Fortunately, he'd at least stopped long enough to assess the situation.

Just trying to focus his eyes had hurt like hell, but after Chris accomplished it he saw Robbie dusting with more industry than before while Stacy acted as coach and cheering squad.

Yes, she was good with kids. Very good. Chris had to grant her that, and conscientious mothers always impressed him. Perhaps that was the result of his growing up without one.

So he'd stalked back to his room, where he intended to stay unless the house caught fire. He'd made enough people miserable today that he was starting to feel thoroughly ashamed of himself.

"Can you find any common denominator for these attacks?" George kept probing. "Sometimes, for instance, there's a hidden allergen, and something like chocolate or caffeine sets off a headache."

"No, I can't say any one thing triggers mine," Chris had snapped irritably the first time George brought up the subject. At the time Chris had simply been too furious over having headaches in the first place to consider a common cause for them. Headaches—indeed, most physical ailments—seemed damned unmanly to him. He certainly wasn't going to go tiptoeing through life like a nervous high-strung hypochondriac!

But unwittingly he'd found the key, anyway. Tension accompanied by strong, unresolved emotions was an absolutely merciless combination for him.

He'd had his first migraine three days after he'd returned from Europe. That's how long it had taken for his shock and disbelief to wear off. That initial headache began with Chris's gut-deep realization that he had lost Stacy to another man.

For some reason another headache had accompanied his otherwise happy wedding day. His third occurred when it became inevitable that Bonnie Lorio was dying.

The worst headache of his life came on the day of his wife's funeral.

Now that Stacy was back, a torment in various ways, Chris knew he shouldn't be surprised to find himself in pain. The only real surprise was that it hadn't happened sooner.

She still churned up so many emotions in him! Attraction. Anticipation. Excitement. But those, in turn, triggered frustration and depression, because of course Chris couldn't trust her one whit. Now now, not ever.

And beyond that another part of him—strong, proud, aloof—demanded that he never, ever forgive her for having hurt him years ago.

But, damn it, he wanted her. A lot of the tension he was feeling these days was of the purely sexual variety, Chris knew. She was still such a lovely woman. When she walked her feminine hips had a small and gentle sway. And when she turned her head and Chris saw the creamy smoothness of her throat and shoulders, he kept remembering how her skin had felt beneath his hands, his lips, his body. Then the raw, aching hunger in his loins would begin. Stacy...

After several hours had passed, Stacy couldn't help but grow worried about Chris. She rarely ever had a serious headache; still, it didn't stop her from empathizing with someone who did.

She had just about made up her mind to invade Chris's lair and risk his displeasure when Miriam's daughter, Jeannette, called them to dinner. Jeannette usually filled in for her mother on the weekends so Miriam and Preston could have those days off.

Without Chris at the head their table looked oddly deserted. Robbie hardly spoke above a whisper, and Stacy found her own voice hushed. Even the food seemed flat. Although edible, it was neither as well cooked nor as tasty as Miriam's.

"Good evening."

Both Stacy and Robbie jerked up warily at the sound of Chris's voice. "Well, if I make *both* of you jump I guess I behaved even worse than I thought." He sighed.

"Are you feeling better, Daddy?" Robbie said anxiously.

"Oh, I'll be all right, sport." As Chris paused by the boy's chair, he punched Robbie lightly on the arm. Apparently this masculine gesture meant affection, Stacy deduced, since Robbie's face began to glow.

With a few pleasant words murmured to Stacy and Jeannette, Chris sat down and began to put food on his plate.

But Stacy noticed that he was taking dabs instead of helpings. She also noticed that he still held his head in an unnaturally stiff position, and she knew that while Chris might be feeling a trifle better he still wasn't well.

"I'd like to see you after dinner if you can spare a few minutes," she requested.

"Sure," Chris agreed.

Tonight he declined both dessert and coffee, which was atypical behavior, although he waited patiently until Robbie and Stacy had finished eating. Then Chris arose and gingerly inclined his head in the direction of the staircase.

"Let's go to my study, Stacy. Robbie, why don't you watch TV in the family room, okay?"

"Sure," Robbie said, casting an uneasy look at his father.

Chris's study was a handsome room, and tonight Stacy was better able to appreciate it than the first time she'd been in it. The furniture was large and ornate, the desk and tall bookcases made of rich polished wood. There was also a sofa with matching chairs, as well as several small tables. Photographs and pictures hung from plum-colored walls. Chris's personal computer dominated one corner of the room; a lighted globe commanded attention in another.

Chris slumped into the chair behind his desk and turned on a tabletop lamp to a low setting. Stacy took the same chair that she'd occupied several nights ago.

Now that she sat close to Chris, Stacy could see the pallor beneath his tan. His eyes were faintly pink and his head seemed almost rigidly attached to his neck, as if he were afraid to allow it motion in any direction. Clearly he was still suffering, so Stacy determined to be brief.

"Chris, I just wanted to clear up a couple of matters," she began swiftly.

"Oh?" One eyebrow went up, then he lowered it quickly, as if even so small a gesture had hurt.

"I gave Robbie permission to stop calling me Miss Stacy. I think he's gotten the idea by now that he's to show respect for all us elderly people," Stacy explained with a smile.

"Okay, just as long as it was your idea," Chris said and only his black eyes and white lips moved fractionally in his still face.

"Also, Robbie doesn't bother me being underfoot," Stacy went on. "I know he asks a lot of questions, but I don't mind. Of course, a lot of the time I don't know the answers, but I always say so frankly." She felt a little discomfited by Chris's steady, unvarying stare.

"Robbie's getting very attached to you, you know," Chris said flatly. "That's one reason I more or less told him to cool it."

"I understand," Stacy assured Chris. "But don't you think it's natural under the circumstances?"

"Probably. But I don't think he needs to lose a *second* mother, do you?" Chris probed.

"Well, why would he have to lose me completely?" Stacy fired back. "Why, he'd always be welcome to come visit Taylor and me in New Mexico—"

"That's not wise, Stacy." Chris's voice flatly denied her plea. "I can understand why you'd want to be close to *Lynn's* child. But, frankly, once this last matter of her personal possessions has been resolved I can only see our paths diverging."

Although Stacy had suspected in her heart that Chris probably felt this way it was still a shock to her to hear him say it so bluntly. Nor was she prepared for the unexpected pain that suddenly knifed through her.

"You don't really want me around Robbie at all, do you?" she asked, her voice bitter.

Chris didn't even blink. She wished he would and make his head hurt more, she thought vengefully. But as she stared at him his face became increasingly drawn.

"Stacy, let's try to look at the situation in a different, kinder light," he suggested. "I honestly feel that you have enough problems, since you've shared some of them with me, without taking on Robbie. I don't think you need to be burdened with the responsibility for staying in touch with him or occasionally caring for him. Tell me, do you really have the time or money to become kindly Aunt Stacy?''

"I guess you know the answer to that one," Stacy said, but her voice was still faintly bitter. She didn't believe for one minute that this reasoning was Chris's honest opinion.

"Stacy, I'm not deliberately trying to be...nasty," he said, as if reading her mind. Now he swiveled half around in his executive chair and she saw his eyes close. Politely he inquired, "Was there anything else?"

"Yes, as a matter of fact," Stacy said, steeling herself for battle. "Betty Thackery mentioned to me that Robbie's absence from church had been noted by various people, especially since he always enjoyed Sunday school."

Chris muttered an unprintable word but since the oath didn't seem personally directed toward Stacy she forced herself to go on. "I didn't assume Betty was correct, Chris. But today Robbie brought up the subject himself, and I asked him how he felt."

"What did Robbie say?" Chris asked, his voice hard.

"That he likes Sunday school because he has a lot of friends there and his teacher tells some keen stories. I think he also likes to sing, but he didn't admit to that. He finds church a bore, except for the pipe organ. Oh—and Mrs. Glover, whoever she might be, drools on him, which he doesn't care for.'' Stacy stopped, drew a breath and fired her last volley. "Robbie asked if I would take him to church tomorrow. But I guess that's out, right?"

"Oh, for—" More unprintable words followed until Stacy's hands knotted together tightly in her lap. Then Chris sighed. "Hell, I forgot all about Sunday school! Robbie's never mentioned it to me. I'll admit I'm not keen on church doings, but I'm not such a louse that I won't let my son attend his mother's church. If you're willing to take him, Stacy, then Robbie has my permission to go this Sunday— or any Sunday."

With that Chris swiveled his chair completely around, presenting Stacy with the back of his head.

She was so surprised at his swift capitulation that, for a moment, she couldn't move. But she knew that Chris was anxious for her to leave and let him suffer in private.

Stacy also guessed from the way he cautiously lowered his head and began to massage the back of his neck that even the light from the lamp on his desk was killing him. Pain rather than outright rudeness prompted his presenting her with the back of his head. His rather shaky looking hand rubbing his neck was evidence to the fact.

"Thanks, Chris," Stacy said, rising to leave. But suddenly she just couldn't do it—not when she knew how badly he must be hurting.

His low sigh decided her to risk another of his snubs. "Chris, I think I could help that headache." Stacy spoke rapidly, before she could lose her nerve. "Come over here and sit on the sofa."

Slowly he swiveled back, his eyelids lifting reluctantly to peer at her. "Nothing ever helps one," he said in a fatalistic tone. "The son of a bitch just has to wear off gradually. Meanwhile I'm so sick I can't eat or sleep for a couple of days."

To hear such an admission of weakness from the usually invulnerable Chris Lorio only made Stacy all the more determined. "Has anyone ever tried Oriental massage on you?" she asked.

"God, no," he answered wearily. "Is that hokum what you have in mind?"

"Don't be so cynical." Stacy found herself scolding Chris, much as if he were an irascible child. "These ancient methods are still around because generally they work. What I plan to do is massage various pressure points. They'll probably feel quite sore when I first begin but as they loosen up you'll start to relax. That relaxation, plus additional massage, will work together to banish the headache."

"You sound like a saleswoman for snake oil," Chris said skeptically. "Are you sure you don't want to add leeches, too?"

But even as he denigrated Stacy's unorthodox healing methods he was rising carefully from his chair, she noticed. "The sofa, you said?"

"Yes. And while I don't have any snake oil or leeches, I really do wish I had a certain herbal essence to apply. Oh, well," she shrugged, "we'll make do without it."

"Just where are these so-called pressure points?" Chris asked a trifle warily.

"There are two at your temples and two in the back of your neck, which are crucial for headache control. Now just lie down here on the sofa, Chris—"

"You said sit. You didn't say anything about lying down," Chris complained. "Do you plan to join me, Stacy? Not that I could do anything for you right now, I'm afraid."

She bit her lip, deciding to ignore the sexual allusion. "I'll just draw up a chair and sit here."

"Oh, all right."

Grumbling and obviously highly dubious of this whole unorthodox procedure, Chris stretched his long body on the leather sofa. When Stacy drew closer to him she could smell his pleasant natural aroma, enhanced by shaving soap, after-shave and clean clothes. But mingling with it was a faintly acrid scent that she associated with severe pain.

"Now don't talk and just try to relax, Chris. I'll start behind your neck," she said soothingly.

First, Stacy flexed her hands a couple of times, then she dropped them down into his fragrant, soft black hair. Her sensitive fingertips probed, seeking the various pressure points.

"Ouch!" Chris complained.

"See, I told you they'd be sore. Now just relax. Take slow, deep breaths, Chris," she instructed.

He opened one eye to glare at her but then did as she instructed. Slowly, repetitiously Stacy rubbed—gently at first and then with increasing pressure. Finally she felt the two tensed-up knots, which had previously felt as firm as kernels of frozen corn, start to yield a little.

After Stacy thought she'd managed to ease some of the pressure in those areas she turned her attention to Chris's temples. The contact with his warm vibrant skin made her fingers tingle.

"Where in the hell did you learn Oriental massage?" he asked abruptly.

"No talking!" Stacy commanded, her tone stern. "You relax, and I'll talk. Advertising people will try anything. A few months ago our boss got the idea that this would help several of us to be less uptight. We had a day-long seminar and spent lots of time practicing on each other."

"Frankly, it's starting to feel good," he admitted.

"Don't talk!" she snapped again. "You tighten up with every word you utter."

She thought that might provoke an argument, but after a moment she felt Chris's muscles relaxing even more deeply than before.

Stacy knew that her hands were unusually strong for a woman, and she worked to utilize them to their fullest. Before her eyes she could see Chris growing drowsy. Well, sleep would be the best thing for him, she thought.

"Stacy?" Chris's voice was barely a whisper. "Mrs. Glover, who drools over Robbie, is the Episcopal parson's wife. She's the woman who introduced us."

For a moment Stacy froze. Then she resumed her repetitious motions designed to ease and relax. "Oh," was all she said, in a voice as soft as Chris's.

A moment later she realized he was asleep.

Carefully Stacy rose and pushed back her chair. She tiptoed across the room and lowered the light on Chris's desk until it was only a faint glow. Quietly she eased out into the hall and closed the study door with the gentlest of clicks.

Robbie looked up when Stacy entered the family room downstairs. On the television he was watching men run in all directions, trying to dodge a hail of bullets. Over the booming sound track Stacy explained to Robbie that she'd massaged Chris's neck, trying to ease his headache, and he'd fallen asleep.

"That's good," said Robbie wisely, sounding like a little old man. "It always makes Daddy's head feel better when he can sleep for a while."

"Has he had these headaches for very long?" Stacy asked curiously, for the young Chris she'd known had never suffered from them.

"Oh, yes. He's had 'em all my whole life," Robbie said, and Stacy smothered a grin at the thought of such a vast and extensive time period.

She sat with Robbie while he watched the rest of the detective show and a situation comedy that followed. But what Stacy kept seeing on the screen was a scene straight out of her own life.

She remembered being the new girl in town and attending the midsummer's night dance in Langlois. Remembered looking across a room into a stranger's black scowl—and being intrigued by his hard and handsome features as well as by a sudden appreciative flicker in his eyes as he watched her.

Unquestionably Chris Lorio had been the best-looking man at that dance. He'd worn a blue-and-white striped seersucker suit, fashionable summer attire for Southern men in 1976. A white shirt with a deep blue tie and a matching blue handkerchief in his breast pocket also made him the best-dressed.

Politely he made the circuit of sponsors and chaperons, shaking hands with them. He even asked a couple of the older women to dance, which only increased the yearning of younger women watching him. Still, again and again, his gaze returned to Stacy.

She couldn't resist looking at him, either. She tried to distance herself from the giggling girls who'd so annoyed him. But at the same time Stacy kept trying to remind herself that Chris Lorio was not truly eligible because he "belonged" to Cousin Lynn.

Obviously there were two people who weren't completely convinced of that: Chris and herself.

Suddenly Stacy heard a woman's voice behind her. "Hello, my dear. You're new in town, aren't you? Why, you're so pretty I'm sure I'd remember you if I'd ever seen you before."

Stacy swung around to confront a slim attractive woman who looked to be in her late forties. She had cornflower blue eyes and a shimmering halo of silver hair, which she wore in a neat chignon.

"I'm Ellen Glover," the woman continued, extending her hand to Stacy.

"Hello, I'm Stacy Powers but I'm not exactly new in town," Stacy explained. Then Mrs. Glover listened to her tell of her family's connection here with an almost flattering intensity.

"I noticed you and Chris Lorio looking at each other earlier," Mrs. Glover went on smoothly. "Let me introduce you to him if you haven't met. He's a very nice young man."

"No, we haven't . . . uh, met," Stacy stammered. "But I know who he is, of course."

Before she could say anything more, the patrician-looking Mrs. Glover had steered her straight to Chris. Stacy couldn't help but be impressed by the older woman's rather forceful manner.

"Good evening, Chris," Mrs. Glover said forthrightly. "I hope you'll help me welcome Stacy. She's new in town, sort of." With that the Episcopal parson's wife turned and walked away.

Chris looked down at Stacy with not-so-veiled amusement, as if he suspected her of finagling their introduction. "Well, Stacy, would you like to dance?" he asked politely.

A pop tune was wailing from the jukebox, a female vocalist claiming that it would take a lot of love for things to work out. Chris, when glimpsed up close, was so handsome in a brash devil-may-care way that Stacy felt almost breathless. Still, she glided into his arms as if she'd been here a thousand times before. Together they moved easily to the music.

He smelled wonderful, although his fragrance was subtle, and the way his hand wrapped over hers was warm and strong.

"Why are you new in town, sort of?" Chris asked, his lips just inches from Stacy's ear.

"Both of my parents grew up here," she replied, and her voice sounded breathless, too. "I was born in Langlois."

"Oh?" She felt the warmth of his breath near her ear, stirring a curl whenever he spoke. Stacy was aware of his hand resting on the small of her back, its warmth seeming to penetrate through her pretty lilac dress until her skin fairly glowed. "So why have you come back?" Chris asked. "To visit relatives or friends for the summer?"

"No . . . not exactly," Stacy stammered. "I mean, I am staying with my grandmother. But I've really come back here hoping to find a job. I just graduated from high school so I don't have any experience, except for working as a lifeguard and instructor at a swimming pool. But I've studied typing and shorthand, and I'm pretty good. Do you know of anyone who needs a secretary?"

"Not offhand," Chris replied casually. He steered her out of the midst of the crowded dance floor and off into a quieter, darker corner. "I'll ask around, though."

"Thanks," Stacy muttered and wished she could think of something really scintillating to say to him. Chris Lorio was older by five years, she knew. He was also greatly pursued by the town's belles, who found him dangerously fascinating, and Stacy felt sure his minimal interest in her was waning fast. How very dull she must sound.

But whenever Chris glanced down at her he didn't seem to regard her as dull. Rather Chris watched her with a lively interest, as if everything about her was charming.

Rather than taking heart from the warm expression in his eyes, Stacy felt her spirits plunge even lower. Mrs. Glover hadn't mentioned her last name, so Stacy knew she must tell him the truth about her relationship to Lynn.

"Look, Chris, I—I feel like I already know you," she blurted.

It wasn't a very subtle opening. But then, at barely eighteen, Stacy herself wasn't subtle.

"Oh? Is it that old black magic?" The amused look had returned to the depths of his wonderfully deep, dark eyes. "Or is it one enchanted evening, across a crowded room? I saw you watching me earlier, by the way."

Ill at ease as she felt, Stacy still realized he was jeering at her lightly. It wasn't malicious, but it still reflected Chris's underlying cynicism. Her spine stiffened.

"Not at all," she said coolly. "The reason I feel I already know you is because I'm Stacy Powers, Lynn Ashley's cousin. By the way, I saw you watching me, too."

Stacy briefly had the satisfaction of seeing Chris caught off-guard—surprised, confused, even disbelieving. She had the feeling that he wasn't surprised very often.

"You?" he said. "*You're* that Stacy? From New Mexico?"

She nodded. "The very one."

"You don't look a thing like Lynn!" Chris spoke as though he still sought to disprove her claim. "Why, I've seen pictures of Stacy. She's a blonde, too."

"Strawberry-blond when I was little," Stacy corrected. "My hair darkened as I got older."

Chris danced her directly beneath a chandelier, and Stacy saw him scrutinize her hair color. "Yeah, it is red and you have those green eyes that Lynn's mentioned," he muttered, almost to himself. "Well, I'll be damned!"

Several seconds passed while Chris danced rather mechanically as he digested this new information. Then he spoke again. "Lynn never said a thing about your coming here!"

His voice sounded faintly aggrieved, as though he felt he should have been warned. "Lynn didn't know," Stacy replied. "She mailed me a graduation present the first of May, right before she and her folks left for Europe. But I didn't decide to move here until last week. See, there simply aren't any jobs in my town in New Mexico. It's a one-industry place—a copper mine. I thought I might be hired to work in the mine office. Then a couple of weeks ago management started cutting back instead of hiring.''

"I see," Chris said and his voice sounded mechanical, too.

The music ended too soon. Chris thanked Stacy for the dance and said politely that he'd been glad to meet her. And then he turned and walked away through the throng, leaving her feeling suddenly bereft even though plenty of other young men began asking her to dance.

Stacy didn't lack for escorts through the rest of the evening. But she couldn't stop glancing around for Chris Lorio, either. He hadn't looked at her again and Stacy would have said he was paying her no attention at all.

Until the dance had ended . . .

Chapter Six

Hey, that was a neat show, wasn't it, Stacy?" Robbie said enthusiastically as credits began rolling over the TV screen.

"Why, yes it was enjoyable," Stacy replied, catapulted back into the present. She glanced at her watch and informed Robbie that it was time he went to bed. After all, he'd have to rise earlier than usual tomorrow because his daddy had agreed to let Stacy take him to church.

Robbie obeyed immediately. He was half out of the room when he turned and came scooting back, obviously inviting a bedtime hug and kiss. Stacy obliged warmly and Robbie beamed at her.

"See you in the morning, sport," she said, unconsciously using Chris's nickname for his son.

After Robbie had gone, Stacy rose, turned off the TV set and checked all the doors to be sure they were securely locked before she went up to her own room. There she changed into her nightgown, cleaned her face and brushed her teeth. As usual she picked up her book to read herself to sleep. When she found herself yawning, Stacy knew it was time to turn off the light and tuck in.

Suddenly she thought she'd better check on Chris first. Was he still sleeping? she wondered, pulling a light cotton robe on over her nightgown.

Stacy tiptoed out into the hall, then slipped to the closed door of Chris's study. There she pressed her ear to the door, listening for sounds from within. There was only silence, and she debated whether or not to enter.

If Chris was still sleeping she might awaken him when he badly needed sleep's restorative powers. On the other hand, the sofa would probably not be the most comfortable place on which to spend the night. Perhaps Chris would appreciate being awakened so he could go back to his room and his own bed.

Finally Stacy decided to ease the door open just a crack. Even after she'd done that and discerned Chris's long length still sprawled on the sofa, his very immobility disturbed her. What if he wasn't merely sleeping? What if he should have something more serious than a migraine headache and need medical attention?

Worriedly she walked to his side as the slant of light that entered the room with her dimmed and disappeared, the door closing again soundlessly. Now there was only the very faint glow from the single lamp on the desk.

"Stacy?" Chris's sleepy voice drifting up out of the darkness startled her.

"Yes, Chris," she breathed, moving even closer to the sofa. "Are you all right?"

"I don't know yet. Oh, I know I feel better, but I haven't tried moving my head. Well, here goes." Slowly she saw the outline of his dark head lift, then move from side to side.

"Well?" Stacy asked, unable to bear the suspense.

"Yes, I'm better...*much* better," he said in a voice filled with surprise. "Oh, my head still hurts a little but that repetitious bong, bong, bong is gone."

"Good! Let me give you another treatment, and by morning you'll probably be good as new." Even as she spoke, Stacy pulled back the chair that she'd used previously and sank down into it.

"Robbie?" Chris asked as Stacy began massaging again, using a gentler touch this time since the situation was no longer so acute.

"In bed for a couple of hours," Stacy replied.

"Good Lord, what time is it?" he demanded.

"Eleven-thirty," she replied. "Now remember, Chris, you're not supposed to talk. Just take deep breaths."

Even as she continued kneading she could tell he wasn't going to obey her. "Oriental massage, huh? Who on earth would have thought it could possibly help?" he said teasingly.

"A few million Chinese, Japanese, Javanese, Thais, Vietnamese—"

Stacy was still chanting when Chris cut in.

"Okay, Stacy, you've won this round," he said.

Unexpectedly her throat tightened from the same sort of hurt with which he'd stung her earlier. "Is that what we're having, Chris—rounds? Why must we be such opponents?"

Stacy spoke impulsively, without thinking of exactly what she might be implying.

Chris's hard warm hands closed tightly over hers. "Don't you know?" he asked roughly.

"Know what?" she cried, then she felt herself being drawn irrevocably closer by the tugging of his hands.

"This," Chris said before the import of exactly what was happening dawned on her.

Suddenly Stacy found herself lying sprawled across his broad warm chest with his arms encircling her like iron bonds. One of his hands closed around her neck, tilting her head up, and Stacy felt him draw her face to his.

His lips touched hers gently, very gently, and yet never had a kiss felt quite so compelling. In fact, the carefully tender brush of his lips moving slowly back and forth on hers had the effect of inflaming her in milliseconds. All at once Stacy felt herself sagging against him, her bones dissolving and her muscles melting like hot wax. In this molten, boneless state it was easy to allow Chris to pull her entire body up and over his in a total caress.

Her hands, still lost in the thick, fragrant softness of his hair, knotted there while her mouth welcomed his hungrily. Again and again his lips covered hers—lightly, lingeringly, warmly—until Stacy felt the once-familiar heat searing through her body. Its potent pleasure spread along her limbs, not missing a single nerve ending.

As the seconds ticked by soundlessly, Chris's kiss grew deeper. Now his tongue moved in to take sensual possession of her mouth, and one hand glided boldly back and forth over her rib cage. Slowly the audacious hand reached to cup the delicate breasts beneath twin layers of soft, thin cotton.

When he touched her, Stacy's very heart leapt for joy. Her senses began humming, singing their own harmonic melody. And with another kiss, even more encompassing as his lips made music against hers, Stacy felt an ache begin deep inside her, burning emptily, making her aware of being an unfilled vessel.

Abruptly Chris drew back, putting her away from him, even pushing her away as he struggled to a sitting position. In the dimness of the room Stacy could only stare at him, her lips parted in surprised yearning, her emotions shock-torn, her body clamoring with need.

"Now you know the real reason," Chris said, his own voice thick and low with suppressed passion. "I want you, Stacy. I've always wanted you. God help me, I never could leave you alone—and thirteen years later not a thing has changed. I guess I'll always want you...even when it's no good for me and it's no good for you."

"Oh, Chris!" Stacy scarcely recognized that strange hoarse cry as her own.

"I can still make you want me, too, Stacy," Chris rushed on. "You know I can! Just what do you think would happen if we kept lying here another five minutes—hell, even another two minutes?" His hands knotted lightly in her hair, pulling at it a little, just as he seemed to be pulled in two directions at once. "What would happen, Stace, if I made you want me? Would you beg me? Cry for me? Undress me and touch me the way you used to, after I taught you just how to make love?"

"Chris, no—don't!" Stacy gasped, stricken as much by the truth of his words as by his explicit language.

"I can still hear all those things you used to say to me, Stace. They've haunted me for years. Do you know I still dream about it, about making love with you and hearing what you'd say—that it felt good, that you wanted more, much more, and that you loved me—"

"Oh, no, Chris, no!" she cried again. For Stacy thirteen years of regret and reserve and prim inhibitions were crumbling. Somehow she managed to free her hands from Chris's taut grip and she covered her ears, her whole body shaking uncontrollably.

But Chris reached for her hands and peeled them back from her head with those steel-like fingers of his. "You will listen to me, Stace. Together we used to burn like a comet! Why, the way we made love should have lit up the whole sky! Like a comet we almost burned ourselves up, too—at least it nearly destroyed *me*. For years I've thought you got off scot-free. Now I wonder. Did you?"

"No, I didn't!" Stacy heard herself starting to sob. "Oh, God, I didn't! I paid for every single one of those nights, Chris—oh, yes, I paid!"

"You know something, Stacy? I'm still not sorry, even after everything... Hell, no, I'm not sorry I held you in my arms, made love to you for hours. But are we going to hack ourselves up all over again? My God, I've hardly known what to do," Chris exclaimed in baffled tones. "Maybe I've even wanted to ask for your help, because if ever a woman tested my control..."

Now Stacy was trying to free herself, trying to pull away. Tears spilled down her face as though she were eighteen again instead of a mature thirty-one. "I don't want to be cut up all over again, either. I'll help you! I'll *stop* you—"

"Then get the hell out of here right now, Stace, because in another minute I won't be able to stand it. That's just how much I want you lying here beneath me!" Chris blurted.

Stacy backed up and away from him, stumbling over a chair. She stopped, started to right it and then let it fall with a resounding thud as she darted for the door. Still crying—silently now—she ran down the hall until she reached the safety of Lynn's room.

After shutting the door with shaking hands, she sank down onto the soft pale beige carpet and drew her knees up to her chin, hugging them helplessly as she cried. Although most of her sobs were silent, occasionally a strangled sound tore loose from her chest.

Why had Chris said all those things? she wondered desperately. Was he deliberately trying to hurt and humiliate her? That couldn't be true, for he'd indicted himself just as surely.

No, even as those hot compelling words had burst from Chris, Stacy had had the feeling that he was a man desperately struggling to do the so-called right thing. And that meant that Chris Lorio had obviously changed quite a lot from the careless, confident, cocky young man she'd remembered through the years. That young man had taken what he'd wanted, and he'd had the finesse and sexual expertise to do it.

Now, by reminding her so forcefully of just how it had once been between them, Chris had also awakened her fully once again. He had forced Stacy to remember nights and memories she'd hoped to keep locked away safely behind a wall in her mind.

Because bringing them to light was still almost too painful to endure.

Chris had made her want him all over again, too—made her acknowledge it, at least to herself—and Stacy wondered how she could ever bear to face him again.

But as her sobs gradually dwindled and Stacy began wiping at her streaming cheeks, she became aware of a certain alien delight. It stole through her, a single, simple, treacherous thought that made her heart soar.

He still wanted her!

At nine-thirty the next morning Stacy dropped Robbie off at the church's Sunday school entrance, promising him once again that, yes, she would definitely return in time to attend the eleven o'clock church service with him.

The option for adults at this hour was Bible study, which had sounded like more than Stacy could concentrate on this particular morning. She had elected instead to take her car out for a road test since she hadn't had it on a highway following the massive repair job by Floyd.

Earlier Stacy and Robbie had breakfasted together. Mercifully they'd been alone, although Stacy's heart had jerked in painful awareness at every sound, even the occasional creaks of the house settling further onto its foundation. In the bright morning light the scene from the previous night seemed like a lurid fantasy. Still, Stacy knew that it had been no dream, and her mind kept taunting her with thoughts of Chris. She still dreaded facing him, but gradually, as the breakfast hour passed with no sign of him, Stacy began to wonder if he was not grappling with a similar problem and wondering how he could face *her*.

Cold water and several hours of sleep had returned Stacy's eyes to near normal, belying her tears. Still, to have fallen apart so utterly angered her in the bright sunny light of a new day. Unfortunately Chris had chosen to resurrect the most trying and traumatic time of Stacy's entire life—not making love with him, for that had always been exquisite. But facing the aftermath alone, living through the denouement and having to cope with the lasting results of such exquisite passion had exacted a toll she'd barely been able to pay.

Enough of the past! Stacy thought now, pressing down on the accelerator as she left the city limits behind her. She followed an access road that funneled her onto a busy interstate highway. New Orleans, 80 Miles read a huge green and white road sign.

All Stacy cared to know was whether her car could carry her home to New Mexico. She planned to depart early to-morrow morning. By then—if she worked steadily all this afternoon—she could be finished sorting Lynn's personal possessions. Let Chris do whatever he wished about the contents of the attic. She was not going to stay here, Stacy vowed, to be used or manipulated or—

The trouble with those thoughts was that she knew in her heart that Chris had been trying not to use her, even though he probably could have. The way Stacy had responded to Chris on both the occasions he'd kissed her, she knew he was probably right in thinking she could be successfully se-duced. Or could she—really?

The morning sun was now so hot and bright that Stacy fumbled for her sunglasses. Then she rolled up her car windows and switched on the air conditioner.

Outside the world was a blur of green as rampant, lavish, impenetrable vegetation grew high and deep. Sturdy black trunks and limbs of seemingly mile-high trees, all thick with foliage, climbed triumphantly toward the blue cloudless sky. Although grass and weeds growing by the sides of the high-way had been ruthlessly trimmed, a vast Louisiana swamp lay just a few feet away. Through the thick brush Stacy caught occasional glimpses of shining black water, and once she passed a boat with two fishermen seated in it, casting.

Crepe myrtle trees were beginning to bloom, providing an occasional burst of color amid all the greenery. Bright hot pink blooms yielded occasionally to lighter pinks, even to whites and violets. Once again Stacy was struck by the beauty of this lush and extravagant state.

Her car glided along the highway soundlessly. Stacy couldn't recall its ever having run this well, except perhaps when it was brand new, and Gary had driven it then. A sigh escaped her. She still owed Chris for this car.

Well, somehow she'd manage to pay him back after she had returned home, Stacy vowed. Perhaps she could pull

Taylor out of camp, since he wasn't really enjoying it anyway, and receive a partial refund.

It will all work out, Stacy assured herself, since she wasn't up to grappling with practical problems today. She thrust that topic out of her mind, too.

The exotic scent of magnolia blossoms drifted into her car, pulled by the air conditioner. Glancing out, Stacy saw that she was passing a roadside park where the vast trees cast much-needed shade over the hot and humid day. Dotted with huge white blooms they reminded Stacy poignantly of that first summer she'd spent here.

The dance . . . and her first encounter with Chris. He'd drifted away, after he'd learned she was Lynn's cousin, Stacy recalled. He'd pretended to ignore her for the rest of the evening. But then, as Stacy had prepared to leave with her new acquaintances—the giggly girls who'd thought Chris so handsome but so dangerous—he had walked straight over to her.

"Come on, Stacy Powers. I'll drive you home," he said in a low voice meant for her ears alone.

"That's not neces—" She stopped, totally mesmerized by the look in his jet-black eyes, a look so filled with raw desire that Stacy was frightened as well as intrigued.

"Don't you want to come with me?" His voice held a note both silky and alluring.

"Well, I—" Bluntly Stacy blurted out her greatest reservation. "I know you're Cousin Lynn's boyfriend."

Sheer astonishment crossed Chris Lorio's face and lingered for a brief moment. Then one strong hand came up in the stopping motion of a traffic cop. "Hold it," Chris said curtly. "You've obviously gotten the wrong impression. Sure, Lynn is my oldest, closest friend—but I date anyone I choose, and she's certainly free to do the same."

"Well, yes." Stacy sighed, realizing that to an extent what he said was true. In her letters Lynn had often lamented that Chris was sowing more than a few wild oats and hadn't exhibited any desire to settle down as yet. Still, Lynn confidently expected that they'd be engaged one day, and the whole town seemed to agree. Maybe Chris had agreed as well. But, at that dance, Stacy simply lacked the courage to ask. Maybe she was afraid of his frank, honest reply.

"I just...just don't know," Stacy stammered instead. She wanted to leave with him, and yet at the same time she wanted to be loyal to Lynn, too.

"Make up your mind about me while we ride," Chris said masterfully and simply folded her hand in his. Then, before Stacy could protest further, they were outside and climbing up into his truck.

But Chris didn't take Stacy straight home. Instead he drove away from town over quiet, two-lane country roads. When he finally stopped the truck Stacy could see that the setting was blissfully romantic. Moonlight shone on a picturesque lake ringed with magnolia trees. For the rest of her life, Stacy would always remember the smell of magnolias when she thought of Chris Lorio's first kiss.

Up to that point Stacy had been kissed plenty, usually by Gary Thomasson. But no man's kisses had ever made her feel like Chris's—hot and cold all at the same time, willing and weak-kneed and *wanting*. She was immediately hungry for him and avid for anything he could give her.

She yielded, melted, letting her tongue duel with Chris's until she heard the satisfying sound of his gasp and felt a new sudden urgency in his hands. Then, all at once, she grew afraid.

"We'd better stop this," she said, and heard her own voice sounding like that of a breathless stranger.

"All right," he agreed, still in that smooth and silky voice. Immediately he started up the engine of his truck and turned around, heading back toward the Langlois city limits. But he also kept an arm around Stacy as he drove, and his long fingers caressed her bare arm, then glided beneath the loose sleeve of her thin summer dress. His fingers were hot and his touch exciting—an excitement that ignited when those fingers roamed slowly to the slope of her breast. There they rested, just barely moving, their gentle pressure far more inflammatory than any grabs or tugs by less adept men had ever been.

"Chris, uh...tell me what—what you're doing this summer," Stacy stammered, trying to talk to him on the return trip. Perhaps she'd also been trying to escape the distraction of those long warm fingers that, for some reason, she just couldn't push away. "Are you working at—at a service station?"

"No. This summer I'm working as personal assistant to Knox Kinard. He's a local attorney who has a law firm here with Congressman Hamilton Bainbridge. Usually Bainbridge is in Washington, but he's been back and forth a lot this year. He'll be leaving on a fact-finding trip to Europe later this summer. He and Lynn's parents are friends, so they're all planning a get-together in Paris." Lightly his thumb grazed her nipple, setting it ablaze.

"Lynn's mentioned the congressman occasionally," Stacy said, soaking up Chris's words like a sponge so that later she could remember not only his exact phrasing but also their tempo and tone. "How nice that the congressman and the Ashleys will see each other."

"It would be even nicer if I could finagle a way to go along," Chris muttered.

Yet even as Stacy listened intently to Chris, as he began sharing a few of his plans and dreams, the physical part of her was aware of little except the glide of his fingers up and down her breast, tantalizing and teasing and gradually growing bolder.

It seemed forever before they stopped, this time in front of Stacy's grandmother's dark house, and Stacy could melt back into Chris's arms again.

Later, as she tried to sleep in her narrow bed in a small bedroom sticky-hot, because her grandmother could not afford air-conditioning, Stacy's whole body tingled and burned with a new expectancy. She'd been awakened to new desires and she tossed restlessly on her sweat-dampened sheets, her tongue occasionally licking her lips where *his* had so recently been pressed.

Stacy had never had trouble resisting a man before. But from the very beginning Chris Lorio had known her body and its responses even better than Stacy herself. Indeed, all she knew on that sultry summer night was that he was the most physically exciting man she'd ever met and she was falling madly in love.

The organ music built to a powerful crescendo. Stacy, staring down at the rapt face of the child seated on her right, knew that whether or not Robbie had inherited Lynn's musical talent, he definitely had an inborn love for music. The stirring, triumphant processional as Father Glover marched in along with the acolytes and choir was a stirring spectacle even in a small-town church like this.

Before I leave Langlois tomorrow I'll urge Chris to keep exposing Robbie to good music, Stacy decided. Then even if Robbie does insist on dropping piano lessons now he may return to music when he grows a little older and wiser.

A strange pang shot through Stacy as she thought of leaving young Robbie alone and motherless once again. She would keep remembering this child, she knew, with deep concern for his welfare. He was already very important to her. And as for leaving Chris again—

Suddenly Stacy felt Robbie nudge her gently. Everyone was moving onto the kneeling hassocks and Stacy hadn't even noticed. She dropped down obediently beside Robbie as he chanted words familiar to him and to the rest of the congregation.

Soon they stood to sing a hymn. Just as they started into the second stanza, Stacy's startled eyes saw the handsome, dark-haired man who suddenly materialized at the end of their pew. He slipped past an elderly couple with a softly murmured word of apology to them, and moved down to join Stacy and Robbie.

"Daddy!" Robbie whispered to the tall man on his right as his face brightened with surprise and joy.

Over the child's head Chris's stark eyes met Stacy's for a fleeting minute, then he reached to take a hymnal that the elderly couple pressed into his hands.

Her heart pounding, Stacy bowed her head over the hymnal that she and Robbie shared. Chris...*here*? Her senses swam with amazement for she knew he was no churchgoer. And just what had that naked expression in his eyes really meant?

Today Chris looked his most distinguished in a perfectly tailored navy suit, which definitely hadn't come off of a rack. A pale blue shirt lay beneath, topped with a subdued foulard tie.

When the congregation sat again to listen to Father Glover announce church events for the coming week, Chris drew a pen from the inside pocket of his coat. Rapidly he jotted a few lines across his church bulletin. Then he passed the bulletin over Robbie's head to Stacy.

Bewildered, she turned it to read Chris's note, written catercorner in the margin. *I chose a poor way to thank you for curing my headache,* said the bold, black words. *Please try to forgive me.*

Try to forgive me... Those were not the words of the proud and arrogant Chris Lorio that Stacy had once known. That man would have strangled on such words. He would have cheerfully died before ever uttering them!

Unless this was a clever act, then Lynn's influence on Chris had been even greater than Stacy had suspected. But what should she do now about his request? Did she dare to believe he meant it?

At just that moment, like a synchronistic bell chiming right in her ear Stacy heard Father Glover announce that today his sermon topic was forgiveness.

Startled, Stacy wondered if God could possibly have a sense of humor.

Whether the Almighty did or didn't, Stacy determined to concentrate on the sermon that followed. Maybe there was another message for her. She listened attentively to Father Glover, a quiet-spoken man in his sixties, who seemed to understand that base human instinct was to stay mad, strike back whenever you could and always wish the very worst for your so-called enemies. But there was a higher, better way, he stressed, warming to his topic.

The others in the congregation appeared to listen, too. Then Stacy was momentarily distracted by a movement from the first pew, where a familiar-looking woman with a silvery chignon stirred restlessly.

"Furthermore," the minister continued, trying to make another point for the nearly superhuman virtue of forgiveness.

Stacy found her attention moving to the man seated on the other side of Robbie. She darted a quick look at Chris and found him listening dutifully to the sermon. But as Stacy kept staring at him, unable to look away, his black eyes swung toward her. Now they looked baffled and even held a glint of pain.

Was Chris still hurting? Stacy wondered. No, he'd said that she'd cured his headache. Was he in mental or emotional pain?

She swallowed hard, bowing her head with the rest of the congregation for a prayer. All right, she would try to be forgiving even though she couldn't begin to understand Chris's incomprehensible behavior toward her.

When the service ended a few minutes later Stacy glanced casually around the church. Chris was unquestionably the best-looking man in this gathering, she had to admit. Next to his natural male magnificence, all other men paled.

Suddenly Stacy's mouth felt dry. Longing filled her like water running into an empty cup until she stiffened, wondering how she dared feel anything of this sort at church. Then Stacy realized that her deepest longing right now—sparked by Chris's own words requesting forgiveness—really had little to do with physical desire. She wanted just to be held close to Chris's heart for a few minutes. Wanted to share long-bottled-up words of her own. She even longed to confide the oldest and most precious secret of all.

The moment passed. Stacy grew aware of a curious wash of eyes sweeping over them as she filed out with Chris and Robbie to a triumphant swell of organ music. She also saw that Father Glover's silver-haired wife was making her way toward them.

On the church steps Father Glover stood, shaking hands with his parishioners. Stacy found herself funneled into line, wedged between the two Lorios.

"Hello, Chris... Robbie. How good to see you both!" Father Glover's mellifluous voice washed over them first, then he turned to Stacy. "Hello, my dear. I don't believe we've met."

Chris presented Stacy to the minister with an economy of words. By that time Mrs. Glover had arrived on the scene.

"I remember you!" the attractive woman cried triumphantly to Stacy. "Oh, I don't exactly remember how many years it's been, but I know your name is Stacy. You were from—where? Arizona? New Mexico?"

Still chatting effusively, Mrs. Glover linked her arm through Stacy's and drew her away from the crowd. "My goodness, but you're just as pretty and young-looking as ever! What brings you back to Langlois?"

Stacy explained about Lynn's request and saw Mrs. Glover's blue eyes cloud briefly. "Oh, yes, we all miss poor dear Lynn. Such an exemplary wife and mother... for all that she really wasn't right for Chris, you know."

Stacy couldn't stop her start of surprise. This was the last thing she had expected to hear on the church steps from a parson's wife. "Oh?" she said, adding loyally, "I've never heard that comment before."

"But Lynn really was wrong—for both of them, actually. Robbie as well as Chris. She was just too frail... too gentle and ethereal. Why, just look at how vigorous they both are—how full of life and vitality—"

"They've never complained about Lynn," Stacy cut in coolly. "Just the opposite, in fact."

"Oh, dear, I didn't mean to offend you." Despite her apologetic words, Mrs. Glover spoke quite briskly. She was blunt and plain-spoken, Stacy realized, and suddenly she knew, as if by empathy, that being a parson's wife had never come easily to this woman. "What I really meant—" Mrs. Glover stopped, then plunged ahead. "Actually, you know, I always expected you to marry Chris."

"Me!" Stacy cried, amazed that anyone else had ever shared her one-time dream.

"Yes. Because I never saw Chris look at any woman the way he looked at you. Oh, here come my daughters. They're visiting for the weekend. Stacy, have you met Caroline and Elspeth?"

When she found herself being led forth to meet both of the Glover daughters Stacy glanced back at Chris and Robbie. Chris was deep in conversation with one of the ushers, but he glanced up and his eyes met Stacy's once again. This time amusement lurked in their dark depths. He knew she'd been captured even before Stacy mouthed, "Help!"

After a couple of minutes he came to her rescue, steering Robbie before him. "Good morning, Mrs. Glover," Chris said coolly, then he turned to the other two women. "Caroline—Elspeth, how nice to see you again."

Stacy wondered if she'd imagined it or if Chris's voice and manner had warmed perceptibly as he'd greeted the two younger women. They were both tall and fair, handsome rather than pretty, and quite pleasant of manner.

"How surprising to see you, Chris," Mrs. Glover said, her tone faintly tinged with acid even as her hand went out to touch Robbie's head. "Your fourth visit, I believe."

Chris blinked. "I'm not sure," he said as he leaned over Robbie to shake hands with Elspeth and Caroline.

"Let's see, you came here to be married and for Robbie's christening. Then there was Lynn's funeral," Mrs. Glover enumerated. "So what's the special occasion today?"

"No particular reason." Chris gave an easy shrug. He managed to snag Stacy around the waist with a casual hand. "Are you ready to go?"

But Mrs. Glover wasn't quite ready to let her conversation with Chris end. "So what do you think of a typical church service?'' she inquired, still in that faintly scolding tone.

"Oh, it's all right,'' Chris said maliciously, "but I wouldn't want to make a habit of it.''

"So what does Dr. Caroline Glover do?'' Stacy asked curiously.

"Research into the physiology of armadillos,'' Chris responded. "Beyond that it's all too technical for me.''

It was an hour later. Stacy, Chris and Robbie sat in the restaurant of Langlois's leading hotel, the remains of a lavish Sunday brunch still before them.

"And Dr. Elspeth Glover?'' Stacy inquired.

"Elspeth's a pediatrician in practice in Baton Rouge.''

"I wonder what their ages are,'' Stacy continued. She wasn't really all that interested in the two Dr. Glovers but this was convenient cover-up conversation to make with Chris.

During the past hour they had spoken only of mundane things, as though both were obviously determined to pretend that the previous night had never happened.

"Elspeth is a few years older than I am,'' Chris replied. "Caroline a couple of years younger.''

"And neither of them have married? That's unusual for women in their thirties,'' Stacy mused. "They're both so nice-looking and intelligent, too.''

"Actually Elspeth married about ten years ago, but it didn't work out,'' Chris explained. "Since she didn't have any children she took her maiden name back. I know because I was in practice with Knox Kinard at the time, and our firm handled her divorce. I think not having grandchildren is a great disappointment to Mrs. Glover.'' Pointedly Chris looked across at Robbie. "That's probably why she makes such a fuss over you.''

"Oh,'' said Robbie unenthusiastically.

Abruptly Chris wadded up his napkin and tossed it beside his plate. "Are you two finished?'' he asked Stacy and Robbie. "Good!'' he continued at their nods, "let's get out of here because I see that wretched Betty Thackery and her whole miserable family getting out of their car. If we hurry we can miss them."

Chris tossed four ten-dollar bills beside his plate, then rushed Stacy and Robbie out the side door.

Robbie giggled at what Chris described as "a close escape," and Stacy couldn't help remarking, "So this is what a fugitive feels like."

"Well, I'm sorry but I really can't stand that woman," Chris explained, bundling Stacy and Robbie into the Monte Carlo. Then he hurried off to his own Mercedes.

They all arrived back at the house at about the same time. There, in the foyer, Chris announced to Stacy in a matter-of-fact voice that he was leaving town that afternoon. He had a court case upstate on Wednesday and wanted to arrive a few days early for adequate preparation. Then, following the trial, he thought he'd enjoy fishing for a couple of days, since he'd be close to a particularly scenic lake.

"You're going to be gone for six whole days!" Robbie exploded, obviously having counted the days while Chris spoke. When Chris nodded the boy's lower lip began to quiver slightly.

"Hey, sport, don't look like that," Chris teased, avoiding Stacy's eyes. "Oh, I guess there's something I failed to mention. I'll be taking you along with me! I'm sure Stacy can work a lot better with both of us gone."

Chapter Seven

God, how he hated to fish, Chris thought.

Never mind that this was a traditional male sport. He'd always hated to fish, finding it dull and monotonous, not to mention usually being hot as Hades, too, when you were out on the water with the summer sun broiling down on you like it was today.

The only thing worse than fishing, in Chris's opinion, was cleaning fish, and from the way those flashing silvery nuisances had been going after the worms on his and Robbie's hooks they now had a whole damned string of fish to clean.

"Look, Daddy, I'm getting another nibble!" Robbie exclaimed excitedly.

At least Robbie was having fun, Chris thought morosely. As for him, he'd rather be back in that courtroom, even though the judge had taken an acute dislike both to Chris and his client and had ruled against them. Certainly Chris knew he'd rather be back home, performing even the most grinding of chores, than to be sweating in this damned boat, which he kept praying would mercifully sink.

"Daddy, can we take Stacy some fish?" Robbie asked.

"I don't know why not," Chris replied. God knows *he* didn't want them. He hated eating fish just one degree less than he hated catching and cleaning them, and never mind that fish was supposedly good for you.

Robbie's mention of Stacy brought her back very keenly into his mind. Not that she'd ever been far away. Chris continued thinking of her even though it irked him thoroughly to do so. She still intruded regularly on his thoughts, not to mention his sleep.

She, of course, was the reason he'd fled his own house.

Even now, days after the fact, Chris was still annoyed that he'd gone. He wasn't used to being driven out by women, beautiful or not, and he still found Stacy so beautiful that sometimes the mere sight of her made his throat tighten up and his chest feel constricted, as if a heavy weight had been resting there.

It was all just a physical thing, of course. Mainly a physical lack. And, if Chris was just half as smart as he'd thought he was, he would have found himself someone else by now to satisfy all those male urges that kept making his life holy hell. Then, with sex no longer such a burning issue, he'd be able to treat Stacy as he wanted to—coolly, indifferently and impersonally, Chris thought.

He had known from the moment he first saw her taut, set face at the church that she intended to trot right back home to New Mexico. The thirty new miles on her car's speedometer were the clinching argument, for as Chris had approached the church earlier that Sunday, hoping to set things right between them and also hoping rather cynically that church might have softened her up, he'd idly dropped his hand on the hood of her car. The heat of a still-hot engine beneath warned him against any quick solution.

He knew at once that Stacy had been out driving, making sure her newly repaired car was roadworthy.

By God, it ought to be, he thought irritably, reaching now to remove the fat and flopping fish that Robbie had swung so triumphantly in Daddy's direction. Chris had paid tha

SILHOUETTE DELIVERS FIRST-CLASS ROMANCE— DIRECT TO YOUR DOOR

Mail the Heart sticker on the postpaid order card today and you'll receive:

— **4 new Silhouette Special Edition novels—FREE**
— **an elegant pen & watch set—FREE**
— **and a surprise mystery bonus—FREE**

But that's not all. You'll also get:

Money-Saving Home Delivery

When you subscribe to Silhouette Special Editions the excitement, romance and faraway adventures of these novels can be yours for previewing in the convenience of your own home at less than retail prices. Every month we'll deliver 6 new books right to your door. If you decide to keep them, they'll be yours for only $2.49 each. That's 26¢ less per book than what you pay in stores. And there is no extra charge for shipping and handling!

Free Monthly Newsletter

It's the indispensable insider's look at our most popular writers and their upcoming novels. Now you can have a behind-the-scenes look at the fascinating world of Silhouette! It's an added bonus you'll look forward to every month!

Special Extras—FREE

Because our home subscribers are our most valued readers, we'll be sending you additional free gifts from time to time as a token of our appreciation.

OPEN YOUR MAILBOX TO A WORLD OF LOVE AND ROMANCE EACH MONTH. JUST COMPLETE, DETACH AND MAIL YOUR FREE OFFER CARD TODAY!

Remember! To receive your free books, pen and watch set and mystery gift, return the postpaid card below. But don't delay!

DETACH AND MAIL CARD TODAY.

If offer card has been removed, write to:
Silhouette Books, 901 Fuhrmann Blvd., P.O. Box 1867, Buffalo, NY 14269-1867

bandit Floyd more than eight hundred dollars to fix up the Monte Carlo and make it run the way it should.

But last Sunday, when Chris had divined Stacy's intent—which wasn't hard to do, considering his own uncivilized behavior—he knew he had to find some way to stop her from leaving Louisiana.

Now, to himself, Chris argued that it was the least he could do for his late, beloved wife who had been so insistent that it must be Stacy, only Stacy, to sort through the possessions accumulated over years and generations.

Could Lynn sleep peacefully if her last wishes weren't fulfilled? For that matter, could *he*?

And yet, because Chris always tried to be truthful with himself, he knew there was that other reason, too.

Inappropriate though it was, his constant, gnawing hunger for Stacy was the real reason Chris didn't want her to leave. Even though he had no intention of satisfying that hunger, having the object of his desire nearby assured him that he was alive and vital once again, and that his time of feeling lost and grieving for Lynn was over.

Also, once Stacy left, Chris doubted if they would ever see each other again. He'd told her so quite plainly. Why it was important that she not leave yet he wasn't sure. He just knew that it was.

Of course the irony was that, thanks to his inability to keep his hands off her, they weren't seeing each other *now*.

Still, he knew she was close by, just a couple of hours' drive from this fish-infested lake where he and Robbie kept casting their worms upon the water and watching two- and three-pound fish come back attached.

At least, too, this time he'd played scrupulously fair with Stacy, Chris thought. There had been no exploitation of her. No manipulation or elaborate seduction or trying to take advantage of her own strongly sensual nature. He'd warned her how he felt, released her and told her to run.

She'd taken off like a scared rabbit, too, he remembered, his lips twisting wryly. Stacy didn't want a sexual involvement any more than he did. At least on that topic they were in full accord for once.

You'd think that merely knowing she didn't want him would have cooled him off, Chris reflected. But it hadn't...not really. Because he still wanted Stacy in the most basic and elemental way, just as he wanted food when he was hungry and water when there was thirst to quench. He wanted her...wanted her...

"Look, Daddy, you're getting a bite on your line!" Robbie squealed excitedly.

Oh, swell, Chris thought, and began dutifully to reel in his catch.

How still and quiet the house was, Stacy thought on the second day that Chris and Robbie were away. Already there seemed to be a deserted air, as if all the home's occupants had fled, never to return.

How fanciful she was being! Stacy scoffed. Miriam and Preston were still downstairs, enjoying a well-deserved holiday, no doubt, so the house was certainly not deserted.

She simply felt lonesome and at loose ends with both of the men away, Stacy tried to tell herself. Yet this ignored another basic reality, too—the fact that she'd always enjoyed having time to herself. Just let the door slam behind the exhausting Taylor and Stacy had been known to fling herself to the sofa, cast her eyes toward heaven and say fervently, "Praise God!" Then she could do her hair or nails in perfect peace. Or she could read a book or watch the cerebral sort of TV show that Taylor could never abide.

Taylor. Stacy tried to fill some of the long quiet hours by writing to her absent son. Even though she longed to hear the sound of his perky voice, Taylor had made her promise that she wouldn't be "phoning him night and day, carrying on like most mothers." Since Taylor's scorn for clinging women was so great, and he clearly wished to avoid the humiliation of being summoned to a camp telephone to talk to Stacy, she tried to respect his wishes. If Taylor should need her he had her phone number here in Langlois. Of course, Taylor rarely needed her for anything.

Now Stacy sighed aloud, dipping into the barrel that Preston had brought from the attic that morning. Missing people—the way she was presently missing Taylor, Robbie and Chris—was not something she'd experienced often in recent years.

Stacy just devoutly hoped she wasn't falling in love with Chris all over again!

She swallowed hard at the thought. But the man preyed on her mind. She kept remembering how handsome Chris had looked in his expensive business suits and then contrasting that with his state of natural male beauty in swim trunks or shorts. She remembered his occasional humorous quips. Most of all, Stacy kept remembering the moment in his darkened study when he'd pulled her down on top of him, and the way his mouth had burned beneath hers. She kept remembering the way he'd aroused her so easily and his own obvious state of physical excitement.

Oh, God, after more than a decade of chaste, careful living she couldn't be setting herself up to make the same mistake all over again, she just couldn't!

In fact, she never should have made the mistake the first time. She'd had plenty of warnings about Chris from the very beginning. Stacy had been warned most rigorously by her grim, disapproving grandmother. Old Mrs. Powers had insisted that Chris wasn't really serious about Stacy and would undoubtedly walk away from her without a backward look—a good thing, she'd added, because he was bad, dangerous, wicked...

"Chris Lorio can't really help it," her grandmother had continued, a fanatic's glow lighting her usually cold eyes. "He's the devil's spawn, you see."

"He's the *what*?" eighteen-year-old Stacy had cried in surprise.

Mrs. Powers had been happy to amplify on her primitive and—in Stacy's opinion—crackpot beliefs. "He's a bad seed. Children born out of holy wedlock always are. Since they were conceived in sin and lust they're easy prey for the devil. Now, nobody knows exactly who Chris Lorio's parents are but plenty of us have our ideas! I don't think he'd be working in Knox Kinard's law office right now if he wasn't Knox's woods colt. And I'm not forgetting, either, how infatuated Knox was once with Kathryn Ann Harper."

"Who was Kathryn Ann Harper?" Stacy had asked her grandmother curiously during that pivotal summer.

"She's the younger sister of the parson's wife," Mrs. Powers had related with relish. "She was a prettier woman than Ellen Glover, but she always wore a lot of paint on her face and she was wild, too. She smoked cigarettes and drank liquor and had herself a high old time! Then there was Knox. He was already engaged to Lottie Ericson, who was plain as a post, but her daddy had promised to push Knox's career along, and Sam Ericson had the influence to do it, too. So the way I figure, Knox had himself one last fling with Kathryn Ann and that's how Chris Lorio was got."

"Did Knox go ahead and marry Lottie?" Stacy had wondered.

"He sure did 'cause Knox knew well enough which side of his bread had butter. Kathryn Ann might have been pretty but she was poor. So off Kathryn Ann and her sister, Ellen Glover, went to tour the Holy Land, they said. A bunch of baloney if I ever heard it! And Kathryn Ann has never been back here to Langlois since. That's 'cause she's got bad memories and a guilty conscience. But you just take a close look at Knox sometimes. See how tall and dark he is. See if you don't see some resemblance to Chris Lorio. And you just remember, young lady, what's likely to happen to any decent, God-fearing woman who gets too friendly with a bastard. You're inviting hellfire and damnation—"

Now why was she thinking of all that nonsense? Stacy wondered. Her grandmother had been dead for several years, and it would have been a lie to say that old Mrs. Powers had been loved or missed by anyone. Fanatics were rarely lovable.

Oh, she'd probably thought of it again simply because she kept thinking about Chris. Also, Stacy knew, she still had Ellen Glover on her mind, as well as the astonishing things the parson's wife had said. Of course, Mrs. Glover's interest was logical if she was indeed Chris's aunt. But was Knox really Chris's father? Stacy wondered. Did Chris himself even know for sure?

Stacy suspected that he did. She couldn't imagine Chris letting anything as important as the identity of his parents escape him.

Sighing, Stacy delved to the bottom of the storage barrel and wished there weren't two dozen more just like it stored up in the attic. Even after she'd finished with the barrels, there were a number of boxes and suitcases to go through as well.

"Miss Stacy?"

At the timid voice behind her, Stacy turned in surprise. Young Ted Thackery stood there, looking at her uneasily.

"Yes, Ted?" Stacy said, not missing a beat in her sorting of tea towels. She'd seen him hanging around the tree house earlier this morning looking forlorn. Obviously he missed Robbie.

"Miss Stacy, I wondered if you'd help me," Ted said earnestly. "I know you can swim real good, but I've never learned how. I took classes twice at the Y but—but I get scared ever' time I put my face in the water. My mom says I act that way 'cause I almost smothered once when I was real little."

"Oh, Ted, I don't think—" Stacy started to produce a glib lie when the real misery in the child's face got through to her. Perhaps if Ted had one-on-one attention from an instructor instead of being just one more kid in a busy, crowded class, he could be encouraged to overcome his fears.

Also, what was she doing that was more important than making a child feel secure and proud of himself? Stacy asked herself.

"Sure, Ted, I'll try to help you," she said, forcing enthusiasm into her voice. "Why, we can get in a lot of practice while Robbie is away."

"Yeah. He won't be there to laugh at me," Ted said in a disconsolate voice.

Stacy made a mental note to tell Robbie to be more sensitive to Ted's various deficiencies. "Well, run on home and get your trunks, Ted," she said aloud, "and I'll meet you by the pool in ten minutes."

Home had never looked so good! After four nights in various motel beds, which in rural Louisiana were never long enough to accommodate his height, Chris found the sight of his large, two-story home beautiful and reassuring—until he noticed the blue bicycle lying in the driveway.

"That isn't *your* bicycle, is it?" Chris said questioningly to Robbie. But he knew it wasn't even before Robbie shook his head. Preston would never have allowed a bicycle to remain in the driveway for days, nor would Stacy have been riding Robbie's bike, since it was too small for her.

"Looks like it's Ted's," Robbie volunteered.

"What's he doing over here when you're away?" Chris said crossly. He was sick to death of sun and water. Sick of being in the exclusive company of a talkative eight-year-old, even though he loved Robbie with all his heart. Certainly he was sick of handling fish...more and more damned fish. Four days' catch, frozen into icy blocks, were layered into his ice chest right now. Chris knew he'd probably never get out the stench of them, but Robbie had been determined to bring back all his fish for Stacy.

Chris hoped *she*, at least, could eat a few and make Robbie happy.

Now that pesky little Thackery kid was over here, which scarcely boded well, Chris thought darkly. Preston wouldn't be on the lookout for him, as he was whenever Robbie was home. Nor did Chris have to specialize in personal-injury cases to realize that it could cost him an arm and a leg if Ted

tumbled out of the tree house or fell into his swimming
pool—

Oh God, the stupid kid couldn't even swim!

With his heart suddenly knocking against his ribs, Chris
flung open the door of the Blazer, his recreational vehicle,
and started running toward the pool. The patter of steps
behind him told Chris that Robbie was hot on his heels.

*What if the kid is lying on the bottom of the pool? What
if he's—*

Chris's worried flow of thoughts were cut short as he
rounded the corner and skidded to a breathless stop. A
healthy thrashing sound came from the water. Also, there
was Stacy serving as a responsible lookout, Chris saw with
relief.

She was crouched on the edge of the pool wearing a pale
lemon-colored bikini that was light-years away from that
dark, dowdy tank suit she'd worn before.

The wet bikini showed off each ripe luscious curve. The
scanty material clung to her high full breasts and cupped
around her delectable little bottom. It displayed those long
tanned legs of hers just the way such works of art should be
shown.

Chris felt his body give a throb of arousal even while he
was still half a football field away from her.

"That's it, Ted! Now you're really moving!" Stacy called
enthusiastically to the splashing child.

"Well, I'll be damned," Chris mused as Robbie came
panting up behind him. "Ted's swimming!"

Somehow she had taught the kid how to swim after every
other instructor in town had branded Ted a hopeless case.
Not that he'd probably ever be Olympic material. What he
lacked right now in form and grace, even doing the basic
dog paddle, was considerable. Still, he was managing to
keep himself afloat, and considering his consistent record of
failures, that was quite an accomplishment.

"Stacy's a real good teacher," Robbie said loyally, then
he dashed past his father crying, "Stacy! Ted! I'm back and
I've caught lots and lots of fish!"

Stacy turned at Robbie's shout, and her arms opened instinctively to the child. When Chris saw her bright smile and
the way she simply folded Robbie tight against her, the stab
of hunger shot through him again, even stronger than before.

He remembered being in the cabana with her years ago
and how they'd lie exhausted after making passionate love.
Remembered his head pillowed on the soft warm mounds of
her breasts and how her gorgeous, shapely legs had still been
locked around him tightly.

Chris wanted to be just where Robbie was right now, held
against that gorgeous body. His desire to be close to Stacy
once again, joined and linked with her, was suddenly so
overwhelming that Chris turned away swiftly.

Yes, what he needed was a long cold shower. The thought
of dousing his passion was far from pleasant, but the alternative was having Stacy leave, and for reasons he still didn't
understand, Chris was no longer eager to see her go back
home.

"Stacy, Stacy!"

"What is it, Robbie?"

"Aren't you coming out to see the 'clipse?"

Stacy sighed, her hands deep in barrel number eight. Or
was this one number nine? Sometimes she thought they
multiplied like toadstools—each time she had a barrel
moved down from the attic, two more seemed to sprout behind it. She'd been here in Langlois for almost four weeks,
but she was still a long way from being through with the
contents of the attic.

Now she looked up at the excited little boy framed in the
doorway. "I don't think so, Robbie," Stacy sighed. "I
watched an eclipse of the sun last year in New Mexico. We
couldn't use a telescope. In fact, we had to watch it through
a piece of camera film so we wouldn't burn our eyes."

"But this is a moon 'clipse and we can use a telescope!
And the earth's passing 'tween the sun and the moon,
Daddy says. Anyway, he told me to come fetch you."

Stacy's wayward heart gave an unguarded lurch as it always did on matters concerning Chris. "He did?" she asked dubiously.

"Yes, ma'am. He says since the moon's full it's gonna be a spectacle and you oughtna miss it."

"All right," Stacy decided quickly, rising from the carpet. "Let me rinse the dust off my hands and then I'll be down. Where are you guys? In the garden?"

"By the pool. That's the best place 'cause there aren't any trees and bushes to get in the way of the sky. Preston and Miriam are coming, too!" Robbie added.

Again Stacy felt her heart knock against her breastbone. The pool. She never went there at night. But, at least, she wouldn't be out there alone with Chris. No, tonight she would have plenty of company, and Chris would be preoccupied with the telescope that he'd brought home to use in instructing Robbie and Ted about eclipses.

Actually Stacy wondered why she feared being with Chris at all. Since he'd returned from his fishing trip with Robbie he'd been polite but distant, indeed almost aloof. They'd scarcely spoken a single private word. They were always with Robbie and Ted or Miriam and Preston, or some combination thereof.

Of course, Stacy had been just as scrupulous as Chris about keeping them apart. Yet, paradoxically, the more careful she and Chris were to avoid dangerous situations and compromising positions, the more she, at least, yearned to be alone with him again. Something still happened to Stacy each time she glanced up and met Chris's black, usually inscrutable eyes, and despite everything their gazes met often. Deep inside, in a vital area that Stacy couldn't quite identify, something seemed to be tearing loose, slowly rent apart, thawing and melting...

"I want you, Stacy."

She kept hearing the words Chris had spoken in the dark soft quiet of his study. And each time they played through her mind Stacy's body seemed like a delicate instrument that vibrated in response.

He stalked her dreams—a tall, dark presence who would have seemed menacing if he had been any other man. In Stacy's dreams Chris boldly invaded her room, her bed, her body. But in all the fantasies and dreams Stacy could only welcome him, her body twining feverishly around the strong, rock-hard length of his.

Now she hastily splashed water on her face, added fresh lipstick to her mouth and put a single drop of perfume behind each ear. Then she smoothed her casual shorts and camp shirt, thrust her feet into sandals and dashed down the stairs to join the group by the pool.

As Stacy sped through the gardens she happened to think of Taylor. Would he be watching the lunar eclipse tonight?

How she wished for some further word from him. But there had been nothing but an ominous and probably surly silence since his single postcard. Stacy had written him a number of gung-ho letters about giving camp a fair chance and learning to adjust to and endure his tent mates and how it was costing her a bundle to keep him there. Unfortunately for his mother, Taylor rarely succumbed to guilt.

If the little wretch doesn't write or call me by tomorrow then I'm calling him—and I don't care if it embarrasses him, Stacy thought, her familiar exasperation at Taylor peaking once again.

He was so strong-willed—so utterly independent and self-reliant, too. In temperament as well as looks, Taylor was so very, very much like his father!

Stacy reached the pool area, then turned to greet everyone. Preston and Miriam were sprawled comfortably in lawn chairs while Ted managed to nervously crawl all over his Robbie stood at Chris's elbow, looking anxiously from hi father to the telescope that Chris was attempting to assemble.

Chris, sprawled on the concrete apron of the pool muttering imprecations, was sweating as he struggled with the unfamiliar instrument. He glanced up at Stacy as she passed by, his face level with her knees, and she intercepted a black and baleful look.

Hadn't he been the one to send for her? she wondered indignantly. "Am I intruding?" she inquired, her voice fairly dripping icicles.

"No!" he snarled in a far from reassuring voice.

"Well, if you're mad at me—" Stacy began spiritedly.

"I am not mad at you, damn it! I'm mad at this—" He spewed several unprintable words at the telescope.

"Chris! Not in front of the children," Stacy cried, shocked.

What he muttered about kids wasn't much better, so Stacy moved off huffily to take an empty chair. Her lips tightly clamped, she sank down and glanced over at Preston and Miriam. The staid elderly couple were pointing to the full round moon and marveling at the dark rim just beginning to shadow it.

Robbie was twitching by now, growing just as antsy as Ted. "Hurry up, Daddy, or we're gonna miss it!" he urged, which prompted another lengthy blast of curses from Chris.

"Robbie, come over here and leave your father alone," Stacy instructed, speaking before she thought.

But this time the look Chris tossed in her direction was pure gratitude. "Look, why don't you and Ted race down to the streetlight, then back to the tree house and let's see who can get up there first?" she suggested. "I'll pay the winner fifty cents."

The two boys were off like a shot on a nearly equal contest. While Robbie's legs might actually be a bit longer, Ted could climb trees with the agility of a monkey.

With the two young boys out of the way for five minutes, Stacy was finally able to concentrate her attention on the frustrated Chris. Even in faded navy shorts and an equally faded red polo shirt he was still an arresting sight. His shirt had pulled loose from the waistband of his shorts and lay twisted awry, exposing several inches of his brown corded belly. His long muscular legs were akimbo, and a light sheen of sweat plastered his dark hair to his forehead and made his face glisten as he wrestled with and heartily cursed the obstreperous telescope.

Just the sight of him—of all that raw male beauty on open display—made Stacy's limbs feel heavy while her breathing grew almost painfully labored. She couldn't help but be aware of every erogenous zone in her entire body. They each seemed to be throbbing in lack, in emptiness and in blatant need.

Stacy had given up wondering why Chris, of all men on earth, should still affect her so. He just did. He always had. It was that simple.

Now he gave a grunt of triumph and sat up. Automatically he straightened his legs and tugged down his shirt, tucking it into his shorts. "Robbie! Ted!" Chris yelled to the boys. "The telescope's ready."

One by one Chris helped them peer through it and demonstrated how to adjust its focus for their own particular eyesight. Now that the blasted thing was up, the cries of surprise and exclamations of delight that the telescope elicited made his struggles to erect the new toy worthwhile, he decided. Everyone exclaimed over the suddenly visible pits and craters on the moon's surface; everyone eagerly anticipated the large darkening shadow that was rapidly creeping over and covering the bright full disc.

Stacy was the last to take a look, having thoughtfully hung back to allow the children, then Miriam and Preston to go first. She was always thoughtful, Chris realized, and again he felt ashamed for having glared at her.

She just hadn't known what she was doing to him, of course, or how nearly visibly she had affected him when she'd dropped her dimpled knee down about two inches from his rapacious mouth. The desire to taste, touch, lick, kiss and caress had been almost overpowering, causing another layer of perspiration to break out all over him. He remembered once when he'd done just that, feasting on her lovely, tempting body. This time he'd either had to get so angry he could think of little but his rage or suffer the inevitable consequences of becoming aroused in front of everybody.

Sometimes it was a hell of a thing just being a man, especially when you kept trying to be the right sort of guy and set a proper example for a worshipful young boy to follow.

It had been one thing for him to go slam-banging through life years ago, Chris reflected. But everything was different for him now.

Except for the way he felt about Stacy.

She came over now to where he stood, the last to take a look. "See, here's the focus knob," Chris explained as she bent slightly to look. He waited for a moment. "Can you see anything?"

Puzzled, Stacy shook her head and Chris swore under his breath even as he stepped forward to help her. Preston was the only one who'd gotten it right on the first try.

"Look, Stacy, stare through here—" automatically Chris slipped his arms around her to guide her "—and look through the telescope while I slowly turn the focus button—"

"There!" she cried in excitement, unconsciously dropping a soft hand down on his arm. "Oh, Chris, I see it! It's marvelous. Oh, how exciting!"

It sure as hell was, he could heartily agree, but *he* didn't mean the moon. He meant her pert little fanny burning the back of his thigh every time she moved. He meant the soft fragrance that wafted toward him on seductive undulations of air. He meant her clean profile, her smooth soft cheeks and gentle brow, her huge eyes and delicately outlined lips.

She'd worn lipstick, too, Chris noticed, frustration rising in him like bile. She probably had no idea what she was doing to him. Not this thoughtful, maternal Stacy who had only acted like the girl he'd remembered on two brief occasions, when her lips had heated and parted beneath his.

Brusquely Chris turned and walked away, striding off through the flower-bright gardens. He'd gotten the damned telescope set up, now let them enjoy it. But he had to get away from Stacy before he did something ridiculous. Before he caught, stroked, held and even begged for what she once couldn't wait to give him.

Actually Stacy had been pretty innocent at the start of her eighteenth summer, Chris recalled. Although she'd looked plenty sexy, and acted it, too, in the way she'd let her kisses inflame Chris, she'd been anything but experienced. Not that he'd realized it at first, for she was definitely a graduate student in kissing, using her tongue to trace the outline of his lips, or biting gently on the corner of his mouth or drawing his lower lip between her own soft two.

Neither was she averse to letting his hands roam and wander from the waist up. But let his fingers linger and caress one inch too far up a silken thigh and Stacy would freeze. Always.

Chris hadn't understood her sudden coldness until he'd identified it as fear. In fact, at Stacy's stammering, stumbling confession—"Oh, Chris, I'm still a virgin!"—his heart had practically stopped beating from surprise. He'd had a moment of doubt, even disbelief.

But then, as she'd sobbed that she was scared, desire had struck Chris again. With Stacy, even the realization of her sweet innocence and inexperience had been erotic. Of course, everything about his reactions to Stacy had always been extreme. But twenty-three-year-old Chris, in his physically inflamed state, had vowed possessively that no other man would take her first.

Even now Chris still didn't quite see himself in the role of cad seducer, he thought as his path ended on the patio where Miriam frequently served lunch. Stacy could have said no. As a matter of fact she did say no on quite a few occasions—at first. But she'd wanted Chris, too, and ultimately that had become his biggest ally—Stacy's own very natural and healthy desire mixed with curiosity about the mysterious and forbidden unknown.

Now a different sort of pang went through Chris as he sat alone on the patio, idly shredding a leaf between his fingers. He was thirty-six now, while that young girl he'd been so determined to possess had been exactly half his present age. It seemed awfully young to Chris now. In fact, it seemed too damned young. How could she have held out against the worldly, determined and somewhat cynical young stud he'd been?

Of course, he'd also been insane about her. Still, the scales no longer seemed quite so evenly balanced to Chris. Frowning, he reached for another leaf and shredded it, too. At least he'd always taken care to protect Stacy, he remembered with an almost virtuous pride. With his own particular heritage Chris had always made certain to avoid the sort of accidents that could turn into people.

Now, from inside his house he heard the ring of the telephone. It continued persistently, if faintly. After a moment Chris sighed and got to his feet. He was not eager to talk to anyone, so the phone had shrilled five or six times before he finally reached the wall extension in the kitchen.

"Hello?" Chris said just in time to hear that unmistakable click that meant the caller had hung up.

He slammed the receiver back with annoyance. It was probably just Betty Thackery, wanting to check on Ted. If she was really curious she'd soon be over. Betty wasn't the type to let her curiosity go unchecked.

At least the phone had provided a distraction from his thoughts of Stacy. His desire had dwindled enough now to allow him to rejoin the group at the pool, he decided. But Chris didn't kid himself. His reactions to Stacy were still extreme—and that fiery desire he felt for her was just barely banked. With the least encouragement it would blaze out of control once again.

Chapter Eight

Stacy was keenly aware of Chris from the moment he returned. She'd been secretly watching for him, she knew. When he'd gone striding off so abruptly she had sensed the extent of his frustration, although she wasn't sure of the cause.

She'd tried to get interested in the eclipse, sharing her own scanty bits of knowledge with the two excited young boys. No, she'd never seen a lunar eclipse before but at the solar eclipse a year ago... Stacy's voice trailed off as Chris rejoined their group. His arms were full; he carried a carton of ice cream, a sack of cookies, six Styrofoam bowls and a handful of plastic spoons.

"I hope everybody likes chocolate," he said in a friendly voice, his good humor apparently restored.

They ate the ice cream between taking turns at the telescope. Excitement built to a peak when the moon was finally almost totally obscured. But then, just when it seemed as if it might be blotted out entirely, the alignment of the planets shifted and the moon began to increase in size and glow brightly again.

By now it was well past bedtime for the two boys; they were sleepy and trying to muffle their yawns. "Ted! Ted Thackery!" Betty's shrill voice came drifting over the wall by the pool. "You come home right now!"

Ted thanked everyone for a super time and made his departure. "See you tomorrow, Ted," Robbie called, and Stacy wondered if Ted was proving a more satisfactory companion of late or whether Robbie had just gotten used to his limitations.

"Good night to you, too, Robbie," Chris said pointedly to his son as soon as Ted had gone.

Robbie was too tired to argue. He allowed both Miriam and Stacy to give him a kiss on the cheek, then endured his father's arm around his shoulder before he went sauntering off toward the house.

Meanwhile Preston was starting to collect bowls and spoons. "Leave that," Chris told him. "Stacy and I can gather up everything—right, Stace?"

"Oh—sure, Chris," Stacy agreed. She felt surprised, and dubious, too. But what else could she say?

Miriam and Preston thanked Chris for the enjoyable evening, then they, too, started up the path toward the house.

As they disappeared, Stacy's nerve endings began to tingle, both in warning and in anticipation. She darted a wary look over at Chris and found him scowling. "Gum wrappers!" he snapped in exasperation. "I didn't know those damn kids were chewing gum."

"What's the harm?" Stacy asked mildly. "We can gather them up."

"It's not the wrappers I'm worried about. It's where they parked the chewed gum. Uh-huh, just as I thought. Well, Robbie will clean it off the bottom of the table tomorrow."

Lulled by his apparent anger and preoccupation, Stacy continued to gather up the scattered Styrofoam bowls and plastic spoons. She glanced up again when Chris brought over the litter basket that he customarily kept by the pool.

It was hard to see its slotted opening since the moon was not yet fully out again. Stacy bent over, feeding debris carefully into the basket when she felt the warm hard length of Chris pressing against her back and legs.

"Stace—"

She knew that tone in his voice and it rendered her immobile. But her heart began such a frenzied pounding that Stacy wondered if she could even hear any further words that Chris might say.

"Stace, do you remember the first time?"

Although his voice was soft and low she could hear him, after all. Just as she could feel him moving even closer, pressing against her knees, her calves, her thighs.

Her eyes fell closed for just a moment, then she made herself turn around and look up at him in the dim reflected light. "What first time, Chris?" she asked distinctly, hoping he didn't really mean what she thought.

"You and me. The first time we made love."

Rapidly Stacy lowered her gaze. Although she couldn't see his scrutiny, she could *feel* his eyes burning down on her.

"Do you remember, Stacy?" Chris persisted.

She cleared her throat nervously. "It's not the sort of evening a woman forgets, Chris."

"So you remember, too." An echo of satisfaction, possibly even triumph was in his voice.

"Oh, yes, I remember well," Stacy blurted. "Because you said you were through being teased, Chris. You said kisses weren't enough anymore, and maybe we'd better forget the whole thing. I went into Grandmother's house crying—"

"That really wasn't the night I meant," he interjected softly.

"Oh," Stacy cried, her hands balling up into fists. But that was just because she wanted so badly to reach out and touch him. "You were such a *bastard*, Chris!"

"No one's ever disputed that fact," he said whimsically. His head had bent down toward hers, and she felt his breath, warm and sweet on her face.

If only she could touch him, just for a moment. "You know that wasn't what I meant," Stacy replied fretfully. Then the rest of her words died, and she swallowed hard. His large, warm hand had lightly cupped one of her cheeks, his thumb resting just below her chin. The opposite side of her face suddenly felt numb by contrast.

"I cried, Chris. I couldn't eat, I couldn't sleep. I almost lost my crummy typing job at the courthouse over you. And the day you came in to file some papers for Knox Kinard and didn't even glance at me, I thought I'd die." At last Stacy could accuse Chris. At last she could beat on his chest with her fists, the way she'd wanted to do long ago. Now maybe she'd stop thinking about his shirt having slipped outside his shorts again and how, if she slid her fingers beneath the shirt, she could feel his firm vibrant skin. "Oh, yes, it was blackmail."

"That's because any time I even looked at you, Stace, I could barely talk or walk. That's how much I wanted you. That's what bad shape I was in, always aching for you. Maybe I didn't cry, but I sure as hell went through everything else. I couldn't eat, couldn't sleep, couldn't concentrate on work.... And you knew it, you little witch. You knew just what you were doing to me!"

"You wore me down, Chris—"

"No, I didn't. I just waited for you to come to me. And finally you did, because you *wanted* to!"

"You didn't play fair!" she accused.

"I suppose *you* did? Why, I can still see that white swimsuit you wore with all those little revealing cutouts. And you had the gall to claim you'd just dropped by Cousin Lynn's house for a swim. Baby, a swim wasn't what you came for, and we both knew it." His voice was hoarse now with remembered passion, and his hand glided down to rest at the juncture of Stacy's neck and throat, setting a pulse there to throbbing wildly.

"I just wanted you to kiss me again, that's all!" she protested.

"Bull. The way you twined around me like a vine—you
wanted it all just as badly as I did."

"I was frightened, Chris—"

"That sure didn't last long."

"It was all so strange, so new—"

"I didn't hurt you, except maybe for a second."

"No. You—" Words failed Stacy. She stopped, shaking
her head. If only she could dare to touch him again!

"We were born to be together. Then. Now. It's every bit
as bad for me now, you know. The feel of you, the taste of
you—that's all I've been thinking about all night," he admitted, his voice low and shaken. "I guess it's why I asked
you to stay and help me clean up. And I think it's why you
wore perfume and lipstick."

"No—" Stacy choked. But her hand leapt forth of its
own volition to deny her words. It moved to his taut belly,
which twitched at her touch.

"Stace, we agreed we didn't want this. Tell me to go away!
Make me leave now, Stace," Chris urged.

"I can't!" she gasped, tears stinging her eyes. But they
were tears of longing as his hand touched her with such
gentleness.

"Then you leave. Just turn and go up to the house," he
instructed.

Her own wayward hand crept under his shirt. At last she
touched his bare, warm flesh. "Oh, Chris, I can't," she
whispered.

"It's a mistake."

"I know," she agreed.

"We'll both be sorry," he warned.

"Yes, that's true," Stacy admitted but she wanted him so
badly she could scarcely breathe.

Now his roving hand had found her breast and tightened
around it slowly while his other hand tangled in her hair,
raising her face to his. His lips met hers, sweet and wild, and

his tongue plunged inside. She twisted frantically closer, desperate to be nearer to him, next to him, one with him.

As he continued to caress her breast Stacy's whole body came alive. A warm current ran zigzagging along all the pathways of her body.

"Why do some of us keep playing with fire...when we know we'll just get burned, Stace?" Chris asked, his voice sounding choked.

"I don't know, Chris," Stacy replied, her own voice a half sob, and then, as thirteen years of longing and barren emptiness ended, she went up on tiptoes to meet him. Their mouths crushed together, their bodies came close, grinding against each other. Chris was already fully aroused, ready for her—even desperate for her, as Stacy could tell from the sound of his breathing. A triumph of her own soared through her even as another part of her, tired and jaded, hissed that she was embarking on another exercise in self-destruction.

But even if the voice had told her she would burn on a pyre tonight Stacy couldn't have turned back. All she could do was twist more closely in Chris's arms and let her hardened nipples agitate his chest, let the juncture of her legs and pelvis mold to his excitement, offering, needing, wanting...

"Oh, Stace! My God, Stace!"

The sound of his delight fueled her own. Suddenly Stacy discovered her shirt unbuttoned, her breasts bare for his marauding lips and tongue. She sagged against him, almost too weak to stand.

"I think this time we...we can skip the swim," Chris choked, each word spoken with difficulty.

Dizzied with desire, Stacy still caught his meaning. Their first time she had dived into the pool defiantly, trying to prove the lie that she'd come here just to swim. But when she'd surfaced at the far end of the pool Chris was there, too, naked and wet, waiting for her. He'd caught her in the water, stripped off her bathing suit and pinned her against him. Then, for the first time, Stacy had allowed her emotions full sway as she'd wrapped her legs around Chris's body, finally allowing him the secret access he'd sought. He'd taken her then and there, the warm water lapping around them, an accompaniment to their eager gasps.

Now Chris half led, half carried Stacy toward the cabana, which she had so scrupulously avoided until now. It was dark and very warm as she remembered, damp-smelling from rain and humidity. Chris closed the door behind them, and Stacy swayed, reaching out to the wall to steady herself.

"Last chance, Stace," he said, his voice husky with passion. Then she heard the slap of waterproof cushions striking the cabana's concrete floor.

She couldn't see Chris, but she didn't have to. Her hands found him as if they'd been equipped with radar. Then Stacy was helping him remove his shirt and tugging down his shorts. She reached and found the sheer male magnificence of him.

Chris gasped beneath her touch, then bore her over until the waterproof cushions were squishing beneath Stacy's back, the only sound in the cabana except for their labored breathing.

Now Chris tore away her few clothes and Stacy lay back to the bold invasion of his hands and lips. She had never encouraged such intimacy with any man except this one.

But Chris's own need was too great to delay for long, as he told Stacy in a half-apologetic whisper.

She drew him closer, knowing that her complete self-gratification could wait. Right now the emptiness within her yawned, yearning to be filled. "I don't want to be alone any more," Stacy said to him urgently. "I want you, Chris, I want you—"

"I want *you*, Stacy," he said, taking up her ecstatic, almost anguished chant.

Then his body was piercing hers, sending a cry of mingled delight and pain to Stacy's lips. It had been so long—oh, it had been much too long!

Chris recognized the sound of pain and stopped. *"No,"* Stacy said to him fiercely, her body twisting beneath him, then moving to meet his. She didn't care about her brief discomfort from years of self-denial. The pain was a burning brand that she accepted gladly, and soon all discomfort disappeared and there was only pleasure—exhilarating, perfect pleasure that swirled higher and higher.

"Talk to me, Stace. Tell me what you want," he said in her ear.

"I want more," she gasped. "I want every bit of you, Chris! Oh, I want it all!"

She felt him going crazy then, skyrocketing out of control. His mouth covered hers, his tongue deep within her mouth, and his hands aroused and stroked her in rhythm to his thrilling movements. He carried her higher and higher, until she was swimming in a sea of waves that surged and crested then surged anew. Stacy barely heard her own sharp cries, muffled by his lips, until together they found the highest, strongest wave of pleasure and, like erotic surfers, rode it all the way in.

At the wave's culmination Stacy gave a cry so sharp and intense that it trembled, vibrating against Chris's lips. Then she heard and felt his own shaken cry.

For long silent moments they lay close, both gasping for breath. "My God, woman, what you do to me," Chris sighed.

"Better now?" Stacy couldn't resist asking.

"Well, that knocked off the rough edges," Chris said, starting to laugh. "Another five or ten times with you, and I might actually be satisfied!"

Content, Stacy lay beside him, resting, her arms still linked around Chris's warm sweat-damp neck. His heart, beneath her cheek, continued to pound like a runaway engine.

Yes, what they did for each other was still just as fantastic as ever. But now Stacy knew that she, at least, was driven by more than physical desire. No mere sexual episode ever left a woman feeling this blissfully replete or quite so com-

pletely whole. Sex for sex's sake, or to perform one's wifely
duty—any of the various reasons she'd made love with
Gary—had never once left her feeling even remotely like
this.

No, a woman only found a man absolutely irresistible
when she loved him madly. With the renewed realization of
her love for Chris and all its awesome implications, Stacy
felt tears gathering behind her eyes. No wonder the wild yet
tender lovemaking they'd just shared was as great as ever.
Love was the reason she'd kept feeling drawn to Chris,
thinking about him, needing him, wanting him. Yes, I've
always loved him, Stacy admitted to herself. I never really
stopped. Now, as far as her heart was concerned, the inter-
vening years might never have happened.

"How about that swim?" Chris said softly, slowly peel-
ing his body away from hers. Stacy welcomed the diversion
as she struggled to adjust to the amazing, incredible fact of
being in love with Chris Lorio all over again.

They went skinny-dipping, not swimming with vigor but
just drifting languidly together in the moonlight where they
could see and enjoy the sight of each other's body.

"You're a beautiful man, Chris," Stacy said softly, letting her hands outline the fan-shaped design of hair on his
chest. She followed that hairline all the way down below his
waist, finding it coarse and curly, springy to her touch.

"You're a lovely woman, Stacy." His hands went to her
body. As she stood waist-deep in the warm, rippling water
Chris sought her rounded curves and softly cushioned areas
until they were clutching each other tightly once again.

"Let's go up to my room," Chris whispered. "Making
love in the pool or cabana is fine when you're young. But
right now I want you stretched out on my big, soft, comfortable bed."

"Your room sounds delightful," Stacy admitted, and
their lips caught again and clung.

The master bedroom was a wholly masculine room of
heavy, oversize furniture dominated by the king-size bed.
Thick, tweedy drapes hung over the windows, and the

room's colors were a harmonizing blend of maroon, gray and brown.

Chris threw back the spread on the bed, then drew Stacy down beside him. He reached out and turned his bedside lamp low, so there was light enough for them to see each other.

"Come here," he whispered, wrapping himself around her in a melee of long, taut limbs. "Satisfy me!"

"How will I do that?" Stacy asked, her voice suddenly tremulous.

"Just the way you always did," Chris said softly, then slanted his head for their lips to meet. "Give me everything."

There were so many ways in which she and Chris could make love, and Stacy began rediscovering them all. Chris moved her atop him first, letting her take command until rapturous fulfillment followed by exhaustion left her lying limp on his chest. Then Chris rolled her over swiftly and reclaimed the lead, driving into her until she was fully aroused once again and clutching his damp back, moving beneath him to his tempo.

"Talk to me," Chris said, his eyes closing, while on his face ecstasy and agony mingled. "Tell me what you want . . . tell me how you feel with me so close . . . oh, Stace, just talk. . . ."

His need to be wanted, to hear the sound of her voice, sent the old love words bubbling softly to Stacy's lips. As she watched ecstasy gain supremacy, lighting Chris's face, a new, poignant awareness went through Stacy. Clearly Chris had not been getting what he needed, probably not for a long time indeed.

Then as the delicious hours gradually slipped past, hours in which they often rested replete in each other's arms, Stacy began to suspect that it had probably been longer than Chris would admit since he'd had any woman at all. His need seemed insatiable, and his hunger for her went too deep.

"When you said you wanted five or ten more times with me I didn't know you planned on all of them tonight," she quipped.

He grinned—a rakish grin—for despite the intensity of their feelings they had always been able to laugh and joke together, too.

"Come back here and I'll show you number whatever," he flashed right back.

Finally they were both so tired they lay on their sides, facing each other, and now his deep love strokes were slow yet almost unbelievably sweet. "There hasn't been anyone for you in a long time, has there, Chris?" Stacy finally dared to whisper.

She could tell his guard was down as passion slowly built within him anew. "No," he admitted. Then his dark beautiful eyes sought her face as he made an even deeper admission. "But there's never been anyone else like this, Stace. Not like I am with you. Not ever."

"Oh, Chris!" Then words failed Stacy. She wanted to tell him that the same was true for her, but emotion tightened her throat until speech was impossible. Instead she pressed a kiss on each of his eyelids and clutched his black head between her breasts, covering it with more kisses, sending flames sweeping over them anew.

Spent at last, they slept in each other's arms, and Stacy was no longer haunted by phantoms or troubled by dreams. All of her tumultuous emotions were stilled at last.

Peace was also what she saw on Chris's sleeping face when she awoke early the following morning.

Amazingly she didn't feel especially tired, although the ache of various muscles and a special soreness between her legs reminded her that once again Chris's tender vigor had won over her innate resistance. Still, Stacy couldn't feel sorry. How could she regret hours so passionate and blindingly beautiful that just recalling them made a lump rise in her throat?

Chris's head lay on her shoulder; his relaxed arms encircled her. For a few minutes Stacy felt too happy to move and risk disturbing him. But then her need to look into Chris's face overcame her contentment.

He frowned just a little when she drew away, then his breathing resumed its steady rhythm. His hair was tousled and mussed, his thick eyelashes almost brushing his high cheekbones, the hard lines of his handsome face softened. The long sculpted mouth was parted slightly, allowing her a glimpse of gleaming white teeth within.

Chris looked almost exactly like Taylor looked when he, too, was fast asleep.

No, Stacy thought, swallowing down the increasingly large lump in her throat and daring to touch one tendril of Chris's soft black hair, Taylor asleep looks almost exactly like Chris.

As she continued to awaken, Stacy knew she might as well get up. In fact as she became aware of the tumbled condition of the bedsheets she knew she herself probably suffered from a similar disarray.

Blushing, she located her clothes by the side of the bed, but they felt too damp and clammy from her impromptu swim to put back on. Fortunately long thick towels hung in Chris's bathroom, so Stacy borrowed one, wrapping it around her.

It was another stroke of good fortune that no one was up yet. Stacy dashed across the hall, then sped past Robbie's door and turned into Lynn's bedroom.

A long shower did wonders for Stacy's various aches and dispelled her last twinges of sleepiness, as well. Soon the two men in this household—two men she loved, she realized with wonder—would be waking, and Stacy wanted to surprise them. She would have fresh hot coffee waiting for Chris and a breakfast more elaborate than cold cereal for Robbie. Cinnamon rolls? Stacy thought as she flew happily down the stairs clad in one of her nicer slacks outfits. The olive-green pants fit her smoothly and emphasized her long legs. Topping the slacks was an expensive summer sweater of Aztec Indian block design.

I'm through hiding my light under a bushel, Stacy thought as she put the coffee on and began stirring up cinnamon rolls from a box of mix she'd found in the cupboard. She was still a very attractive woman, and from now on she was going to dress the part. Instead of worrying about arousing Chris with lipstick and perfume and smart clothes, she frankly intended to arouse him at every opportunity, until all his love-starved needs had been met. Mine, too, she decided happily.

Humming, Stacy sipped at a cup of black, dark-roast coffee and idly fluffed her still-damp hair. The delicious aroma of rolls baking and spicy cinnamon began to seep through the kitchen, and suddenly she felt hungry, just as she felt alive and glowing in every pore.

Was it possible that she and Chris could have a future together? Stacy found herself wondering. Or was always and forever too much to expect?

Whoa, lady, she warned herself. You're moving much too fast. And don't forget that a lot will depend on Chris's reaction to Taylor.

That thought was sobering. But then the natural ebullience she felt asserted itself again. Today Stacy felt *loved*, and it had surely been an eternity since she'd last had that feeling.

She checked on the rolls again and had just closed the oven when an unexpected tapping on the kitchen door swung her around sharply. Ted—already? But surely it was too early for Ted, Stacy thought, bewildered. The tapping—louder and more impatient—came again.

Chris woke, just moments before the telephone rang, to a hundred surprised and startled thoughts dashing through his mind.

Had that wonderfully incredible night with her really happened?

Chris's own deeply sated body answered in the affirmative. Well, if he'd ever wanted to test the health of his heart, last night should have done it. At the same time, Chris couldn't remember when he'd felt this content, this relaxed—this blissfully complete.

There was something about Stacy—there had always been something about her—that fed even his most primitive desires and shamelessly met all his needs. With Stace there had always been a mutual understanding in their lovemaking and an abiding passion that was completely reciprocated.

For years Chris had tried to tell himself she was just another woman—nothing special. But those had been necessary lies he'd had to devise to survive without her. Stacy *was* special.

Love... well, of course that was something quite different from sexual desire, Chris thought. Love was what he'd always felt for Lynn and Robbie—deep, compassionate, protective love. With Stacy he could simply never wait to get her clothes off, to feel her body moving beneath his until he blazed out of control, his mind, body and soul thrilled by almost unbelievable rapture.

That wasn't really love, of course. That was just damned good sex.

And yet, all during those weeks when he'd been in Europe with Congressman Bainbridge and, later, with Lynn and her parents, thoughts and memories of Stacy had obsessed him. He still remembered Lynn clutching his arm as they'd walked along the Seine at dusk, and Chris knew she was finding Paris so romantic—while he yearned for Stacy, not Lynn. And he remembered a gondola ride in Italy and how Lynn tilted up her face to him, inviting his kiss. But even as Chris obliged he desperately wished he was kissing Stacy.

By the time they'd sailed back to the States, Chris was trying to get up his nerve to tell Lynn the truth. To confide that he'd gotten all hung up on her sexy younger cousin and couldn't wait to get back and hold Stacy in his arms again.

But he *hadn't* spoken, even though he'd had a couple of golden opportunities. Like those moments when he and Lynn had strolled around the deck together and he'd seen her studying him thoughtfully. Or that last night on board when Lynn had said lightly, yet with a little catch in her voice, "Oh Chris, I keep feeling like you're miles away!"

He'd cared so much for Lynn that he hadn't ever wanted to hurt her... That's what it had come down to in the end. She had always been there for him, even when no one else was. All through the years she'd been his friend, his champion, and once they'd been grown, how obviously she had longed to be his wife and lover. To Lynn those two were utterly inseparable. In fact she had told Chris once that she couldn't imagine ever giving herself to anyone, even him, without marriage.

That was Lynn: idealistic, romantic and very moral. No, she couldn't really understand what he'd had with Stacy, Chris had thought, his own discomfort increasing proportionally as they'd neared the U.S. coastline. Since he had spent much of the summer in hot pursuit of Stacy, taking her to movies and parties and for long night drives, someone in Langlois would be bound to tell Lynn.

What would happen to Lynn then? She was so fragile and delicate, anyway, with her circled eyes, too-slim body and occasionally blue-tinged lips. What would pain and disappointment do, Chris had wondered, if he told Lynn he intended to marry Stacy?

Losing Lynn would mean relinquishing a lot more, Chris had thought candidly, prowling the deck of the *Queen Eugenie*—not only her dearness and devotion. Chris knew he could use Lynn's family's help to establish a law practice when he graduated next year. He knew further that Lynn's own social connections would finally guarantee him acceptance in a town that had always looked on him askance, endlessly debating his paternity. And Chris knew that to succeed in his chosen profession he needed the help of other influential and well-placed lawyers, men such as Knox and Bainbridge. Both were friends of Lynn's parents; both had the highest regard for Lynn herself.

Was he prepared to throw all that away? Chris had asked himself.

But whenever he thought of Stacy and his almost desperate need for her Chris knew there was really no choice. Why, his first night back in Langlois—no, the very first hour he was back—he knew he'd be seeking her out, trying to slake two months' hunger and thirst for her. How could he ever be Lynn's faithful, loving husband in a town where there was Stacy?

Still, he decided to put off telling Lynn for as long as possible. So she knew nothing until they were back home and Chris was decked by the news of Stacy's impulsive marriage to Gary. Then Lynn had heard plenty! Worried and frightened, she'd come to Chris's bleak rooming house, where he lay immobile and half blind from the first migraine headache of his life.

And half out of his mind because the woman he'd really wanted was gone, irrevocably gone—

The telephone shrilled, and Chris scooped it up before it could awaken the rest of the household. Of course Stacy was already up, and Chris wondered where she was as he listened to a woman's voice calling from a children's camp in New Mexico.

"I'll have Mrs. Thomasson call you right back," Chris said automatically, seizing a pen and jotting down the phone number on the pad he always kept by the bed. Stacy might be anywhere—her room or bathroom or the kitchen. She could even be outside taking a walk or a swim.

Replacing the receiver, Chris jumped naked out of bed and went straight to his walk-in closet hunting for a robe. He had planned to bathe, shave and dress, to look more appealing before he saw Stacy again. But now, with the urgency of this message, even toothpaste was a luxury for which there was no time.

Stuffing his feet into bedroom shoes and knotting a robe around his waist, Chris struggled to still his whirling mind as he tried to think of the best way to tell Stacy that her son, Taylor, was missing and had apparently run away yesterday from his summer camp.

Chapter Nine

Stacy swung open the kitchen door then reeled with surprise at sight of the dirty, shaggy, unkempt but totally familiar figure. "Taylor!" she gasped in disbelief.

"Hi, Mom," her son said a little warily before pushing his way past her into the kitchen. He sniffed the various aromas with appreciation. "Look, I'll explain later. Right now I'm about to starve to death! Can I have something to eat?"

"Oh, Taylor! How— What?" Stacy stopped, knowing that remonstrances were useless. He was already *here*, the little scamp. Suddenly she was absolutely appalled at the predicament in which he'd just placed her.

The moment Chris saw Taylor he would know the truth! And now Stacy wouldn't have time for a build-up-to-it-gradually sort of explanation.

Meanwhile, her twelve-year-old son stood staring at her expectantly. "How on earth did you get here?" Stacy blurted even as she dragged Taylor toward her. Affectionately she hugged him and pressed a kiss on his forehead.

"I hopped a freight coming east. Man, it's really fun to ride the rails! Only this was a fertilizer car."

Even before the import of his words dawned on Stacy her kiss ended with her wrinkling up her nose. The dirty, disheveled Taylor stank—and as for his horrible-looking hair—

"You didn't get your hair cut while you were in Santa Fe!" she accused, her mind seizing on these trivial, mundane things to avoid confronting the real truth of her predicament. "The very last thing I told you and Gary was to be sure you got your hair cut." Stacy stopped, her voice threatening to wobble out of control.

"Aw, Gary didn't have time. He's too busy chasin' this twenty-year-old fox to bother about me. But, man, he and the fox sure had time to drive me up to that godawful camp you picked out." Then, as if sensing that the topic of the camp was a touchy one to Stacy, Taylor went on quickly. "Please, Mom. *Food!* Can't I have some of what's baking? And could you throw a few eggs in a skillet? You know the last time I ate anything except green apples? Yesterday at breakfast!"

"Oh, my God, Taylor!" What Stacy really longed to do was spirit him out of the house immediately, before Chris came downstairs.

And then do what with him? Just how did you hide a live, hungry, energetic twelve-year-old? No, even as Stacy turned automatically to the refrigerator to get out a carton of eggs she knew that her concealment of Taylor's identity had finally ended. Now she would just have to face Chris—and whatever scathing words he might choose to say.

Stacy was in the kitchen. Chris could hear the low murmur of her voice as she talked with someone. Was Robbie up this early? He thought the young voice responding to Stacy sounded rather like Robbie's. And yet it didn't, too.

The air was filled with readily identifiable smells: eggs, cinnamon rolls, coffee. It was too soon after rising for Chris to feel hungry just yet, but undoubtedly Stacy had wanted breakfast to be a real feast.

How was he going to tell her about Taylor? *How?*

She would probably go crazy. Any mother would, thinking of all the perverts and murderers that preyed on children.

Was something else wrong? Or did she already know? The distress Chris heard now in Stacy's voice was unmistakable. He hurried toward the sound, wanting to comfort her.

Instead he skidded to an abrupt stop as he came through the kitchen door.

He took in the scene at a flash: the ragged, dirty little boy cramming food into his mouth as if he hadn't eaten in a month, and Stacy sitting across from the child, white-faced and stricken. Both of them glanced up at Chris, and then to his amazement, Stacy paled even more.

The young boy groped for his napkin and swiped it quickly across his mouth. His black eyes met Chris's with interest; his small but handsome face tightened with a look much like respect—or was it calculation?

"Who are you?" Chris blurted, but he knew at once. Before he even spoke the words, he knew. He had looked at his own face in a mirror every day of his life, and he could certainly recognize that familiar configuration of features.

"Chris—" Now Stacy was trembling as she pushed herself up and walked over to stand beside the ragged little urchin. One of her shaking hands touched the kid's bony shoulder. "This is my son, Taylor." She swallowed hard. "Taylor...Thomasson. Taylor, this is Mr. Chris Lorio. You've heard me..."

Chris wasn't surprised when her voice trailed off. Still, she nudged the boy, and at her prompting, he seemed to regain a rudiment of manners. He stood, wiping one grimy hand on his napkin before he extended it to Chris. "Please-to-meet-you-sir," he muttered all in one breath. Clearly he was more intent on getting back to his breakfast than anything else.

Chris heard himself murmuring something as he took the warm but dirty little hand, which had an amazingly tough grip. *The very first touch of my son,* Chris thought numbly.

His words to Taylor must have been socially acceptable because the boy sank back down at his place and resumed eating hungrily.

As total realization struck Chris, the realization that Stacy had once borne him a son that he hadn't even known existed, Chris sagged against the doorway, and for the next few minutes it was all that held him up.

When his mind finally began to function again Chris glanced anxiously at Taylor, wondering if the boy had experienced a similar recognition of *him.*

No, he saw with momentary relief. Although the boy was an absolute living replica of him at the same age—could even have posed for those childhood pictures hanging over Lynn's bed—Taylor was not yet able to look ahead and project the appearance of the man he would become.

But Chris could certainly look back and remember, and he did so now with fury, outrage and total condemnation of Stacy swelling through his soul. Not only had she kept Taylor's identity a secret all these years, but she'd let the child go around looking just as neglected, just as ragged and shaggy as "that woods colt who lives with Bonnie Lorio" had ever been.

My son—*my son*—is this famished, smelly, deprived little boy. Oh, my God, she's let him suffer just the same way I did, the way I vowed no child of mine would ever suffer, Chris thought through a blinding red haze of rage.

Utter fury seared his soul. And if Chris had been able to move he would probably have strangled Stacy on the spot.

What expressions were on his face? Chris had no idea. Stacy kept staring at him, growing visibly more nervous by the second. Only the boy kept eating with perfect aplomb. *At least he seems to have my knack for survival,* Chris thought, and a little relief started to seep through the violent fury still gripping him.

Finally, too, Stacy began to find her tongue. "Taylor ran away from camp yesterday," she said to Chris through white, bloodless-looking lips. "He—he—oh, I can't believe he really did this . . . he hitchhiked to El Paso where he caught a freight train—"

"Yeah, I rode in this fertilizer car all the way to Baton Rouge," Taylor chimed in. "It didn't smell too great, either. Then a truck driver gave me a lift here to Langlois. He kept smoking cigars, so I guess the fertilizer didn't bother him. Say, Mom, how come something pronounced Lang-wa is spelled so funny?"

"It's French," Stacy said. "Oh, I still can't believe what you did, Taylor! You could have been mugged, robbed, murdered—"

"Aw, all they'd have got is my threads. I don't hardly have any money. Gary, that cheapskate, only gave me a couple of bucks—" As Stacy went even whiter the boy glanced cautiously at Chris and picked up the final cinnamon roll. "Say, you guys aren't looking too hot. Is something wrong?"

"Where are your clothes?" Stacy shrilled, seeming to awake to the boy's wretched appearance. "My God, I spend a fortune on you and you turn up looking—" She stopped, her eyes closing almost helplessly.

"Hey, no sweat, Mom. They're outside. I knew you'd have a conniption fit if I lost 'em. That and my toothbrush, after a thousand visits to the dentist. I stuck my bag in a bush." Agilely, the boy bounded to the kitchen door, darted through it and was back a minute later with a name-brand suitcase that now looked battered. "See, I brought all my good threads. You want me to go get washed up and change?"

That he just might be in serious trouble was obviously beginning to dawn on the confident Taylor.

"That suitcase was brand new," Stacy said, her voice sounding shaky again.

"I know. I'm sorry, Mom. I had to throw it in the boxcar and it got a little bit bent."

"A little bit—" Stacy stopped, biting her lip.

"Uh-oh, she's pretty P.O.d," the boy said confidentially to Chris. "Say, can I take a shower? Where's a bathroom?"

Chris, who couldn't recall ever being at a loss for words before, had to try twice before he could give Taylor adequate directions.

"Oh—and, say, thanks, sir. I sure 'preciate your hospitality and the breakfast 'n' all. Real nice place you got here." The boy cast a last anxious look at his ashen-faced mother, then fled with obvious relief.

Chris was beginning to feel a little relief, too. At least the boy had some manners and a few clothes, and he seemed to know what a dentist was. He even appeared fond of his mother. Still, the realization of Stacy's duplicity left Chris's head reeling.

"Chris..." Stacy began.

At last Chris was able to push away from the doorjamb, no longer needing its support. Angrily his eyes met Stacy's.

"You *bitch*," he snapped.

The pain that slashed over her face would have rent him, too, if he'd seen it last night when they'd been so close and Stacy so dear.

Now, as Chris watched, her chin came up and her lips tightened. She'd always had plenty of spirit and spunk. "Before you start throwing names around, Chris Lorio, just ask yourself where the hell you were when I first found out about Taylor!" she flared back.

Chris couldn't bear to think about all that right now. He couldn't bear to talk about it. There was simply too much he had to adjust to.

That he, of all people, had once had a birth-control failure seemed particularly ironic to Chris. That Stacy had borne his son, his first-born son, as a result of those uninhibited nights by the pool or inside the cabana...

His thoughts suddenly narrowed to follow one very important thread. "Lynn shouldn't have died," he whispered. Then another spasm of rage seized Chris, squeezing his heart as his fists balled at his sides. "Damn it all, Lynn risked her life to give me a child—and all the time I already had one." Chris swung on Stacy again, and only the iron control he'd learned through the years kept him from slapping her.

She faced him squarely, although her green eyes were wide with fear. "Can you really wish Robbie gone?" she asked.

Chris felt his own eyes closing. No, of course not. He could not live without Robbie... not after eight vital years. But, damn it all, Stacy had cheated him of twelve years with Taylor!

He would never, ever forgive her, both on Lynn's account and on his own. And he'd never forgive her, either, for letting his son run around looking like a ragamuffin, hitching rides and jumping onto boxcars. What the hell kind of mother had she been to Taylor? About as good as Bonnie Lorio?

The rage he felt so threatened to consume him, coming in remorseless waves one right after another, that Chris turned away blindly. Slap Stacy? Hell, he had to get out of here or he was liable to kill her!

"We'll talk later," he said stiffly. "Right now I'm going to get cleaned up myself."

She started to say something, her green eyes shooting off sparks, but the phone started ringing. In the tense silence the noise was as grating as a fingernail scratching over a blackboard.

"Answer that," Chris directed Stacy. "It's probably Taylor's camp again. They called earlier. A Mrs. Stephens said they kept trying to reach you yesterday evening, but of course we were out by the pool."

Then Chris turned and walked out of the kitchen, not even waiting to see if Stacy would obey or not. Frankly, he didn't care. All he cared about right now was that he had a brand-new son that Stacy had concealed from him for twelve years, and the shock of it all had started lights flashing behind Chris's eyes and a dull throbbing in his temples.

All the classic signs of a migraine headache were beginning.

She'd always been able to give him pain.

A shower helped Chris a little, and the beta-blocking drugs and black coffee that he gulped also helped to forestall the virtually inevitable headache. Clean-shaven and dressed in business clothes, Chris phoned his office and told Janice he'd be late. He also instructed her to cancel any appointments that weren't dire life-or-death emergencies.

Then he crossed the hall to the room that Stacy occupied. Her door was standing ajar so Chris simply walked in.

Stacy and Taylor were over at Lynn's dressing table, too occupied in their own conversation to notice Chris at first. Taylor sat fairly twitching on the vanity stool, a towel clutched around his neck, while Stacy whittled at his black hair with overlong scissors.

The boy's suitcase lay open just a few feet away from Chris. He saw with relief that the kid actually did have quite a few decent-looking clothes. And Taylor had changed into a coordinated outfit consisting of khaki slacks and a red and khaki shirt.

"You're gonna cut too much off," Taylor grumbled to his mother. "I know you are—you always do!"

"*You* be quiet!" Stacy said, half-threateningly.

"Anyway, I'm too big for you to still be cutting my hair," Taylor went on, seemingly unconcerned by his mother's threats.

"I agree. That's why I told you and Gary both to be sure and have your hair styled before you went to camp. No wonder you didn't get along well with the other boys! I'm sure they all looked like proper young gentlemen while you look like some punk out of a ghetto," Stacy said grimly, whittling at the child's thick jet hair.

"Listen, I could make every one of those sissies holler!" Taylor said with grim satisfaction.

"Why are you always fighting?" Stacy cried. "Oh, Taylor, sometimes I don't understand you at all!" All at once her voice broke on a sob.

"Hey." Hastily the boy swung around, wrapping long skinny arms around his mother's waist. "It's okay, Mom. I just didn't fit in at that camp very well, but, man, I sure do like it here. I've never seen trees so big—and everything's so *green*."

Stacy was frankly crying. "You could have been killed, running away like you did. And you're all I've got, Taylor! Oh, God, if anything ever happened to you—" She caught the boy's head to her breast in a gesture that suddenly squeezed at Chris's throat, it was so akin to the way she'd hugged him the previous night.

"Nothin' gonna happen to me," the boy said confidently, patting her on the back. "Hey, Mom, don't worry so. You always worry too much, even when everything's cool—"

Abruptly his voice broke off and he pulled away from Stacy in embarrassment. He had just seen Chris.

Chris, much calmer now, was grateful he'd been able to witness the revealing little scene. At least Stacy seemed to love the kid, and Taylor obviously loved her, too, for all that he tried to con her. Chris wasn't quite sure why Stacy's love for the child was so compellingly important to him, but it was . . . it was.

Meanwhile the boy watched Chris carefully. *He's quick and he's shrewd,* Taylor's father found himself thinking. *He's a lot like I was at his age except that he's less angry.* Admiration and concern for Taylor mingled in Chris's still turbulent heart.

Aloud he spoke quietly. "Taylor, I just remembered that I need to get my hair trimmed today. Maybe you'd like to go to the barbershop with me."

"I sure would," the boy said with visible relief, tugging off the towel wrapped around his neck. "Otherwise Mom's gonna *murder* my hair. She always does."

"I'll be ready to go in five minutes, Taylor," Chris went on, trying to keep his voice friendly and even-toned. "First, I need to talk to your mother. I think you'll find my son Robbie in the kitchen by now. Why don't you go down and get acquainted with him? You guys will probably be swimming together and doing a number of other things as well."

"All right!" said Taylor fairly beaming at the prospect. Chris could tell he loved to swim. "Bye, Mom."

"Hold it!" Stacy snapped, and both Chris and Taylor looked at her in surprise. "Listen, Taylor, Robbie is eight years old, and in case you've forgotten, he lost his mother a few months ago. He likes fun as much as any kid, but he's also a sensitive little boy. If you do anything mean or act overbearing I'll have your hide—okay?"

"Yeah—okay," Taylor agreed, then he darted past Chris and out the door.

As it closed behind him, Stacy looked at Chris bleakly. Angry though Chris still was with her, a shaft of sorrow pierced him, too. Last night with Stace—which had seemed so absolutely marvelous—might have happened a thousand light-years ago.

"Why did you tell Taylor that?" Stacy demanded of Chris, her voice curt.

"What?" Chris asked irritably.

"You as good as promised Taylor he could stay here and swim in the pool when—"

"Because he can and he will!" Chris roared.

She looked as if she was about to throw something right back in his face, but then she pressed her lips together determinedly. It was not the sort of gesture Chris liked to see. He didn't really trust a Stacy who was obviously trying to stifle some remark. He'd rather she'd just go ahead and scream at him. But how funny he'd had any thought of trusting her at all, he thought suddenly and bitterly.

"Look, Stacy," Chris said, dragging a hand unconsciously across his aching forehead. "Can't we sit down and talk like two sensible adults? There are some rather obvious questions I want to ask."

For a moment Chris thought she might refuse. Then, with a sigh, Stacy sank down on the vanity stool that Taylor had just vacated. "What do you want to know?" she asked, her voice defeated.

"Anything about Taylor," Chris emphasized, dropping down into an armchair opposite her. "Anything at all!"

"You don't have to be concerned, Chris. He's mine—all mine, and always has been," she said tautly.

Now he identified her expression as the maternal instinct at its most fierce. "Look, Mother Tigress, nobody's trying to steal your baby away," Chris said wearily. "Although he seems to be pretty good at running away. You're going to lose control of him soon, if you haven't already. He's almost exactly like I was at his age—reckless...independent..."

"Taylor is not your concern, Chris!" she flared.

"Then just whose concern is he—Gary's?" Chris shot back at her. "From what I've seen and heard, I don't think Gary's very interested in being a father." Chris drew another breath and rubbed again at his forehead. "For God's sake, Stacy, the boy's the very image of me. You can't deny that he's my son!"

"No," she admitted and looked down at her hands clenched tightly together in her lap.

"Look, just tell me a few things, okay?" Carefully Chris adopted the placating tone he often used with recalcitrant witnesses. Even when you wanted to stomp them to pulp and grind them into the ground, a smart man and a shrewd lawyer always extracted the necessary information first. His own father—definitely a wily legal mind—had taught him that.

"What do you want to know, Chris?" Stacy asked wearily.

"First, why you didn't tell me when you found out you were pregnant," he said, even-toned despite the anger that arose in him with the question.

"Just how could I do that?" she inquired, throwing the question right back to Chris.

"Why, I—" He stopped. *Oh, God.* Remembering those impulsive months in Europe, he felt his headache tighten viselike on his temples.

"You were the big macho man, taking care of everything, weren't you?" Stacy went on, her voice pure acid. "*I* wasn't going to get pregnant. *You* weren't going to be away in Europe very long. It was all going to be fine—just fine. Well, something went wrong, Chris—something went very badly wrong indeed."

"Surely you could have written me—" Again Chris stopped. He remembered now that he'd had no fixed itinerary.

"Sure—care of American Express at all the foreign capitals," she gibed. "I'm sure you checked in regularly for mail."

"No, I didn't," he admitted. "But I'll bet you didn't write, either."

"No. Frankly I was too sick, Chris. I threw up the whole nine months—everything but my toenails! I had morning sickness a dozen times a day...or so it seemed. Actually, I can't say enough bad things about being pregnant!" She stopped, her eyes taking on a faraway, haunted look.

Chris found he couldn't simply sit still and listen dispassionately, as he'd thought. The look in her eyes was getting to him. Restlessly he got up and walked toward the window.

"I lost my job," Stacy went on. "They fired me three weeks after you left, Chris." Her slim shoulders gave a shrug. "It was just as well. I was too sick to sit in that office and type."

"Oh, God, Stacy!" His hands clenched over the curtains at the window, unconsciously crushing their delicate lace.

"It's true!" she cried as if Chris had disbelieved her.

He stared out the window without seeing a single thing. "Why didn't you stay at home with your grandmother and wait until I came back?" he asked hoarsely.

"Grandmother threw me out as soon as she discovered I was pregnant. Maybe you remember how so-called reli-

gious she was. She had a few thousand things to say about
fallen women and spawn of Satan, as I recall.'' Stacy's voice
was completely dispassionate now.

"Why didn't you—'' Chris stopped. He remembered that
her parents' financial situation had been critical.

"Go home to my folks in New Mexico?'' she supplied, as
if her thoughts had tracked his. "They couldn't even feed
me, that's why I came to Langlois in the first place—remember? They certainly couldn't take care of me and a
baby.''

God, she'd been so young, he remembered again. Barely
eighteen. Only half his present age. "What did you do?'' he
said through lips that were starting to feel stiff. Then he
swung around from the window to face her again. "Never
mind. I know. You called Gary.''

Chris was starting to understand. He hated what he was
understanding, but still he was beginning to comprehend
what Stacy had faced.

"No, I didn't,'' she said, surprising him. "I went to stay
with Joannie Hopkins first.''

"Joannie—?'' A plump, wistful, not-very-pretty face
formed in Chris's mind.

"She was a friend I met, typing at the courthouse that
summer. She had a tiny apartment with a Pullman bed that
came out of the wall. I stayed with her almost a month, just
because she felt sorry for me.''

"I'm sorry I don't remember her better,'' Chris muttered.

"Joannie was nice—but I was imposing, and I knew it,''
Stacy continued. "Of course, I kept hoping I'd hear from
you, that you'd write me a long letter, Chris. I kept hoping
you'd say—well, all the things girls always want guys they
love to say, so I'd know that you really were coming back
and everything would be all right. But you know what?
Even though I got up early every single day and waylaid the
postman before he got to Grandmother's house, all you ever
wrote were two postcards. 'Wish you were here—Paris is
great,''' she said, her tone mocking.

Chris had always hated writing letters. As a practicing attorney it was a quirk he'd had to overcome, but listening to Stacy, Chris was feeling sicker by the moment.

A thought occurred to him. "The first night you were back here this summer...that scene by the pool...you said I'd left you holding the bag. I didn't know what you meant, but you were talking about Taylor."

"Yes." Now Stacy stood up and turned away from him. "Frankly I never meant to say that. After I had, I was afraid you'd figure it out."

"No, I didn't figure it out," Chris admitted, his own voice turning bitter. "It never occurred to me, ever, that you might have gotten pregnant. I thought I was being—"

"Careful...I know." She shot him a mirthless smile. "I guess nothing's foolproof."

Chris hadn't understood, when he'd left for Europe, why Stacy had carried on like it was the end of the world. "It's not like crossing the Atlantic with Christopher Columbus!" he remembered arguing with her. But she'd known intuitively that he shouldn't leave her. If only he'd listened.

On the other hand, he'd had a darned good reason for going, and it wasn't just to have fun, as he'd always implied.

"Let's go back to when you were staying with Joannie," Chris said, his attorney's mind striving to get everything in its proper time sequence. "You finally called Gary?"

"No. I never did. But he'd grown very disturbed when he couldn't reach me. And Grandmother wouldn't tell him where I was staying but kept raving about the wages of sin...you know she went quite mad before she died, or maybe you didn't know." Stacy sighed.

"I didn't know," Chris said tonelessly.

"So Gary borrowed some friend's car and drove all the way over here to see about me. I was ashamed to face him, Chris—but I was very relieved to see him, too. Gary and I had always been very special friends—almost like you and Lynn—at least we were until we made the fatal mistake of getting married." Idly Stacy walked back to the vanity stool and sank down again.

"Tell me about that, Stace," Chris urged. "What happened after Gary came here to Louisiana?"

"Well, he was shocked—but he had quite a lot to say. Starting with how he *would* marry me—and you probably wouldn't. In fact Gary predicted you would utter that immortal line that goes, 'How do I know it's mine?'" Stacy's eyes met Chris's levelly. "Frankly, I think you probably would have, too."

Chris opened his mouth to protest, then closed it abruptly. How the hell did he know what he might have said or done thirteen years ago? That selfish, inconsiderate and totally arrogant young man he was beginning to see through the young Stacy's eyes had probably been capable of anything!

"So I married Gary at the courthouse here and we went back to New Mexico," Stacy continued. "I think we both had the best of intentions, but we were too young and idealistic to understand all we'd have to deal with."

"Such as?" Remorselessly Chris continued with questions that he knew were probably none of his business. He simply had to know.

"Very little money, since Gary was working as a waiter in a second-rate restaurant. A hot upstairs apartment. A bride so sick with another man's child that she wasn't interested in making love even—" Stacy stopped.

Chris supplied the words she didn't say. "Even if you'd been in love with Gary, which you weren't."

She nodded. "That was the situation when Lynn called me in tears and despair. She'd just heard about you and me. She asked me if it really was, as *you'd* told her, just 'a summer thing.' That's the only way I knew you were back from Europe, Chris. And that's how I knew what your opinion of our love affair had been!"

"That wasn't my opinion," he confided, his voice low. "I was angry. I was... very angry. I'd gotten home and found out that you'd married Gary—and I was hitting back."

"Well, that's when *I* got very angry, too," Stacy went on. "So I took great pleasure in telling Lynn that I didn't give a damn about you, either, and that I was happy to be married to Gary."

Chris's hands tightened again on the lace curtains. "Yeah, I heard your version, too. I think that's all that convinced Lynn to ever give me another chance."

Stacy looked at him curiously, those green eyes suddenly filled with a strange glow. "Chris, you were angry I'd gotten married because . . . you really didn't want it over between us?"

"That's about it," he said, admitting something that slow torture couldn't have extracted from him once. "That's why I shot off my mouth to Lynn, claiming you didn't matter to me—that and the fact that I didn't want to hurt her any more than she'd already been hurt. But I don't want to talk about Lynn, Stacy. Let's get back to you and Taylor."

"Well, finally, the worst was over. Taylor was born—a healthy eight-pound boy. I weighed ninety pounds and looked like a concentration-camp victim." That haunted look returned to her face. "It was very, very rough, Chris." He knew it must have been, and a hundred more questions occurred to him. Why had Stacy ever put herself through such an ordeal? Why hadn't she simply gotten rid of his baby? Legal abortions weren't that expensive. Or had she or Gary held convictions opposing abortion? But those were questions any judge would consider irrelevant. The boy existed and was safely here, thank God!

"What day was he born?" Chris asked instead. He felt stung by the realization that he didn't even know his first son's birth date.

"April 20," Stacy answered. "At 4:20 a.m. That wasn't particularly easy, either, since he was a forceps delivery."

"Considerate just like his old man, right?" Chris said, then suddenly realized to his horror that not only was his head splitting, making every thought a painful and difficult process, but he was actually—incredibly—on the verge of tears. He never cried. He hadn't cried in years—not even at Lynn's funeral, grief-stricken though he'd been.

Of course, it wasn't every day that a man learned he had a handsome, intelligent twelve-year-old son by a woman he'd once been absolutely crazy about.

Blinking hard, Chris turned back to the window and battled away the offending moisture gathering in his eyes. "Do you love Taylor?" he asked, determined to have the answer verified from Stacy's own lips.

"Of course!" Stacy said, sounding shocked.

"Why, of course, for God's sake, after all you went through? Why?—when the boy looks almost exactly like me?" Chris asked roughly.

"I don't know," Stacy said half defiantly. "When you carry a baby for nine months you naturally learn to love it."

"Didn't Taylor wreck your marriage?" Chris demanded.

"Not really. By the time he arrived there wasn't much left to wreck. Gary already knew he was in over his head. He'd started to look elsewhere for consolation. And I—well, I was so terrified of another pregnancy that I didn't fight for my husband the way I should have."

Chris swung around in time to see Stacy draw a deep breath. "Gary rescued me. He gave Taylor his name, and considering the circumstances, he's taken a fair amount of interest in him since. I'll always be grateful to Gary."

Chris knew it was churlish of him, but he was not grateful to Gary. He didn't want his son carrying some other man's name or believing Gary to be his father, either. But now wasn't the time to go into all that.

Chris had just one question left, but it loomed large and important to him. "After your marriage sank, you...you still never thought of getting in touch with me and telling me about Taylor?"

"No," Stacy said levelly. "As you've pointed out, Lynn had already been hurt once. Anyway, by the time Gary and I officially gave up, you and Lynn were expecting Robbie."

Suddenly some of Chris's very real and deep anguish seemed to penetrate the cloud of memories in which Stacy was submerged. Her face grew concerned. "Chris, what possible good would it have done for you to know?" she asked gently.

"I could have at least supported Taylor," he blurted, haunted by a sense of déjà vu. "Then he wouldn't have had to grow up the way I did!"

"He hasn't grown up the way you did," Stacy said distinctly. "Oh, Chris, I never let you know about Taylor because you would have been the one to damage him, not me."

"What are you talking about?" he demanded.

Her face grew wise. "You would have wanted it all...you always do, Chris. You would have wanted Taylor living right here in Langlois, Louisiana—you know you would! And what would have happened to him then? Could you have foisted him off on Lynn? Not without breaking her heart! So I guess you'd have farmed him out to another Bonnie Lorio and let him grow up with a whole town knowing he was illegitimate?"

"No," Chris hissed through clenched teeth.

Unexpectedly Stacy walked over and took Chris's hands in hers. At her touch, at the closeness and fragrance of her, his body responded almost as it had last night—almost as if it had heard none of the ensuing conversation that made the reaction inappropriate.

"Chris, it's been all right," Stacy said softly. "Taylor isn't you reborn. He hasn't ever been deprived of anything he really needs, and very little that he wants. I did tell him to forget about a motorcycle—"

"How about a father?" Chris cut in.

"Well, yes," she confessed. "Taylor could have done with a better one than Gary."

"Well, he's got one now!" Chris snapped, and walked out of the room to take Taylor to the barbershop.

At least Stacy had opened his eyes to the reality of Taylor, Chris thought in hindsight. He'd been making the mistake of reading much more of himself and his early life into the boy than actually existed.

While Taylor wasn't talkative like Robbie, neither was he given to the sullen monosyllables that Chris had used to respond to adult questions when he'd been Taylor's age. And Taylor laughed when something struck him as funny. Unhappy children lacked a sense of humor, Chris knew. They didn't laugh.

Otherwise, Taylor was shrewd and streetwise, just as Chris had been at his age. The boy's eyes swept back and forth like a radar scan, taking in everything around him. When Chris drove Taylor around after the haircut, showing him the town, its schools and football field, he knew this sharp young guy wasn't missing a trick.

Nor had Taylor missed any signs of Chris's own financial status. Surreptitiously he stroked the expensive leather seats in Chris's car and examined the cassette player and elaborate radio. He toyed briefly with the push-button windows.

"I can drive," he volunteered suddenly.

"You can?" Chris said in surprise.

"Yeah, but don't tell Mom 'cause she'd stroke out and die," Taylor added casually. "I learned from this old guy who lives down the street from us in Albuquerque. He's a big bore, but he's kinda lonely, I guess, 'cause he lives all alone. So I asked him how to drive and he showed me. He's just got an old pickup truck, and it isn't automatic or anything like this car. I had to scrunch down to reach the pedals and I had to learn how to shift gears."

"Well, you need to learn how to shift," Chris remarked. "Someday you might want to drive a sports car. You'd need to use the various gears for that."

"Yeah, I'd really like to have a sports car!" Taylor agreed enthusiastically.

"So you learned to drive while you were with this old guy. But, of course, you haven't tried it on your own yet?" Chris said knowingly.

Taylor shot Chris a look of surprise, as if the older man were clairvoyant. "Yeah, I've tried it," he admitted. "While Gary was busy with his little fox, I snuck his car keys. Then, soon as I heard the bedsprings bouncing, I took out that lemon Gary drives."

"Well, listen—you are never, ever to drive alone again," Chris said, pinning the boy with his fiercest stare. "I won't have you getting yourself killed. Is that understood?"

Taylor's black eyebrows shot up in surprise. How annoyed, arrogant and supercilious he looks, Chris marveled and wondered if *he* ever wore such expressions. He watched the boy's inner debate. He knew Taylor was wondering whether to tell Chris to go to hell or to accept his authority.

The boy's chin came up. It was the first gesture Chris had seen that reminded him at all of Stacy. Taylor's black eyes were hard as marbles, but there remained in them an unwitting gleam of respect. Or maybe every boy in the world just wanted a grown man to like him and be concerned about his welfare.

"Yes sir," said Taylor.

Chris dropped Taylor off at the bottom of the driveway. "Tell your mother I'll be home in a couple of hours," he said. "Now why don't you go enjoy yourself in the pool with Robbie and Ted Thackery?"

"All right!" Taylor exclaimed with enthusiasm.

Chris drove immediately to his office. He sent Barney off on an errand, then asked Janice to come in for dictation. Chris's first order of business was to change his will. The second was to dictate a premarital agreement.

Chapter Ten

They were actually going to get married!

It seemed so completely unbelievable that sometimes Stacy felt like pinching herself just to be sure she was really awake.

Was she really going to marry Chris Lorio at last?

Sometimes she felt so excited, so filled with anticipation and happy dreams of the future that she had to stop, swallow hard and remind herself of one pertinent and less than flattering fact: this wasn't exactly the love match of the century, as Chris had made clear to her.

In fact, when you got right down to it, the real reason for Stacy's second marriage was exactly the same as her first: Taylor. She didn't kid herself that Chris would ever have proposed otherwise, and if Stacy hadn't loved her son so much, Chris's newfound determination to hang on to the boy—whatever the cost—might have made his mother resentful . . . or jealous.

Getting married had been the last thing on Stacy's mind that all-important day when Chris and Taylor had first discovered each other. In fact, Chris had arrived home from his office barely in time to stop Stacy from driving off for New Mexico with the sulking Taylor in tow.

At the time, once again, flight back home had seemed Stacy's only solution to an impossible dilemma. She had almost finished packing the Monte Carlo, utilizing Taylor's and Robbie's reluctant help, when Chris wheeled up behind them. Robbie immediately dropped a box and ran to his father, sobbing that Stacy was leaving "right now."

"Like hell she is," Chris replied calmly.

Then, before Stacy could marshal her arguments, Chris reached into the Monte Carlo and calmly pocketed the car keys that Stacy had been naive enough to leave dangling from the ignition. Next, Chris seized Stacy by the elbow and marched her straight upstairs to his study.

She knew right away that arguing with him in his present mood would be dangerous. Chris held his head too rigidly, and his eyes were starting to look strained—tip-offs to another severe migraine. Still, Stacy talked nonstop all the way up the stairs, her voice low but urgent. This was the best thing for all of them, and the sooner she and Taylor left the better. Couldn't Chris understand that?

"Shut up, Stacy," he said wearily, slamming the door to his study behind them. He winced at its bang. "You and my son Taylor are not going anywhere," he announced. "So forget it."

She gasped at his feudal audacity. "What do you think this is, the eighteenth century?" Stacy cried defiantly, her chin jutting out. "We're not your chattels, Mr. Lorio! I'm taking *my* child and I'm going home right now, and you can't stop—"

"Oh, no? Just watch me." Although Chris collapsed into his chair behind the large, imposing desk his voice held a silky edge that made it sound all the more dangerous. "This is south Louisiana, where we have our own quaint way of doing things. You try to leave, Stacy, and I'll pick up this phone—" deliberately he pointed to the silent instrument on his desk "—and when I finish telling Sheriff Grady Bourg, who plays poker with me, how you've absconded with *my* kid and some of my poor late wife's personal property—why, honey, you'll be lucky if all Grady and his deputies do is run you off the road and shoot out all four tires.''

Stacy gasped again, then recovered quickly, fresh anger stiffening her spine. ''You wouldn't!'' she dared.

''Try me and see,'' Chris threatened through gritted teeth. Stacy almost called his bluff because she didn't believe him for a minute. Chris certainly had his flaws—*worlds* of them—but she didn't think breaking the law he'd sworn as an attorney to uphold was one of them. But as she glared at Chris she saw him rub his forehead as if he felt thoroughly miserable.

So instead of continuing to yell and storm she dropped down into the chair before his desk—a seat that was beginning to feel quite familiar to her. ''Why are you doing this, Chris?'' she asked quietly.

He didn't reply immediately. Instead he reached into the pocket of his sports jacket, pulled out several long legal sheets and tossed them across the desk at her.

Two amazing words, *Premarital Agreement*, leapt up at Stacy, but before she could begin to digest them Chris answered casually. ''I'm doing it because I want Taylor to live here with me. And I believe I owe you a lot as well. It's obvious I once left you in a hell of a mess. I can't undo that, but I'd like to make life better for you now. I think we ought to get married, Stacy.'' After a stunned silence, he finally showed her the courtesy of adding, ''What do you think of the idea?''

She continued to gape at him in speechless confusion, which Chris appeared to enjoy. Then, as it dawned on Stacy that Chris was serious, a wild thrill shot through her, firing her emotions and shredding her common sense. Nevertheless she gulped and managed to reply spiritedly, ''Frankly, I think it's a lousy idea.''

''Why?'' Chris inquired. Carefully he made a steeple of his hands and regarded her over the top of them. ''You've said yourself that all you have in Albuquerque is a job that's unraveling. Also, you need financial help with Taylor. He'll be ready for college in a few years."

"But people don't get married because of things like that!" Stacy blurted, her heart pounding in double time.

"No, generally they aren't so reasonable," Chris agreed readily. "Instead they get married in a state of feverish insanity, which is somehow supposed to be better. C'mon, Stacy—" his voice turned soft and coaxing "—Robbie was in tears when he thought you were leaving him. He's deeply attached to you."

"I know—and I'm equally attached to him," she admitted.

"I don't always understand Robbie very well," Chris surprised her by adding. "I know I need help with him. And, God knows, *you* need help with Taylor!"

"I've done okay," Stacy said, stung. "Taylor's never been in any real trouble except for fighting at school and—"

"Yeah, I can tell he was the real charm boy of summer camp," Chris said, lacing his fingers together even more tightly while Stacy glared at him. Just the word *camp* had the power to rub her sensibilities raw, especially since she'd spoken with Mrs. Stephens and learned that she couldn't have her money refunded.

"Taylor needs to learn other ways to settle arguments than with his fists," Chris continued calmly. "Also, he told me something that I don't think you know about. He recently learned to drive. While he was in Santa Fe he took Gary's car out all alone for an evening spin."

Stacy felt her mouth fall open in astonishment.

"Taylor asked me not to tell you that—but you really must know," Chris continued. "He can't go around driving cars and hopping freights."

The world seemed to be spinning around Stacy. Almost frantically she groped for the corner of Chris's desk and held on tight, feeling as if she were about to drop into a bottomless abyss.

"I wasn't kidding when I said you were losing control of him, Stace. You've done a great job so far, and I can't begin to tell you how grateful I am. But Taylor's turning into a young man now and that's one thing you've never been. Although he's smart as a whip and a daredevil to boot—I doubt if he can think of much that I didn't try, too. Anyway, the first-born son is one I can read like a book.''

"That doesn't surprise me," Stacy managed to say, sniffing. "Taylor's exactly like you. He always has been."

"I know, you poor woman," Chris said, smiling thinly. Then after a minute, he continued, "I'm not so concerned with what he's done so far, Stacy, as I am with what he's liable to do next, especially in a big city. At least the amount of devilment I managed to get into was limited to Langlois's city limits. I'd like to see those same boundaries imposed on Taylor—at least until he grows up enough to have a little more sense. Also, two parents presenting a united front is a lot more convincing to a kid than one. That's another reason I want us to get married."

So it was concern for the boys, Taylor in particular, that had prompted Chris's astonishing proposal. Stacy could almost taste her disappointment even as she wondered why she was surprised.

She drew a breath and gripped the desk edge even more tightly. "Chris, I'm sure all your reasons are . . . quite reasonable," she said pleasantly. "But I don't consider that you owe me any debt to pay off. I love Taylor and I'm very glad he was born. But I consider looking after two boys a ridiculous reason for marriage. Now, if you'll excuse me—"

"I will *not* excuse you," Chris interrupted imperiously. "Besides, you haven't heard what I have in mind for you."

"Well, this ought to be interesting," Stacy said aloud. She leaned back in her chair and crossed her arms. The only trouble with her oh-so-casual pose was that her hands were shaking.

"Aren't you advertising people always secretly hungering to write your own poetry and prose?" Chris inquired. "Well, you could certainly do that right here, Stacy. There are several rooms in this house where we could set up an office for you.

"Or, if you'd prefer a job full or part-time, the local newspaper is always in need of reporters," Chris continued. "I know the editor, and right now he's hunting someone to write a series of articles on local historic sites and buildings."

Stacy glanced down and studied the carpet as if it were fascinating. She'd always had a not-so-secret love of history and Chris—blast him!—had obviously remembered. Fiercely she clenched her hands together, forcing herself to decline again.

"Sorry, Chris—although I appreciate the thought you've obviously given this whole matter." Then, with a little laugh to belie her true feelings, Stacy added, "You know, there's an old saying out West about buying a calf to get the cow, but this is the first time I've ever seen it reversed. Unfortunately, I'm not impressed with your classic and extreme case of being willing to buy the cow to get the calf."

Chris's face darkened with anger. "Damn it, Stacy, that's a complete misrepresentation of the facts," he snapped and came charging up out of his swivel chair even though the abrupt movement made him wince.

"Is it?" she challenged, staring up at him defiantly.

In a flash he crossed the space between them and snatched her up out of the chair. Then, as Stacy's head reeled with surprise, Chris caught her so close and tight that she feared he might snap her spine.

"I want you, too, Stacy Thomasson," he said to her huskily. "You know I want you—I always have!" Angrily he ground his body against hers, making her aware of his quick response to her. "Last night I didn't even know Taylor existed, and I still wanted you so much I didn't let you go until daylight. Don't tell me you've forgotten about that."

Stacy felt her body, too, quicken in response as he held her so close, reminding her vividly of their recent uninhibited hours. But even as Stacy felt her cheeks growing hot and desire beginning to unfurl deep inside her, she spoke disparagingly. "Oh, Chris, that's just sex—"

"'Just sex' is damned important, Stacy," he said, his large knowing hands beginning to trace patterns across her back while his lips moved slowly from her temple toward her ear.

"So that's what you want from this marriage?" Stacy said, her voice beginning to waver, for he'd set her emotions on a mad up and down seesaw once again.

"You're right," he whispered, pressing a kiss against her hair. "You'll have to sleep with me, Stacy. In fact, since I've had the experience of separate bedrooms during my first marriage I can definitely tell you I won't do it again. I'll want you right there beside me in bed every single night. But is that really such an awful price to pay?" he went on coaxingly. "I mean, you were certainly willing to be with me last night."

Again Stacy felt a revealing flush stain her face. And his sheer nearness affected her like black magic. Unconsciously Stacy found her hands stroking Chris's broad shoulders.

"It just wouldn't . . . work, Chris," she said with a sigh.

"It might," he said persuasively. "We used to have a lot of fun together, Stace—and not all of it was in bed."

"Sex often creates more problems than it solves," she protested, but she still couldn't manage to draw away from him, either. After the long difficult day of painful revelations and even more painful accusations it was so wonderful just to be held close to Chris once again.

"Well, I can absolutely guarantee that no sex causes worse ones," Chris retorted. "I'm getting an annulment for a young wife right now who's had a purely platonic marriage for over a year. And poor Lynn's illness caused us some problems along that line. She used to feel so guilty, and she shouldn't have. I always understood."

Chris paused. "I was happily married, Stacy. I liked the closeness, the togetherness that the three of us had. I was *proud* of my family. I want all of that again. You say I have a hell-bent determination to get it all, and maybe you're right. Maybe I do."

Without warning Chris tilted Stacy's head back and kissed her with such passion that her ears rang. For an endless time their lips clung, then parted reluctantly. "I'll make sure you and Taylor have a good life," he promised. "I'll always be faithful. And I'll defend you and support you in . . . well, almost anything. Now, will you marry me, you difficult, contrary, sexy woman?"

She loved him—was there really any choice? "Yes," she whispered and felt tremendous joy and relief surge through her.

She saw a light leap to life in Chris's dark eyes. Saw his head move down toward hers again. Their kiss this time was surprisingly tender and gentle. It was also far too brief, interrupted by a hard knock on the study door.

"Hey," Stacy heard her son call in to them. "Are you guys okay in there? Rob's starting to get worried."

"Remind me to put deadbolt locks on the doors," Chris whispered to Stacy. "Taylor also knows about bouncing bedsprings."

Stacy couldn't help laughing at Chris, then she called to her son. "We're okay. So why don't you two quit dripping all over the hall carpet? Get out of your swim trunks and come join us."

"Okay, Mom," Taylor called back.

Chris looked at her in astonishment. "How did you know they were standing there dripping?" he asked.

Stacy shrugged. "Mothers have eyes in the backs of their heads; didn't you know?"

When the boys came tumbling in, Robbie promptly announced that his was a "baby's name" and that Taylor thought he ought to be called Robert or Rob instead. Already the subversive influence of an older brother had begun.

Stacy signed the premarital agreement after her lawyer in New Mexico, a woman who had handled Stacy's divorce, said it was that true rarity, a generous one. That had been

Stacy's own impression, but she was glad to have it verified.

Stacy's appointment with her lawyer came while she and
Taylor were back in Albuquerque for a week. They were
there to move out of their apartment, close bank accounts
and get Taylor's school records. Stacy's former co-workers
gave her a bridal shower that emphasized sexy lingerie, but
she stayed so busy she scarcely had time to dwell on many
aspects of her forthcoming marriage.

When she agreed to marry Chris he'd set a wedding date
just three weeks away. Now Stacy was having to hurry to
meet it as she disposed of her run-down furniture and most
of their other possessions as well. Since, at Chris's insis-
tence, Stacy and Taylor had flown back to New Mexico,
Stacy knew that anything she wanted to keep would have to
be shipped. That knowledge helped her keep the load light.

Taylor had shown a surprising willingness to part with his
own possessions, as well. There were so few items that he
absolutely had to keep that Stacy was startled. She'd been
braced for tantrums and fury only to discover that Taylor's
allegiance to the great American West had diminished
steadily with each day he'd spent in Louisiana.

Taylor might not know yet that Chris was his biological
father and Robbie his half-brother, but he definitely knew
where he felt welcome and appreciated.

On Stacy's next-to-last evening in New Mexico she left
Taylor playing at a friend's house and drove up alone to
Santa Fe. There she met Gary for dinner to broach what she
feared might be a ticklish subject. But Chris had insisted. He
wanted to change Taylor's last name to Lorio immediately—and to do this painlessly required the agreement of
the man who was legally Taylor's father.

To Stacy's surprise she found Gary in a jovial mood. "So
you're getting married?" he asked over their appetizer of
nachos as he selected one. "What a coincidence, Stacy. I
am, too."

"Oh?" said Stacy, feeling less than enthusiastic about his
news. She really liked Gary—she always had—and she was

sorry to see him marry a giddy, shallow young girl. Taylor had not characterized "the little fox" in a flattering light. "Well, Gary, I certainly hope you and your fiancée will be happy."

"Relax, I'm not marrying who you think," Gary said, popping the nacho into his mouth. "I guess Crystal was my last crazy fling. I'm marrying Norma Atkinson."

"That schoolteacher who lives across the hall from you?" Stacy said excitedly. Norma was Gary's age, possibly even a year or two older. "Oh, Gary, I really liked her."

"Yeah, I'm lucky she'll still have me. I woke up one morning, and I guess I'd come to my senses. Anyway, I no longer needed to keep proving how desirable I was to women."

"I feel partly to blame that you ever had such a feeling," Stacy said quietly.

"Well, that's life, Stacy. Always full of unexpected twists and turns, isn't it?" Gary said, passing her the plate of nachos.

"Yes, it is," Stacy agreed, wondering how to lead into her topic. Gary had always been so wonderful about everything that she wished she didn't have to do this.

But once again Gary made it easy for her. "Anyway, Norma and I agreed we wanted kids as soon as possible. At our age we'd better get started."

Stacy blinked, amazed at this latest stroke of luck. "How wonderful!" she breathed, reaching over to touch Gary's freckled hand. And then she made her request.

"I'll really have the Lorio name, too?" Taylor asked Stacy suspiciously.

"You sure will. Chris wants to adopt you, and now Gary has agreed. I hope the idea pleases you, Taylor," Stacy added anxiously.

For a moment the boy frowned. "Yeah, sure. Oh, I know I wasn't in Louisiana with Chris for very long, but he told me then that he wanted me to be his son. I didn't know he really meant it, though."

"Chris doesn't say things he doesn't mean, Taylor," Stacy continued gently.

"Yeah? Well, that'll be a welcome change 'cause I don't think Gary ever said anything to me that he really meant!"

Stacy stared at Taylor thoughtfully. Well, what better time to try and tell him the truth than right now? *"Let me tell Taylor,"* she had insisted to Chris, and for once he had readily agreed that this was a task for the mother Taylor trusted.

"Taylor, would it bother you to know that...well, that Gary isn't your actual father?" Stacy inquired gently.

"Bother me? I'd be downright thrilled!" her son exclaimed.

"Then let me explain—"

Taylor took the news with perfect equanimity, amazing Stacy once again. But then she'd always been amazed and surprised by his unpredictable reactions.

Later that night Chris phoned Stacy from Baltimore. He and Robbie were there, visiting with Lynn's parents, who were presenting a well-received exhibit at a Washington museum. Chris had wanted to tell them personally of his plans for remarriage, especially since Lynn had only been gone for seven months.

"Things here are wonderful, Chris," Stacy said, being determinedly cheerful. "Taylor is tickled to death to get a new dad and a new last name, and Gary's relieved to be rid of the responsibility." Quickly Stacy filled Chris in on the details.

"Things here are great, too," he replied encouragingly. "I can't believe how understanding and supportive Ruth and Bill have been. Ruth said that Lynn would undoubtedly approve of this wedding. Then Bill added his two cents' worth and said that he and Ruth had both been worried about Robbie, being so young and not having a mother. It was quite a relief for them to hear of the rapport that you and Robbie have."

"Goodness, everything really is wonderful, isn't it?" Stacy said brightly. "Do give Aunt Ruth and Uncle Bill my love."

"Now, you and Taylor are flying back day after tomorrow, right?" Chris said, reconfirming their schedule.

"I am if I can possibly get everything done by then," Stacy said, but she was angling just a little, too. She needed to hear more encouragement and enthusiasm from Chris about marrying *her*.

"Hire someone to help you, but get it done," Chris ordered. "I know our wedding is just a small family affair but it's all set and I don't want it postponed." He paused, then added warningly, "No last minute jitters, either, Stacy. And don't you dare try running out on me again. I'll track you down if it takes the F.B.I., Interpol and the Canadian Northwest Mounties to do it!"

Stacy started to smile again while a weight over her chest began to lighten. "Yes, sir!" she agreed, mocking a soldier snapping to attention. Then, more quietly, she added, "Chris, who exactly in Langlois knows that we're getting married?"

"Just a very few people," he said, his voice surprised. "Miriam and Preston, Knox and his wife, Lottie, and Judge Danforth, who'll be performing the ceremony. All of them know that they're not to mention it, too. In deference to Lynn's memory I want this wedding done as quietly and tastefully as possible. Why?"

"Oh—" Stacy bit her lip to stop herself from saying any more. She didn't want to worry Chris and she didn't want him flying into a black rage, either. "I was just curious," she said lightly. "I—I guess Robbie knows, too?"

"I thought I told you last time I called," Chris said, his voice sharpening. "I didn't tell Robbie until we were on the plane, flying up here to Baltimore. He's absolutely thrilled. Stacy what's this all about?"

Once again she bit her lip. "Oh, just—just bridal nerves." She laughed, the sound hollow.

"Well, forget being nervous! You don't have to do a thing but show up. Now, since your plane arrives before ours will, Preston will be in New Orleans to meet you—" Accepting Stacy's explanation without further comment, Chris began to outline their travel arrangements.

After Stacy hung up she went to sit on a packing case in her darkened living room. The room had a large picture window that looked out on the lights of Albuquerque, and many, many nights Stacy had sat here, simply gazing and thinking, especially when she'd had something pressing on her mind.

And she certainly did tonight. Indeed, it had been a busy, exhausting evening following an equally exhausting day. Stacy had been so worried that Gary might give her problems that she'd completely forgotten to check her mailbox until after she'd gotten back from Santa Fe.

When she did get around to checking it, there on a cheap white sheet of paper tucked inside a small cheap white envelope she'd found a warning written in a large, ragged hand: "Chris wants your son, not you. If you marry him you'll lose your life."

It was signed, as such anonymous letters often were, "A Friend," and it had been postmarked in Langlois, Louisiana.

Stacy had hoped that it was merely a juvenile prank in abysmally poor taste. Had hoped that Robbie might have confided in Ted Thackery, for instance, and that Ted had either sent the note or had told someone who had.

That had never been a very rational explanation, Stacy knew. The someone who had written this anonymous letter either knew of, or had guessed at, the very special bond between Chris and Taylor.

And now, according to Chris, Robbie had not even known that Stacy was going to be his stepmother until he was flying away toward Baltimore.

This meant that someone whom Chris had trusted to keep quiet about his and Stacy's wedding plans had not done so.

This same person was now trying to frighten Stacy into—what? Calling off her plans to marry Chris? In that case, it was someone who certainly didn't know *her* very well. Stacy wasn't about to be intimidated by a coward writing letters he or she wouldn't sign.

Why hadn't she told Chris tonight about the letter? Stacy wondered. True, she'd hated to rain on his parade when he'd sounded so buoyant. But this concerned him every bit as much as it concerned her.

I'll tell Chris just as soon as I see him again, Stacy vowed. Handling the letter with distaste, she drew it out of her purse and started to rip it in two. Then, at the last minute, she realized that it wouldn't be a very good idea. As much as she longed to shred the loathsome letter, she smoothed it out again instead, carried it back to her bedroom and tucked it into her suitcase.

Then she crawled wearily into bed and fell sound asleep.

Chapter Eleven

Stacy and Taylor returned to Louisiana on schedule—unlike Chris and Robbie, who had trouble getting home when the Memphis airport, where they were scheduled to change flights, was closed for several hours because of dangerous wind shears.

"First they said our flight was delayed. Now it's been cancelled," Chris said long-distance to Stacy. "You and Taylor go on to bed. We'll be there in the morning."

"You'd better be," Stacy threatened, feigning anger to hide her dismay. She had really hoped to talk with Chris before their wedding tomorrow afternoon. He needed to know about the nasty anonymous letter that kept preying on her mind. But with other stranded passengers in a jostling line behind him awaiting their turn to use a pay telephone, it didn't seem right to tie Chris up any longer than necessary.

No sooner had Stacy hung up and creamed her face in preparation for bed than the telephone rang again. Ha

Chris forgotten to tell her something? she wondered, scooping up the receiver.

"Hello?" she said expectantly.

Only silence greeted her. It continued for so long that Stacy was about to hang up when suddenly a message spoken in a monotone began.

"Don't marry Chris," said a low husky voice that could have been either male or female, "or you'll be taking your life in your hands if you do. Chris doesn't want *you*," the rasping voice continued. "Once he has Taylor he'll get rid of *you*."

Abruptly the voice ended, and a moment later the phone line went dead.

Stunned, Stacy sank down on the edge of Lynn's antique bed. Her legs felt about as sturdy as water. The anonymous note had been disgusting, even infuriating. But a telephone call—with an actual person, however shadowy, on the other end—was downright menacing.

Or had that actually been a human being speaking? Stacy wondered. As her heart pounded and a sick feeling of absolute fear made her stomach churn she pondered what she had just heard. The message hadn't sounded like a live voice at all; it had a canned, tinny quality like that of a cheap recording.

Still, live human hands had dialed the telephone and set the recorded tape to playing. With the room whirling around her, Stacy squeezed her eyes shut and tried to think calmly, rationally.

Who on earth would do such a thing? she thought, incredulous. What kind of mind was capable of tormenting a woman on the very eve of her wedding?

Was it some misguided friend of Lynn's who thought Chris's remarriage was too precipitous or who disapproved of his choice of a bride? But then who on Chris's very small guest list knew her at all?

Nervously Stacy pushed her hair back from her face. It was imperative now that Chris know about these incidents, for there was someone out there—someone he trusted—who was not a true friend after all, but a warped enemy instead.

As soon as she considered her legs reliable enough to stand, Stacy walked down to Robbie's room, which had been thoroughly cleaned and aired by Miriam in the child's absence. Twin beds provided a place for a friend to sleep over.

Now Taylor lay sprawled on the spare bed. Although he was listening to a ball game on Robbie's radio, it was barely managing to keep him awake. He looked up in surprise at the sight of his mother.

"Taylor, I think I'll sleep in here tonight," Stacy said and reached behind her to punch in the button that locked the door. For a moment she considered confiding in Taylor—but he was still a child, a child who was going to have to adjust to two other men in his mother's life. She had no right to burden her son further.

It was better that Taylor think what, from the expression on his face, he already did: that his about-to-be-married mother had gone completely crazy.

Shortly before dawn Stacy jerked awake. Beneath the sheet her feet were still moving frantically, just as they had been in the nightmare from which she'd so suddenly awakened.

It had been an unusually vivid and frightening one, and her heart continued pounding sickly while a sheen of perspiration covered her body. Being in the narrow unfamiliar bed in the unfamiliar room added to her overall feeling of disorientation, even panic.

While she lay still suspended in that gray half world between sleep and waking, the dream drifted back to her making her shudder.

She'd been running for her very life, running through dark spooky woods to try to escape a figure who was chasing her. She knew the man would kill her as soon as he caught her, for she was just so much excess baggage that he didn't need cluttering up his carefully planned life. But Stacy also knew her chances for escape were nil. He was so tall, so strong and fleet, and in her nightmare he'd been gaining steadily on her. Just when he'd seized her and she'd felt the clutch of his remorseless iron hands she'd jerked awake, terrified.

The man, of course, had been Chris.

Thank God for bright sunlight, for the cheerful, ordinary clatter of dishes and smells of breakfast, Stacy thought. Thank God for the hurrying, scurrying feet that delivered flowers and brought Chris's best suit from the cleaners. Thank God for the excited voices that quarreled as the photographer tried to get all set up for the ceremony while Miriam tried to give the formal living room a final vacuuming and dusting. And thank God for Taylor, who stared at Stacy in sheer horror, saying, "You mean for this wedding I've got to wear a *tie*?"

The golden summer light, the excited voices and, yes, even Taylor's vast indignation soon swept away all vestiges of Stacy's ridiculous nightmare. And that's all it had been—absolutely ridiculous. By daylight Stacy was furious that her subconscious mind had ever yielded, even briefly, to that cowardly, mechanical-sounding voice that had tried to terrify and torment her.

Today she was marrying the man she loved—the one man she had always loved—and she was positively delighted to be joining her life with his!

In fact, as the morning grew steadily later, Stacy's major concern was simply that Chris and Robbie still hadn't arrived. But their plane from Memphis had finally set down in New Orleans and Chris had phoned Stacy from the airport to say they were on their way.

By midmorning when Stacy occasionally thought about the caller who had triggered her wild dream all she felt was mad as hell.

Still, how odd it was that this anonymous figure had so unerringly found Stacy's one area of genuine weakness. That he or she had pinpointed the fear, which still hadn't entirely gone away, that all Chris really wanted was Taylor.

It's not true, Stacy argued with herself. *Chris does care about me—there's no reason for him to marry me if he doesn't.*

To strengthen her resolve, Stacy began laying out her pretty new wedding clothes on Lynn's bed.

A car skidded up the driveway, and a moment later a joyful commotion arose from below. Dashing to her window Stacy saw that Chris and Robbie had finally arrived and were being greeted by Miriam, Preston and Taylor. *Oh, thank God,* she thought in relief.

Just for a minute Chris's eyes flashed up to Stacy's window. He grinned and threw her a wave. How happy he looks, she thought, surprised. She started to wave back to him but at just that moment the telephone began to ring.

"Chris, I've got to talk to you," Stacy said urgently through her bedroom door. He was holding it firmly closed from the other side.

"You can't back out now," he called, his voice teasing. "It's too late."

"Chris, this is serious!"

"What, Stace?"

She heard a matching seriousness in his voice and knew she had his full attention. "Come in and I'll tell you," she said urgently.

"Don't you know it's bad luck for the bridegroom to see the bride before the wedding?" he flashed right back. But his voice no longer sounded teasing or particularly happy, either.

How Stacy hated to upset him on this day of days! "Then just listen to me," she began, and quietly, with the door still serving as a barrier between them, she told him.

Chris was quiet for so long that Stacy began to grow troubled. "Chris, did you hear what I said? First, there was a letter sent to me in New Mexico and now there have been two phone calls—the last one just a minute ago. It's a recorded message, too, I'm sure of it. The words were identical both times and the person talking has this slow, raspy voice."

"I heard, Stace." The taut fury in his voice chilled Stacy's blood, though she knew the fury wasn't directed toward her. In fact, as Chris spoke again his tone warmed steadily. "Look, don't let it bother you, Stace. Every lawyer handles his share of nut cases—that's all this is. Just some crank trying to cause trouble."

"But you said very few people knew we were getting married," Stacy protested. "Oh, don't you see—" She stopped, her already high-strung emotions beginning to get the better of her.

"Stacy, maybe you should open this door, after all," Chris said.

She bit her lip, trying to get a grip on her runaway nerves. "What? And risk bad luck? No, sirree!"

"You'll be all right?" Chris asked, his voice concerned.

"Absolutely—now that you and Robbie are here," she assured him.

"That's my girl!" he cheered. "Say, do you still have that letter you received in New Mexico?"

"Yes. I thought you'd want to see it."

"I do, Stace." That grim inflexible note returned to his voice. "Just slide it under the door. Good! Okay, I'll see you in a couple of hours at a wedding downstairs. And, remember, we Lorios are far too tough to let a crank bother us."

That particular Lorio was also too tough to let a matter like this go unavenged, Stacy knew with absolute certainty. While she didn't have the least idea who might have been trying to frighten her, she realized that Chris probably had a very clear idea. And despite his chin-up words to Stacy she also knew that he was almost mad enough to commit murder.

"Chris, do you know who's making these calls?" Stacy implored.

"Yeah...somebody who'll never have a migraine," he said mystifyingly.

Twenty minutes before his second wedding Chris Lorio strode into his law office. Although the office should have been locked tight for the weekend, he was not surprised to find the front door unlocked and all the lights on.

Nor was he surprised to find his efficient, long-time secretary, Janice Clayton, seated at her desk. "Chris!" Janice exclaimed, looking up at him. Clearly she was startled.

Rapidly he crossed the reception room to slap down before Janice the letter Stacy had received in New Mexico. Wordlessly Janice stared at it. A long, long minute passed before she finally looked up at Chris. He saw her eyes then, red-rimmed but wary. "What's this about?" she asked, trying to bluff.

"You know. I made the mistake of confiding in you because I thought I could trust you. Get your things and get out of here right now, Janice," Chris said in a voice of ice.

"Chris, please..." Janice began.

Chris leaned back against the wall and crossed his arms, his posture inflexible. "I'll wait until you've left," he said softly. "After that, Floyd, my mechanic, who's also a pretty good locksmith, will change the locks."

"Chris—"

"One last thing, Janice. Using a mentally retarded person to do your dirty work is especially contemptible. It was unfair to Barney as well as Stacy. Don't ever do it again or I'll see that you never get another job in this town."

They'd planned the wedding to be brief but nice. Initially Stacy had been disappointed that Chris didn't want a religious service but he'd explained that he preferred not to involve the Glovers. Since Stacy was virtually sure by now that the overly concerned Ellen Glover was actually Chris's aunt—and that Chris knew it—she could accept his feelings in the matter without understanding the reasons behind them.

In any event, tall and distinguished Judge Lawrence Danforth was an excellent choice to perform the ceremony. Chris was fond of the older man, he'd explained, and the extroverted judge clearly enjoyed his role in weddings. He came up to Stacy's room to meet her and absolutely charmed her with his Southern courtesy.

"Chris tells me the two of you are leaving tomorrow for a week in Mexico," the judge remarked.

"Yes. Chris thought we needed some time alone—and he also thinks I'll enjoy learning to scuba dive," Stacy explained. "Since I've spent most of my time in the desert I've never done any ocean diving."

"Well, just as soon as you lovebirds are back, my wife and I want you to come to dinner one night. Mrs. Danforth's downstairs now, and she's certainly looking forward to meeting you." The judge paused, glancing at his watch. "My dear, it's almost time."

Then, just a few short minutes after that, Stacy and Chris were standing side by side before the judge, their small group of relatives and friends clustered around.

"You look beautiful," Chris managed to whisper to Stacy as they came down the stairs together. She had worn a simple but elegant peach linen dress, a color that reflected the red glints in her dark hair. The bouquet she carried, which Chris had selected for her, consisted of small white orchids.

She also wore a gorgeous strand of creamy pearls and matching pearl earrings that Robbie had delivered, as a gift from his father, less than ten minutes before the wedding. Chris's intense black eyes, drinking in every detail of Stacy's appearance, had brightened with pleasure when he saw her wearing them.

Stacy, in turn, thought that Chris looked incredibly handsome in a formal-looking black suit and quietly subdued tie. He had the flair and good looks to wear the very familiar and carry it off—indeed, to stamp it with his own identity. Then the judge opened his book and began.

Chris's voice was firm as he recited the wedding vows. Stacy's voice was less steady even to her own ears, but equally resolute. Once, many long years ago, she had dreamed of a golden day with Chris as her bridegroom. It felt strange to have that dream come true the way it had, but it also felt good and right. She was finally marrying the man she loved and for the brief few minutes of the ceremony that was absolutely all that mattered to her.

When the judge pronounced them man and wife Chris and Stacy turned to each other spontaneously. Their lips met and clung until mutual desire began to flash. It's been so

long since he touched me last! Stacy couldn't help thinking, even as they reluctantly broke away to accept kisses and
handshakes from the others. Then they pulled their sons
close, making the boys part of the wedding pictures that the
photographer snapped hastily.

After the photo taking they all went into the large dining
room. The immense table looked festive, covered with a lace
cloth and decorated with a bowl of flowers, and Miriam had
set out a small wedding cake, champagne and coffee.

Soon Stacy was trying to talk with everyone at once as she
sipped champagne and took bites of the rich cake, but all the
time the thought uppermost in her mind was simply that
soon, very soon, she would be alone with Chris.

"All best wishes, my dear." The tall dark man who was
Knox Kinard, Chris's mentor and friend, brushed Stacy's
cheek with his lips. Stacy glanced up at the distinguished-
looking Knox and wondered briefly if he really was Chris's
father, as most people in town seemed to think. The two
men were of a similar height and build, but Knox's shoulders were rounded in a somewhat defeated-looking slump.

When Knox's wife, plain and portly Lottie, linked her
arm firmly through her husband's, Stacy suddenly wondered if Lottie explained Knox's subtly defeated air. He had
never come close to achieving the eminence of his late law
partner, the less attractive but still dynamic Congressman
Hamilton Bainbridge. Today, when love was uppermost in
Stacy's mind, she wondered if Knox had ever missed a lively
pretty girl named Kathryn Ann, with whom he'd supposedly once been in love.

Chris had mentioned years ago that Knox really should
have gone further, considering his powerful political connections. But apparently Lottie had always resisted Knox's
ambitions, so he'd resigned himself to being a big frog in his
small hometown pond. Or was that his real reason? Stacy
considered on her wedding day. Might there have been
something in Knox's background, like a love child, that he'd
feared to have revealed?

I'll never oppose Chris, whatever he wants to do, Stacy found herself vowing, even as her eyes once again sought wistfully the tall, handsome figure of her new husband.

Pleasure and delight filled Stacy in waves when she saw that Chris was looking straight at her, too. His eyes, holding an openly hungry desire, telegraphed a simple message: I do wish our guests would go home!

Stacy knew that her own eyes were returning the same message. They hadn't made love since that wildly abandoned night of the moon eclipse, their restraint due both to lack of opportunity and to Taylor's acutely observant nature. But now, following wedding vows, making love was not only legal and acceptable but highly approved of by society. The delightful tension that Stacy felt when her eyes met Chris's created its own magical force field. How she yearned to be in his arms!

"Mrs. Lorio, we'll be taking the boys and leaving now," Preston, ever the perfect butler, interjected quietly.

Stacy turned, smiling, at the sound of her brand-new name and saw that Miriam and Preston had both boys in tow. Taylor and Robbie looked entirely ready to ditch their dress clothes, constricting ties and company manners to escape to Knox's fishing camp, which was located on the Atchfaylaya River and edged a vast and still primitive wetland.

Chris had arranged for the boys to have a vacation, too, while he and Stacy were in Mexico. Miriam and Preston would care for them at the camp and Ted Thackery had been invited to go along.

Now Stacy gave both her sons a hug, and Chris excused himself to tell the boys goodbye. As he stood beside them, dispensing last-minute fatherly advice about watching out for snakes, swamps and too much sun, his arm went firmly around Stacy's waist, drawing her close.

When she felt the heat that radiated from Chris's body, Stacy's longing for him grew irresistible. After the boys had gone, her eyes and Chris's locked once again. This time their gazes lingered and held. *I want you,* Chris's eyes telegraphed, and he seemed to be removing Stacy's clothes, item by item, in his imagination.

When the mesmerized Stacy finally made herself turn back to their remaining guests she saw that Knox was herding the others toward the front door. Behind their backs he gave Chris a quick thumbs-up signal, and Chris laughed aloud.

Stacy, embarrassed, called, "Thanks so much for coming!"

"Have a good time in Mexico," the judge urged them.

"Drink only bottled water," Lottie warned darkly, "and do be careful!"

"Hell, Lottie, who wants to be careful on a honeymoon?" Knox said in contradiction to his wife and motioned to the photographer to follow them out as well.

The front door closed decisively, and Stacy and Chris were suddenly alone. Slowly Chris drew Stacy into his arms until she was wedged tightly against him. Desire swelled through Stacy's breasts, making her breathing uneven and her nipples tingle. "I'm not going to wait to have a good time in Mexico," Chris drawled, his fiery lips grazing her cheek. "Hell, I'm going to have a ball, starting this minute!" Then he added softly, "With your permission, that is."

How she appreciated his asking! Love almost choked Stacy. "You have my permission," she whispered.

Chris's lips touched Stacy's, and the kiss he pressed there was warmly tender but surprisingly brief. "Upstairs, Mrs. Lorio," he said, giving her a decisive pat on her fanny. "Right now!"

"Chris," Stacy remonstrated, her voice split between a laugh and an indignant splutter.

"Well, you said yes. Or do you want to go for it right here in a dining-room chair?" He laughed, but the press of his aroused body to hers spoke of his serious intent.

"Chris," she cried again.

"Because this is one marriage that is very definitely going to be consummated," he vowed, his hands going eagerly to the soft fullness of Stacy's breasts. "Mmm...that bra you're wearing is going to be the first thing to go!"

She pulled away from him and dashed toward the stairs, knowing—of course—that Chris would follow. She'd just reached the third step when she was hit by a sudden sense of foreboding as she remembered running from Chris in her dream. An involuntary shudder ran through her.

Chris caught her then, swinging her around and holding her so tightly that she gave a small scream. Momentarily Stacy's heart rocked her with its berserk pounding. Then she saw the amorous glow in his eyes, and when his lips lowered to hers, the kiss blotted every thought from her mind but the desirable warmth and strength of him. *How could I have feared him even for a moment?* Stacy thought, thoroughly ashamed of her reaction.

Their arms tightly around each other, they kissed and hugged their way up the stairs. At some point Chris dropped his coat and tie, and at the desirous expression on his face Stacy wanted him so badly her heart pounded anew—this time from excitement.

"My room," Chris said huskily, starting to undo the cloth-covered buttons at the back of Stacy's dress.

All she could think of now was him; all she was aware of was him and wanting to make up to him for her sudden irrational fear. Oh, Lord, she did love him so!

The moment they were inside Chris's room, the door slamming shut behind them, his hands dipped beneath the hem of Stacy's new dress and glided up over her panty-hose-clad legs to slip between her thighs.

Another mixed sound, half gasp and half whimper, escaped Stacy, and she clung to Chris shamelessly. Their lips caught and burned as his hands grew even more reckless and daring. "Do you want me?" he breathed against her lips.

"Yes—I want you, Chris! Now—right now," she replied breathlessly.

He went a little crazy then, but so did Stacy, kissing frenziedly. They just barely managed to kick off their shoes before, in a careless tumble, heedless of their wedding finery, they fell together in a heap on Chris's bed.

Rapidly Chris reached around to Stacy's back and unfastened her bra so he could feel her unfettered breasts through the expensive linen dress. As he touched them, first with his fingertips, then with his lips and tongue dampening the peach linen, Stacy cried out and clutched him even closer.

Rapidly he pushed her skirt to her waist, then struggled to slip off her panty hose. But the natural slickness of Stacy's passion-glazed skin combined with the clinging material made them resist Chris's impatient tugs.

"What the hell?" he muttered in typical male frustration.

"Just a minute and I'll—" Stacy's offer ended as he recklessly shredded her undergarment. As panty separated forever from hose, a thousand runs suddenly zigzagged downward, tickling her legs, and Chris successfully bared the specific area of his objective.

He made a murmured sound of triumph while Stacy gasped yet again, half in horror and half in sheer admiration for his tenacity. Then, all at once, she was the one who could wait not even one second longer.

"Now, right *now*, Chris," she said urgently, tugging at his shoulders.

"Just let me get out of these—"

"Now!" Stacy cried insistently, arching beneath him as need swept through her like rapidly fanned flames. Never in her life had she been more aroused—but then never in her life had she had as her husband a man she loved so utterly and burned for with all the passion of her soul.

"Oh, Stace!" Chris tore open his own clothes and then he was plunging into her as Stacy uttered a wild, ecstatic cry.

It was fast and furious but loving and wonderful, too. Chris kept on kissing her—again and again until his tongue driving deep within her mouth was replicating the driving motions of his body.

Repeatedly he carried her to the very brink, until finally with the shattering fulfillment upon her, Chris's last vestige of control splintered. At Stacy's cry she felt the strongest pulsations of his body and knew his fulfillment was complete, even as she reveled in her own.

For a long, long time they lay still together, gasping for breath as they slowly came back to reality. Then Chris began to chuckle.

"What is it?" Stacy asked, feeling safe and secure as she nestled up against him.

"I'm wondering how much damage we just did—and not only to our good clothes, either. The lady decorator who did over this bedroom for me emphasized that I was never, *ever* to sit on the bedspread, since it must not be crushed."

Stacy laughed aloud, too, feeling happy and replete. "Well, I don't know about your bedspread but these five-dollar panty hose are definitely goners!" She held up one slim leg, its nylon laddered with runs.

Chris bent over and kissed Stacy's knee then caressed her calf lazily. "It was sure worth it," he sighed contentedly.

"You were right, Chris." Stacy smiled. "This is going to be fun!"

It was so much fun that they missed the first two flights to Mexico on the following day, and had to make reservations for a night flight instead.

Finally, in early afternoon, they arose and ate a huge breakfast. Then they showered, dressed and left for the airport. During the drive to New Orleans they laughed and talked, touched and kissed, joked and sang along to the radio.

It was wonderful, Stacy thought. No, it was better than wonderful. It was absolutely, positively heavenly, and she felt overcome by joy.

The trip itself was romantic. There were not a lot of passengers on the last plane and, by 10:00 p.m., more and more of them switched off their overhead lights to doze. Stewardesses moved quietly along the aisle, dispensing pillows and nightcaps, then they, too, retired to their assigned stations.

As the dark quiet slipped intimately around them Chris moved forward, raising the armrest that separated their two seats, and drew Stacy toward him. Gently he began kissing her, and she responded until they were necking like teenagers. And all the while he held her and kissed her Chris whispered that she looked lovely, felt delightful to hold and smelled delicious.

Stacy was a little surprised by his tenderness and pleased at the gestures and the words. She'd never seen this affectionate and gentle side of him before.

Even when Chris finally stopped kissing her, he continued to hold Stacy's hand. Slowly he turned it over, examining her polished oval nails, the knuckles and delicate veins on the back of her hand. His knee pressed companionably against hers and he edged gradually closer until their shoulders were rubbing, too.

Stacy couldn't help but voice her surprise at his loverlike gestures. "I like this," she said softly.

"What, Stace?" Chris whispered.

"You and me...just holding, kissing and touching," she replied, her heart swelling anew with love.

"It is nice, isn't it?" he agreed.

"Oh, yes," Stacy said feelingly. "And I'm very glad I married you yesterday. I'm having such a lovely time!"

"I've rather enjoyed it myself," Chris said.

In the soft darkness Stacy could just barely make out his teasing grin. *"Rather?"* she said pointedly, yielding to the impulse to drop her head on his chest. "Is that all you can say?"

"Oh, I expect I'll enjoy it more when we can go back to bed," he whispered. He raised his arm and put it lightly around Stacy's shoulders. Briefly he squeezed her. "Now go to sleep. You'd better get some rest while you can!"

Stacy couldn't help laughing softly even as she slipped off her shoes and curled up against him. Chris was back in character once again.

Chapter Twelve

On their fourth day in Chiapas, Mexico, Chris returned to their suite at the luxurious Spanish Colonial resort where they were staying to find Stacy enjoying a siesta. For several minutes he simply stared down at her, studying her face, soft and flushed with sleep. Then, predictably, his gaze traveled downward to the lithe graceful body he'd been enjoying morning, noon and night, usually in this very bed—although there had been a passionate interlude on the beach late one night, as well as another in the big marble tub in the bathroom.

She wore a loose cotton sleep shirt, which revealed the full length of her long tanned legs, and Chris decided that she should be cited as an original work of art.

Then, reluctant to disturb Stacy's sleep, he turned away smiling and began to shed the business clothes he'd worn today to meet with several local bankers. Had he ever been quite so happy? Chris wondered, his eyes straying back to Stacy once again. Yes, possibly he'd been equally happy on the day that Robbie was born, when Chris had learned that his son was a healthy, squalling seven-pounder and that Lynn had survived the ordeal of his birth.

But Chris had never imagined, when he'd asked Stacy to marry him, that this event might equal the earlier one. Of course, he'd always had a ferocious, driving desire for Stacy, but he'd always attributed that to pure physical attraction.

Their bodies still fit together with awesome perfection, carrying him to new heights of passion. But as great as sex was with Stacy, Chris relished other things as well. Just being with her, sharing a meal or translating her scuba diving instructor's Spanish to English left him feeling happy and somehow complete. In her company he could drop the various personas that life in Louisiana compelled him to assume. With Stacy he didn't have to be Daddy or attorney at law, the ambitious go-getter and the genteel widower.

He could be Chris and feel accepted and desired in the role.

There was an ease and comfort about Stacy and this new marriage that Chris hadn't figured on. Something almost magical kept happening whenever their eyes met, or they found the same situations funny and started laughing together, and he was beginning to realize how he'd underestimated and undervalued his new wife.

Of course, she was still his hot-blooded equal, not to mention being inventive and creative enough to set his senses sizzling! But they seemed attuned at a level even deeper and more basic than the physical.

Only one thing still bothered him: Taylor. Although Chris hadn't let Stacy know, he was still deeply resentful that he hadn't learned of the boy's existence sooner. Damn it, as Taylor's father, he'd had the right to know! But raking over the past could do no good now and could only hurt his relationship with Stacy.

Chris hung up the one business suit he'd brought and dressed again in minimal clothes, shorts and comfortable Mexican huaraches, thinking he might go sunbathe on their patio overlooking the Gulf of Tehuantepec. Then, because he was thirsty, he stopped at the bar intending to pour himself a soft drink over ice. But a large frosty pitcher of sangria, fruit floating on top, tempted him. He knew Stacy had been enjoying the mildly alcoholic drink.

Just as Chris poured from the pitcher, he felt smooth, slim arms encircle his waist. "Hi," Stacy whispered against his bare back.

Her voice still sounded sleepy, but her hands were definitely wide awake, as they gently and provocatively stroked across his stomach.

"Hi, yourself," Chris said casually, taking a sip from his glass. Then he almost dropped his drink as he felt Stacy press even closer to him. When the hard tips of her naked breasts raked his back tantalizingly, Chris began to grin. Obviously she'd dropped her nightshirt somewhere between the bed and the bar.

He hadn't made love to her yet today, and apparently she was now eager and willing to become the aggressor. Even as he felt his body start to respond and his breath quicken, Chris decided to let Stacy take the initiative.

She stroked, she caressed, she pressed a kiss and then another, adding the tip of her tongue against his bare back. Then in a startling movement her slim hands that still encircled his waist slid boldly beneath the waistband of his shorts.

"My God, Stacy!" Chris gasped aloud with delight.

She laughed softly, her voice seductive, her hands having elicited just the reaction she'd sought.

Chris set down his glass with care, then swung around to face her. But he made himself grip the edge of the bar and let Stacy continue to take the lead.

She was beautiful, he thought, his passion rising, when he saw her wearing nothing but a mischievous smile. Just the sight of her creamy soft skin excited him. Her hands continued to stroke and touch him intimately, then she slowly unzipped Chris's shorts and pushed them down.

He was ready for her immediately, even before he felt her body curve, moving against him suggestively. But when he reached for Stacy—lured as readily as moth to flame—she pulled away with a soft low laugh.

Chris liked the variation enough to play along, even when he knew he was being teased. Suddenly she surprised him again, dropping down to her knees and letting her mouth follow the same daring path taken by her hands. A choked sound tore from Chris—although he managed to whisper that it was wonderful. But already Stacy was easing away again. Briefly, playfully, she tantalized him for a few minutes more, but he could see that she was already deeply aroused herself. She reached for Chris's hand and led him over to the immense bed set on a dais at the other end of the room.

There she pushed him onto his back and crouched over him, ready now for long, leisurely kisses and caresses. Chris responded, letting his mouth play over the ripe rosy nipples just above him until he saw her green eyes darken and smolder.

Stacy surged forward, taking him deeply inside her, moving with a suddenness that left Chris gasping again yet consumed by fiery pleasure. And Stacy was ablaze, too, by the novelty of her dominant role.

Not that Chris could ever be entirely submissive. Even as he felt himself straining to meet her sensuous movements he whispered explicit hungry words and watched as they inflamed her further.

The sweetness of sheer satisfaction rushed over her then, a satisfaction Chris shared vicariously as he heard her soft outcries and felt the convulsive movements of her heated body. He fought to maintain his own control even as he soothed and gentled Stacy. It was time she discovered the full outer reaches of her own sensual nature and so, as the wildness left her eyes and her gasping breaths returned gradually to normal, Chris moved powerfully beneath her and slowly began the sweet rhythmic buildup all over again.

They dined in their room that night since neither wanted to dress up formally and socialize with their fellow guests in the main dining room downstairs. For their private meal Stacy wore a long Mexican dress of bright aqua while Chris wore an embroidered short-sleeved Guayabera shirt over slacks.

"How did your diving lesson go this morning?" Chris asked Stacy as he cut into his steak.

"Okay, I guess," Stacy said a little uneasily as she forked up a bite of her succulent-looking shrimp. For a moment she almost told Chris the truth, that her opinion of scuba diving wasn't as exalted as his. For one thing, simply being out in a boat in the vastness of the ocean made her feel distinctly uneasy.

Also, there was so much to remember during a dive: she had to keep watching her oxygen tank and depth gauge—and she couldn't seem to keep herself from watching for hostile jaws. How she regretted ever letting Taylor talk her into seeing so many of those shark movies, although Chris had said that in this area of Mexican waters barracuda were a greater threat. Some difference! Stacy thought.

Then there was the problem of Julio, her diving instructor. He mangled the few phrases of English he knew, and Stacy, who had never had a flair for tongues, couldn't seem to ask the right questions in Spanish. Today had been an exercise in frustration for both of them, she thought privately, and she almost confided as much to Chris. But he was so eager for her to dive with him and she wanted so much to please him, that she bit her tongue to stop the words that would express her doubts and fears. They were scheduled to dive together off a shelf out in the gulf tomorrow.

"What about you, Chris?" Stacy asked, passing him a dish of fresh mangoes and bananas. "Did you find any land you want to buy?"

"Not yet," he said. "But one of the bankers, Antonio Luna Gonzales, thinks his nephew can show me a likely spread tomorrow or the next day. Señor Luna agrees that growth and expansion down here are inevitable unless, of course, Guatemala explodes into civil war, which could affect any border state . . ." As Stacy ate, she listened to Chris intently, determinedly pushing aside her own particular misgivings about tomorrow.

* * *

From the beginning the dive seemed jinxed. Haze from a slightly disturbed weather system out in the Pacific hovered over the area. Although Chris said it wouldn't affect their dive the haze provided a contrast to the usually crystalline days.

There were also too many people along, in Stacy's opinion. They crowded the small boat moving out from shore. They also besieged Julio and his cousin, Juan, with questions and comments. Apparently quite a number of hotel guests had felt as Chris did, that this dive along an ocean shelf was not to be missed.

Stacy sat huddled in one corner of the boat, trying not to think about either seasickness or her own innate fears. Chris, fiddling with a new underwater camera that he planned to use for the first time, seemed oddly oblivious to her silence. Of course, he'd been diving for years.

Then suddenly they were there—although "there" to Stacy just looked like more blue hazy ocean—and she and Chris, decked out in wet suits and air tanks, were being hustled along. Stacy set her face mask and put her air tube in her mouth as she'd practiced. Then they tumbled out of the boat and into the water...and suddenly Stacy felt afraid, deeply afraid.

"Just follow me, Stacy," had been Chris's last command to her, and now she chided herself for cowardice. She also tried to remember the dozen or more things that Julio had attempted, in his fractured English, to teach her.

As they went lower and lower still, stopping at various depths to acclimate themselves, a whole new world opened to Stacy until, for a few moments, she was too entranced to feel afraid. The light down here was eerie, different from any she'd ever seen, and the multitude of coral and fish fascinated her. Here were multistriped and banded fish—fish she'd never seen in the shallower waters closer to shore where she'd made her practice dives. Here, too, were coral in intricate designs and glorious colors. Then a sea horse rode past, and Stacy paused to admire him, delighted at such a close-up view.

She hurried to catch up with Chris, who seemed to be drifting down rather deep, according to the pressure Stacy felt on her ears. As she followed, kicking automatically, she began to feel water pressure being exerted along her body as well. Didn't Chris feel it at all? she wondered as he continued to dive.

Worriedly she looked at her depth gauge. They were now at eighty feet; the maximum dive was one hundred thirty-five feet, she'd been told, although certain people who were particularly sensitive to pressure could get into trouble at a hundred and become disoriented.

At just that moment Chris turned to look at Stacy and made a gesture indicating that he was going to snap a few photographs.

Obviously they weren't as deep as she thought or Chris would feel the water pressure, too, Stacy assured herself. So she drifted along in the general direction Chris had taken, even though she realized it was carrying her deeper. *Ninety-five feet!* As she read her depth Stacy froze, and when she looked around next she couldn't see Chris at all.

Was he gone? Oh, my God, he *was* gone! Anxiety gripped her heart in a vise while the water pressure squeezed her eardrums tight.

Frantically she sought him, following a flash of black that she'd thought was a churning male leg but that turned out to be a strand of seaweed instead. Bewildered, Stacy stopped, staring slowly all around.

She was quite alone and breathing too fast from nervousness. How much oxygen was she using? Her eyes flew to the air gauge as she wondered if she should start up toward the surface. Then, as her anxiety deepened, Stacy couldn't remember how fast she should go up.

Anxiety escalated into fear; fear swelled to terror and terror brought Stacy to near hysteria. Where was Chris? Why had he left her? For that matter, why had it been so important to him that she learn to dive and accompany him to the bottom of the world?

All at once, her terror swelling to monstrous proportions, Stacy knew. *He doesn't want you, he wants Taylor!* The familiar words rang again in her mind.

Oh, God! Chris hadn't brought her down to this relatively remote area of Mexico just for a lavish honeymoon. And he hadn't brought her out here into the Gulf of Tehuantepec for merely a pleasant dive. And he hadn't been spending hours in bed with her ever since they'd married just to get their union off to a rousing good start.

No, Chris Lorio had brought her here to use her until he'd had his fill of her and then to get rid of her. *Well, what better way to die?* Yes—and what better way to kill than with such a seemingly believable "accident"?

Even as Stacy kept turning, twisting, looking again and again in a blindly desperate search for Chris, even as a part of her mind disbelieved the cruel scenario she'd just envisioned, an older and cynical self seriously considered that it was true.

Chris had always been the dark, dangerous one of whom all of Langlois's girls had been in awe. A mysterious and devious man whom only Lynn Ashley could control—and even her gentle restraint had slipped at times. In any event Lynn was no longer here to save Chris from himself or to spare others his wrath.

Long ago Stacy had sensed that Chris would run roughshod over anyone who got in his way, whoever stood between him and what he wanted—and he'd always wanted it *all*. Of course he would want sole custody and complete control of Taylor, the child in whom he saw himself reborn.

It all seemed very logical now when Stacy found herself deserted in a maze of water she'd set to churning in her frantic search, water in which she was presently lost, abandoned and alone. Her heart was beating with a series of slow, heavy, sickening beats and she was definitely beginning to feel strange and disoriented.

I've got to get out of here! Stacy thought desperately. *I've got to get back to the boat—quickly! Chris might come back and cut my air hose! But I mustn't go up too quickly, either, or I'll get the bends. Oh, God!*

Despite her various lessons and the techniques that Julio had taught her during the past few days, Stacy's mind was now a complete blank.

Even worse, as she started trying to make her way slowly back to the surface, she wasn't even sure that *up* was where she thought it was, she'd twisted and turned so in looking for Chris. Now she was desperately unsure and dizzy, too... growing dizzier by the moment.

Two names came to momentarily steady her. *Got to get back to Taylor and Robbie!*

Then all at once even the boys didn't matter. In fact, as her dizziness deepened, Stacy could no longer remember why she'd gotten so agitated, because now she was seeing heavenly visions and hearing a beguiling sirens' song. "Stacy!" the sirens sang, and confused, she began to swim toward the sound. "Stacy! Sta-cee!"

"Stacy! Stacy!"

"I think she's coming back to herself now, Mr. Lorio."

Stacy blinked, coughed, spit out some water. She was back in the rocking boat. Suddenly the recent events below the surface crashed through Stacy's skull like a flash of lightning shattering a tree. Desperately she flailed out at the strong hands that held her. In fear and horror she shrank back from the ashen-faced man who was her husband.

"Don't touch me, Chris! Don't ever touch me again!" she screamed.

"Stacy—"

"You tried to kill me! You brought me out here because you wanted me to drown! Because you don't want me— you've never wanted *me*! It's Taylor, isn't it? He's what you want—what you want badly enough to kill me for!"

Before she'd even finished screaming at him, Stacy's hands became fists that beat against him futilely.

Other hands finally restrained her, not Chris's. He never spoke at all. He just kept staring at Stacy in that frozen, sick-looking, glassy-eyed way, as if she'd gone mad before his very eyes.

Hysteria, the hotel doctor said, and it was practically the only word he spoke that Stacy could understand. The rest of them were delivered in machine-gun Spanish to Chris.

She lay exhaustedly in bed, a sedative the doctor had given her still stinging her arm.

"Nitrogen narcosis, the so-called 'rapture of the deep'?" she heard Chris ask wearily. "Yes, I suppose that's what happened to Stacy. We went too deep. I thought she was right behind me. I guess I thought she was a better diver than she is, too. She's always been a very strong swimmer. She was even a swimming instructor."

"She'll be all over it by tomorrow," someone else in the room said learnedly.

"Yes—but will I?" Chris asked in anguish.

"Now, honey—" the other person was an English-speaking woman with a Texas twang "—you can't hold something like this against her. She was just plumb out of her head. Believe me, she'll be plenty grateful when she understands how you found her going down instead of up and brought her back to the surface."

"Sure," Chris agreed, but his voice still held that bitterly ironic note. "Sure she will. That's why she fought me every inch of the way."

"Look, honey, you go get a stiff drink. Shoot, belt two or three! I'm a nurse—I'll be glad to stay here with her."

None of it really mattered to Stacy anymore. Her eyelids were too heavy to hold open, so she let them drop and she slept, deeply and dreamlessly, until she once again saw heavenly visions and heard sirens sing her name.

Two things Chris had always hated were drinking and fishing. Not that he'd ever tried combining the two before. Well, it was about what he'd expected. Soaking your brain in hundred-proof Mexican joy juice didn't do a thing to make fishing more pleasurable.

But he held the fishing pole anyway, although he suspected the bait on the hook was gone by now. At least fishing gave him an acceptable excuse for sitting alone at the end of a pier getting quietly drunk.

At last the tequila was sliding down his throat more easily. The taste was so awful he kept cutting it with a bite of fresh lime and a lick off the salt encrusted on the back of his hand. Wasn't this the way really macho Mexican men drowned their heartaches?

Hell, he couldn't even remember... which must mean the tequila was doing its work.

But he still couldn't blot out that look of blind horror in Stacy's eyes when she'd recognized him. He remembered her instinctive recoil from him and her accusing words that had pretty effectively finished their marriage before it had truly begun.

Oh, he knew all the *acceptable* answers to explain her behavior, of course.

He knew that the idea behind Stacy's terror had come straight from Janice's hateful letter and poor Barney's phone calls to Stacy.

But Janice had only planted the words. Stacy's own inflamed imagination had nourished and watered them until finally, in extremity, their ugly blooms sprouted.

Of course, Stacy had been scared witless and wasn't responsible. He knew that—logically.

But if there were hidden depths in Stacy, there were even darker depths not so well hidden in him, Chris had discovered. The legacy of being the notorious town bastard still lingered, and when his new wife began screaming accusations at him and all the other occupants of the boat had looked at him so askance, fear and shame had flooded Chris, followed as always by his blistering anger.

He couldn't blame Stacy... not really. After everything that had happened in their shared past—especially after Taylor—she was probably right to distrust him so deeply.

But, God, how it hurt! If he'd been kicked in the chest by an elephant, Chris didn't think it could hurt any worse. To distrust him so much she must never have forgiven him. And if there wasn't any trust, how could the two of them possibly hold a marriage together, even long enough to raise their boys?

He'd bought Stacy, Chris convinced himself. It was time he quit trying to color up reality and accept that he'd gotten her to marry him because he'd offered her money, security and the chance to do what she'd like to do for a change. Plus she'd gotten a father for the headstrong Taylor and some damned good sex in the bargain.

Suddenly Chris's mouth went dry. Had she been faking the lovemaking with him? he wondered bleakly. Had all those abandoned hours yesterday been a sham?

Why not? She'd certainly faked a growing affection for him, cuddling up any time Chris had reached for her, listening so attentively whenever he chose to discuss something, he remembered with a new wave of pain.

As the memory of her bliss-filled face swam before his eyes Chris took another deep pull on the tequila bottle.

Forget about emotions, he told himself harshly. Shelve all the stupid feelings! He'd bought Stacy and, thank God, he could *sell* her.

At least he'd gotten her signature on that prenuptial agreement, which would limit the financial damage. Although the settlement would wing him, Chris intended to offer Stacy an even larger amount in exchange for sole custody of Taylor.

Stacy was sensible. Surely she'd recognize the futility of going on when their marriage was an utter sham. Surely he could work something out with her, Chris thought. But when he considered parting her from Taylor he wasn't so sure.

Leaning down to toss away the empty tequila bottle, Chris thought suddenly of his first wife.

It's no good, Lynn, he said bleakly. *Oh, I know that you set all this up. I guess I saw your fine, sweet hand in this from the very beginning. You wanted Stacy, only Stacy, to handle your clothes, sleep in your house, raise your son and marry your husband. I know you meant well—that you wanted only the best for all the people you loved most—but*

*it just won't wash. . . . There was already too much behind
Stacy and me to forgive and forget.*

*But . . . oh, damn, Lynn, it was such a wonderful, gener-
ous, inspired idea! How I wish it had worked!*

Stacy had apologized in every way she could possibly
think of, but it hadn't helped. All she had to do was glance
at Chris's morose yet icy face to know he wasn't even hearing her sincere, deeply felt and completely abject words.

In many ways he was still the old Chris Lorio, cursed on
the one hand with too much arrogant pride and con-
demned on the other by the insecurities of a once-nameless
and deprived child.

So he simply didn't believe her. Stacy knew she could talk
until she was blue in the face—and still Chris wouldn't believe her.

Why are you punishing us both like this? Stacy wanted to
cry out when she heard Chris making the plane reservations that cut short their honeymoon.

"Do you think I would have married you if I'd really,
sincerely been afraid of you, Chris?" she had already said
to him.

Of course, in the bright light of day with a clear head and
terra firma beneath her feet, it all seemed incredible and
unbelievable. Chris a killer? How could she have ever entertained such a notion, even in dreams or delirium? Only
bad luck and excruciatingly bad timing—Stacy winced when
she recalled the boat full of staring, wide-eyed people—had
confused the fantasy with reality.

She'd embarrassed Chris, and with him presently stony-
faced and hiding his bloodshot eyes behind dark glasses
Stacy didn't dare say too much or pry too deeply.

"Do you have a migraine?" she did ask solicitously at one
point.

"No. I forestalled that by getting drunk," Chris replied
curtly.

"Drunk? *You?*" Stacy's voice was incredulous.

"So now I have a hangover instead. Any more questions?" Chris snapped.

Stacy shut up. His combination of painful eyes, scant appetite and severe depression reminded her of a couple of nights far back in her past when she'd had too much to drink and had lived to regret it.

By the time the car came around, the maid had packed all their clothes and Chris had settled their bill. As they sped over mountain roads, headed toward the airport at Tuxtla Gutierrez, Stacy laid her hand gently on Chris's arm.

"Chris, please—" she started.

"Stacy, not *now*!" he said so fiercely that she was startled into complete silence.

She turned to look blindly out of her window and wonder, if not now, when?

Chapter Thirteen

She might not do another thing right for the rest of her life, but Stacy vowed she would finish sorting through everything in the attic as Lynn had wanted her to do. Before she left Langlois, Louisiana, for the very last time she was going to finish what she'd started and no one, not even Chris, could stop her.

With that determination burning fiercely inside her Stacy had been working away steadily for the past three days. She was finally nearing the bottom of the next-to-last barrel. Already the Goodwill truck had come and gone on several occasions, and a local antique dealer had been here earlier today, viewing furniture brought down from the attic, "Hmm..." the man had said noncommittally, scribbling descriptions of a number of items on a small pad of paper. Finally he'd turned to Stacy and told her that he must confer with his partner, then he would get back to her with an estimate on the lot.

So she was practically finished. Chris would certainly be glad for that, Stacy thought darkly. Then she'd have no further reason to hang around.

Stacy had not seen her husband since they'd arrived home from Mexico, almost a week ago. After that ghostly quiet plane trip, when Chris had appeared to be reading—at least he'd turned magazine pages at regular intervals—they'd endured a long silent drive from the New Orleans airport. Even before they'd reached the house, Stacy had been biting her lip to stem the threatening tears. She couldn't help but contrast their dismal return with the excitement, affection and passion of their departure so short a time before.

No sooner had Chris carried Stacy's bags back into Lynn's old bedroom than he turned to her and announced wearily that their marriage was over.

"Because I was a victim of nitrogen narcosis?" Stacy cried. "Because I got disoriented and confused? Because I accused you of ridiculous, fantastic things when I was in such a mentally muddled state? My God, Chris, serial murderers have been found innocent for being more competent than that!"

"I know," Chris at least had the grace to admit. "But this is a marriage, not a criminal trial, although I wouldn't have known it by all the things you threw at me yesterday. Wait!" Hastily he'd held up a hand as if seeing even more hot, furious words ready to erupt from her lips.

"Stacy, the real problem is that we simply don't trust each other," Chris went on. "I once let you down—badly, I know. You had to marry a man you didn't love and go through a miserable pregnancy because of it. And I don't think you've ever forgiven me for all of that, not deep down inside. I certainly don't believe you've ever trusted me since then."

She turned away to gaze out the window. "Oh, Chris..."

"Well, have you?" he persisted.

"I don't know," Stacy admitted truthfully.

"I seem to be struggling with much the same problems," Chris continued remorselessly. "I hated you for years because I thought you ran out on me. Did you ever know about that?''

"Lynn's letter implied as much," Stacy replied, her hands tightening on the lace curtains.

"I think I'd almost forgiven you for that—almost—and then I found out about Taylor. Stacy, I've lost twelve years with him. Twelve of the most formative years of his life. They're years I'll never get back, no matter how many questions I ask either you or him. And there's a part of me that hasn't forgiven you for it and maybe never will. I should have known my son existed! As a result I don't trust you, either."

Tongs of iron seemed to dig into the muscles on either side of Stacy's throat, making it hard for her to speak. "I . . . see," she managed.

"This marriage is my fault, and I'll take the blame for it," Chris continued, speaking more rapidly. "I leaped for the first easy, convenient, simple solution—'we'll get married and be a family.' But of course it isn't working. I should have known it wouldn't. Anyone who grew up in a shack with Bonnie Lorio should have known to beware the quick and easy solution."

Stacy's grip on the curtains tightened. She wanted to curse and cry. She wanted to reach for the nearest vase and throw it straight at Chris's arrogant black head. She wanted to stun him, surprise him, shut him up—and then, surely, she would want just as desperately to seduce him!

But a tumble in bed was just another quick, easy solution. He was right—this marriage wouldn't work. Not without forgiveness. Not without mutual trust.

So Stacy swallowed hard over the painful lump lodged in her throat. "What do we do now?" she asked of Chris instead.

"Obviously we get the marriage annulled. But, first, let's take a few days to cool off and think things through," he suggested. "I'm going to go down to the camp and stay with the boys. There's no reason for their vacation to be messed up. You stay here, Stacy. Figure out what you want to do and where you want to go."

She swung around, knowing the light of battle was blazing in her eyes. "Just get one thing straight from the beginning, Chris. Taylor stays with me!" she snapped.

She watched an answering battle glint flare in the depths of Chris's dark eyes but, mercifully, he decided to forestall that inevitable fight. "I'll send Miriam back from the camp to cook and keep house for you," he said to Stacy instead.

"That's not necessary," she replied, her voice as world-weary as Chris's had sounded earlier. "I've been taking care of myself and Taylor for quite a long time."

"I know. But I don't want you staying in this house all by yourself. Anyway, Miriam will be glad to come back. She's not that fond of the wilderness or little boys."

So that's the way it had ended. Now Stacy was aware of the baffled looks that Miriam kept casting in her direction, then trying to conceal. The housekeeper was too polite to ask, but clearly she'd never heard of a newly married couple being parted so soon after the ceremony. Certainly she knew that it boded no good.

That the new marriage was clearly on the rocks was made even more obvious by the fact that Chris drove the considerable distance into town each morning and went to his office to work for several hours. Back during their happy days in Mexico, Chris had told Stacy of firing his long-time secretary and why. Now Stacy heard he was using temporary secretarial help supplied by Langlois's one and only employment agency.

As she dipped again into the barrel from the attic, Stacy sighed aloud. She was reduced to listening to gossip—this particular bit courtesy of Betty Thackery—just to glean information about her own husband. And when Taylor had phoned Stacy the night before to tell her they were having "a neat time," Stacy had heard herself asking, "How is Chris?"

She'd wanted to bite her tongue off for that one! But was she supposed not to care? Was she supposed to turn off all the love she'd felt for Chris—a love that had spanned so many, many years—and become indifferent? How she wished she could! And how Stacy wished that the tight band around her chest would ebb and the constant ache in the pit of her stomach would dissolve. All she really wanted to do was curl up in bed and cry until the iron hands that kept clutching her throat finally let go.

But today only young girls in the throes of their first heartache could pause long enough for lengthy tears. Grown women had to keep going because, no matter how bad today was, the sun would still come up again in the morning and there'd be another day to cope with.

She dipped again into the barrel, then felt her fingers glide over something crisp and scratchy. What the—? Stacy thought. Surprised, she pulled out a pale pink envelope, and when she glanced down at it she felt her heart give an even more surprised lurch and thud.

Her own name was on the envelope, and the faded but familiar handwriting was Lynn's.

For a moment Stacy simply sat frozen. Then reluctantly, as if fearing what the contents of the envelope might divulge, she opened it and unfolded the several pages within.

This handwriting looked fresher since the sealed envelope had obviously been airtight, but a glance at the date told Stacy the letter was almost two years old.

"Dear Cousin Stacy," the salutation began rather formally.

Carrying it carefully, even reverently, Stacy walked over to the armchair near the bed where the light was better. She sat down, spread the letter out on her knees and smoothed her suddenly damp palms down the sides of her dusty jeans. A lump rose in her throat as she picked up the pages again and began to read.

If you've found this letter then you're almost through sorting out all the junk in the attic. I intend to stash it in one of the far back barrels. And, if you do get this far along, then it will mean you've been in Langlois for a month at least. Has it been an eventful time? I do hope so!

You see, Stacy, I don't really give a hang *who* sorts through all my stuff. I don't care what happens to it, either. Toss it, burn it or whatever. Things don't matter, just people. Chris and Robbie matter. You and your wonderful Taylor matter, too. Do you know I've never even glimpsed Taylor because you always "forgot" to send me a photograph.

Well, I intend to arrange for you to come back to Langlois in the hope—indeed with the heartfelt prayer—that you and Chris will forgive each other for whatever horrible things you each think the other has done. I hope you'll get back together again. I even frankly hope you'll marry and combine families. You see, the only worry I have about departing this life is, who will raise Robbie? He's so young. It's going to be hard for him. So I want that woman to be you. I think I know what kind of stepmother you'd be.

I also know what kind of father Chris could be for Taylor. He's wonderful with Robbie. He actually likes and enjoys children, and I guess we both know that not every man does.

You'd be very lucky to have Chris as a husband, too. I know he has his quirks and a couple of huge glaring faults as well, but he really domesticated quite easily. He's *very* loyal to his home and family. Just remember that he'll always try to rule the roost, and he always thinks *he* knows what's best, so be warned and prepared to deal quite firmly with him. He really does have a soft and gentle side, which, I must admit, I have been altogether sneaky in helping him to develop. He's especially susceptible to women's tears—just don't overdo them. Remember how intelligent he is—he's quick to see through various female wiles.

Well, Stacy, all my speculation may be totally academic. By the time you read this, if you ever do, you may be happily remarried and Chris may have already run off with a buxom, blond grass widow! But somehow I don't think so. Because deep in my heart I think you and Chris were always meant for each other.

You see, I could never quite believe that bit about a "summer fling." Oh, Chris may have done some tomcatting in his youth, but he never got romantically involved with a woman until you. And you're just not the shallow type to have had a casual affair and then forgotten all about it. I guess I always knew that, about you and Chris both, but it took a number of years for me to finally face it.

My goodness, what an awful lot of positively dreadful feelings I had when I found out that you and Chris had fallen for each other. Mostly, I guess, I just felt betrayed. *My* long-time boyfriend (or so I considered Chris) and the cousin who had been my best friend. How *could* you?! I guess the only reason I didn't scream the roof down, railing at both of you, is that I was always told to avoid heavy emotional scenes lest a good screaming fit be the last thing I ever do. Since nobody really wants to check out that way, I tried to be gracious and good about the whole fling-thing-that-wasn't. I decided to consider it a major test of character—and you know what? After a while, it actually stopped being a test and started feeling real all over again. Until today, when I can say quite sincerely that I love Chris and I love you. Why, it's like those bad weeks and months thirteen years ago happened to someone else.

The bad times don't last. That's another thing I've learned.

Just one last thing, Stacy. It's very important, I think. Chris really did love you once. When we were in Europe together I knew someone was on his mind because he was just going through the motions with me. Then, as soon as we were home from Europe, I found all my friends still buzzing about the two of you, and of course, your sudden marriage to Gary had provided another surprise.

I went to see Chris at that dreadful boarding house where he lived to ask questions about the two of you. I guess I was in shock. Certainly Chris was. In fact, he was lying in bed, totally wiped out by his first migraine headache. I'd never known him to be sick before. And

something else, Stacy. Another first. Even as Chris be-
gàn raging and cursing you he suddenly started crying.
Then, of course, he just swore more violently than ever,
but I'd never known Chris Lorio to cry before and I've
seen him beaten up and I've heard him humiliated. But
it was like losing you had cut the very heart out of him.

Well, of course I probably should have told him to
go find you then and there, except as I've said, I was in
shock myself. And you were married to Gary. In fact,
you said you *wanted* to be married.

What a relief for me! Oh, yes, I wanted you safely
married, hugely pregnant and far, far away! I tried not
to think about Taylor or wonder whose child he might
be. Forgive me for that. We were all young then, and
young people are selfish. Of course, what I'd prayed
for finally happened and Chris *did* turn back to me.
Overall, I really think we've had a good marriage and
that he's been happy, too. And isn't Robbie a real
wonder! Somehow, Stacy, I just know you'll love
Robbie.

That's all, I guess. Except that I hope my match-
making has done some good. I hope you won't let Chris
get away from you again. Remember, sometimes
you've just got to come at him swinging and slugging
until he catches on.

It's late now and I'm tired. Actually it's later for me
than anyone knows. Oh, Chris and the doctors keep
pumping me up with talk of heart-lung transplants, but
I know I'm not strong enough to survive surgery. It's
taken me...let's see...five days just to write this letter.

But don't feel sorry for me, Stacy. Don't grieve and
don't let Chris and Robbie grieve, either, at least not
any more than they have to. I've had such a wonderful, marvelous life! Why, I can't remember ever being
unhappy except for that one brief time—and even that
didn't last long at all. I guess if there's one more thing
I've learned it's that we all do have such a wonderfully
huge capacity to forgive and forget, to love and be

happy. Please do those very things for me. Love, Lynn.

Several minutes passed before Stacy became aware of tears rolling silently down her cheeks and a trembling of her hands. Then she began to shake all over, both from excitement and from hope.

Carefully she folded Lynn's letter back into its envelope, then she tucked it away in the middle drawer of the bedside table. Suddenly sheer jubilation sent her dashing out the door and down the hall, calling for Miriam.

When the housekeeper appeared below, obviously startled at being summoned with a gleeful shout, Stacy leaned over the bannister. "Miriam, can you draw me a map to Knox's fishing camp?" she asked excitedly. "I think it's high time I went to join my family!"

He'd caught another damn fish. Morosely Chris reached up to unhook the thrashing, squirming bass and wondered grimly how Preston would manage to cook tonight's catch. So far he'd grilled fish, smoked them, barbecued them, marinaded and basted them until Chris felt ready to sprout fins. God, how he hated fish! But not the three boys. To Robbie, Taylor and Ted nothing was quite as satisfying as devouring fish they'd personally caught. Obviously it satisfied some young cannibalistic leaning.

Resignedly Chris dropped the bass into the trap that hung over the edge of the pier. It was already full of other, squirming fish that he'd captured earlier. Briefly Chris toyed with the idea of throwing them all back.

Well, it was too late now, he thought, hearing footsteps coming down the pier behind him. "How's the swimming?" he called over his shoulder to whatever boy it was.

"I don't know. I haven't been swimming yet. Frankly, from the looks of this black water I don't want to."

The soft feminine voice—Stacy's voice—absolutely electrified him. In spite of all his gloomy warnings to himself and his dreary, realistic predictions, Chris felt his heart soar.

But as he swung around stiffly to confront her, he kept his facial features similarly stiff. He knew he must keep his guard up around her and be wary or—or— He couldn't let himself finish the thought.

"How the hell did you get here?" he said instead.

Her chin shot up and jutted out. Fire flashed in her eyes, making them grass-green and furious. Granted, it wasn't the most tactful of openings, but Chris had been so thoroughly caught off balance by her he'd wanted to return the favor. Now he felt himself starting to get genuinely angry—just because of what Stace did to him still.

She looked beautiful, so very beautiful to his longing eyes, even though she was just wearing stone-washed jeans, sandals and a casual forest-green shirt. Abruptly Chris felt his emotions going haywire. Felt hunger, passion and tenderness swelling up inside of him at the sight of her fresh, clear face. Could almost feel the softness of her mobile mouth and sweetly curved body. Then, embarrassingly, he felt the swelling of instinctive male reaction to such emotions—and that made him angrier than ever.

"How the hell I got here was by following a map!" Stacy snapped. "It may surprise you to know that Miriam can draw and *I* can read."

"Okay, so you're here. Now what the hell do you want, Stacy?" he snapped right back.

She was so furious at that crack that Chris braced for real trouble. Maybe she'd hired her own lawyer and was going to sue the shirt off his back. Maybe she was prepared to fight him all the way to the Supreme Court for custody of Taylor—and Robbie as well. Or she could be planning to pull out a gun from the waistband of her jeans and shoot him straight through the heart—

Come to think of it, he really hoped that last possibility came true. Let her shoot him; wouldn't he be better off dead?

That's just how miserable he'd been without her.

Her huge green eyes were filling with tears that just made them blaze all the more. Oh, God, if she started to cry he knew he was going to come apart and make a mad grab for her.

"What the hell I want is my *family*," she said in a fierce but tear-choked voice. "I want Taylor... and Robbie... and you! I'm damned if I know *why* I want you, Chris, but I do. I love you. I've always loved you. That's why I had to have your baby, even when Gary begged me to get an abortion or put it up for adoption. I couldn't do either. I couldn't even consider either. And now there are three of you guys to love. So you can just forget about an annulment or a divorce or even a separation because I won't hear of it, not anymore. And don't think you can buy me off, either, because I don't have a price. And don't think you can run away from me because I'll track you down—I'll find you wherever you go even if it takes the F.B.I., Interpol and the Canadian Northwest Mounties. And anytime I catch up with you I am going to damned well be your *wife*! I'm going to eat with you and sleep with you and make love with you because we can make it, you and me! If Lynn could manage to forgive us and love us again—and she did—we can damn well learn to forgive and love each other. Now that's the way it's going to be, and the sooner you get it through your thick, stubborn head the better. You are *not* getting rid of me, and you never, ever will, Chris Lorio!"

Stacy was screaming by the time she finished. Screaming and punching Chris in the chest with one slender index finger. And he just kept standing there, staring at her, dumbfounded by her words and the evidence of his own ears. Did she really say it? Did she really *mean* it? Did she—?

Before he could recover, she had spun on her heel and gone charging up the pier. Then she swung back around. "Where are the boys?" she demanded, and Chris jerked an unsteady thumb toward a path that led off to the right.

"I'll go tell them to get cleaned up for supper. You get cleaned up, too. It's hamburgers and french fries in thirty minutes—I figured you'd be plenty tired of fish by now. Incidentally, I sent Preston home. I'll take care of things now because I am not only your wife but I'm going to be the *woman* in this family and the *mother*, and if you don't like it, Chris, you can just soak your great big head right here and right now. I guess this lake's large enough to hold it!''

Dashing the angry tears from her eyes she stormed off in the direction Chris had indicated, and if he hadn't been stunned into immobility he would have followed that brave, defiant, oh-so-desirable woman. Followed her, hugged her, held her and probably whispered all sorts of mad, extravagant things to her. She'd actually loved him all along! And now she'd declared her intention never to leave him. Suddenly, abruptly, Chris Lorio simply had to sit down. That's how weak his legs felt.

Weak with relief!

Talk about feeling unwelcome and unwanted! A short distance down the path Stacy stopped to dry her wet eyes and to consider the very real and likely possibility that Lynn had been wrong. She'd had good intentions, of course, but Lynn probably hadn't realized how Stacy and Chris could push each other's buttons.

Now Stacy glanced around as she struggled to compose herself. This camp was a rustic place; the path where she stood looked like it had been hacked through deep green jungle. Cypress trees jutted up out of the lake, and the overall wildness of this wilderness made her feel uneasy.

A babble of boys' voices drifted over to her. At least there were two boys babbling—she recognized Taylor's and Ted's voices. Robbie's was noticeably absent.

Suddenly Stacy straightened up, the hairs at the back of her neck prickling warningly. Taylor was not the sort of child who babbled. He was too much like Chris for that.

Stacy's inner alarm rang even louder when she heard panic swelling the two young voices. *Something's happened!* Stacy realized, even as she began to run toward the boys.

Then Taylor's voice rose over Ted's—a panicky, terrified voice, but one that still reflected clear logical thinking. "Get Chris!" he yelled, barking out the order. Then came the most ominous words of all. "I'll go down for Robbie. You get Chris. Hell, Ted, don't just stand there with your damn thumb in your mouth. *Run!*''

Taylor's language is really getting out of hand. Stacy's numb mind seized irrelevantly on the thought even as she was running as fast as she could. Robbie! Oh, what had happened to Robbie?

In her blind haste Stacy almost collided with Ted Thackery, who came sprinting around a bend in the path, his face chalk-white, his eyes wide with terror.

''Run!'' Stacy urged Ted, too, not wasting any time asking stupid questions.

She dashed along the path, vines snagging her and stumbling over stones without feeling any pain. Stacy rounded one bend in the path and then another.

The path ended at a circular pool of dark, murky, churning water. Just as she reached the edge, where she frantically kicked off her sandals, Taylor's head broke the surface and he came up gasping for breath.

''Mom! Down here—quick! I can't find him!'' As Taylor saw his mother his voice mingled relief and terror. Then he called out a last warning to her. ''Don't dive! It's too shallow! That's what Robbie did. He must have hit a stump.''

''Oh, my God,'' Stacy muttered, wading rapidly into the inky-looking water as terrible thoughts of broken necks, severed spines and paralyzed limbs rushed over her. Of course, if they couldn't find Robbie and get him to land quickly, within the next few minutes, he would suffer irreversible brain damage from lack of oxygen.

''Please,'' she prayed as she did a shallow surface dive and then headed straight down.

The pool was thick with water weeds, and its darkness made it difficult for Stacy to see. Frantically she ran her hands along the grassy bottom groping desperately for the small figure of an eight-year-old boy.

She searched and searched, until her lungs seemed to burst. Desperately Stacy went up for air and broke the surface, gasping, just in time to see Taylor's feet and heels descending again in another frantic search as he headed back

down. Stacy gulped air and dived again herself, moving off
a bit to the right this time.

They had to find Robbie—and he had to be all right. He
just had to be. He was all that was left of Lynn, and Stacy
loved him for that, as well as for the part of him that was
Chris. But mostly she loved Robbie for his own bright,
sweet, individual self.

"Please," her mind begged. "Oh, please!" And then as
her frantic groping hands kept finding only emptiness again
and again, a final desperate prayer burned through her
brain: "Oh, Lynn, *help me!*"

At almost that exact moment Stacy felt him.

Her heart gave a great leap of joy as her eager fingers
closed over the firm child flesh. He was here—she had found
him! But was he still alive? Could he possibly recover?

There were still too many terrifying possibilities running
rampant in her head for her joy to be anything but brief.

Even as Stacy wrapped her arms around Robbie and
kicked ferociously, propelling them to the surface as rapidly as possible, she was terrified of what she might find
when she dragged Robbie to shore and examined him.

Just as she came up carrying the child, Stacy felt the water rocked with an enormous splash. She didn't even have to
wonder what it might be. Automatically she knew it was
Chris coming in desperate search for his son.

He was already below the water as Stacy hit the surface
towing Robbie. The moment their faces cleared, she felt
frantically for the child's head, seeking to right his mouth
and nose on the chance that he might breathe on his own.

But he didn't.

"You've got him, Mom!" Taylor was suddenly by her
side.

"Help me get him to shore—quick," Stacy gasped, barely
coherent in her breathlessness.

Taylor was quick. Of course, he'd always been a fast-on-
the-uptake kid. With his help Robbie was towed rapidly toward shore.

As Chris came up, too, splashing not far from them
Taylor began shouting, "We've got him! We've got him!'

and Chris started swimming toward them with swift, powerful strokes. Stacy caught just a glimpse of his face, its color a ghastly gray, and she knew even as her feet touched bottom that the second problem she'd have to confront was Chris.

Robbie came first. The moment they stretched him out on the shore Stacy opened his mouth to check for obstructions to the airway. Finding none, she turned to Taylor. "Start artificial respiration," she directed. Since Taylor had recently completed a course in lifesaving, Stacy knew his technique would be fresher and consequently more effective than her own rusty one. As Chris came surging up out of the water, Stacy ran over to restrain him.

"No, Chris—no!" she screamed, reaching up to seize his shoulders. "Taylor knows just *exactly* what to do—don't interfere!"

Wordlessly Chris struggled with Stacy for a moment in his desperation to get to his son, then her words seemed to penetrate. Clutching her hand with a death grip, Chris rushed over to where Robbie lay sprawled, limp and immobile.

Taylor had already managed to bring up water from Robbie's lungs. Now, as the older boy breathed rhythmically for his half-brother, Stacy felt Chris's grip on her tighten even more with his growing desperation.

"C'mon, Robbie, breathe...*breathe!*" he said in an anguished whisper as more anxious seconds ticked by.

A small whimper at Stacy's side caused her to turn distractedly in that direction. Ted Thackery stood there, his small, homely face streaked with tears while his chest heaved with silent sobs.

"Ted, you did really well," Stacy whispered. She didn't know where she found the strength to restrain Chris, to comfort Ted and to egg on Taylor when she was suffering so herself. That precious child, lying so still on the smooth stretch of sand, could not have been any dearer to Stacy if she had borne him herself. *Robbie,* she thought in anguished yearning of her soul.

Suddenly Taylor rocked back on his heels. "He's breathing, Mom. He's breathing!"

Now Stacy threw off Chris's clutch and dropped to Robbie's side. Yes, he was breathing again, his small ribs moving in and out, but he still lay unconscious.

"No, Chris, no!" she heard Taylor crying. "Let Mom check him over first."

But then Chris was beside her anyway, and the expression in his black eyes—such a tangled expression of renewed hope and desperate, dreadful fear—tore at her heart.

"Chris, I think Robbie has a head injury." Somehow Stacy managed to keep her voice level and devoid of her own wrenching emotions. "We need to take him directly to a hospital now. Lift his body very carefully while I support his head..."

At least Chris was thinking straight enough to do precisely as Stacy instructed. Together they carried Robbie back down the path to Chris's car while the other two boys ran ahead of them to open doors. Chris deposited the child gently on the back seat and Stacy sank down on the carpeted floorboard beside Robbie. Taylor and Ted rode in the front seat as Chris burned rubber in his desperate dash to town. Then, and only then, could Stacy let down her guard enough to touch Robbie's hair that felt so like Chris's and allow herself to cry.

Chapter Fourteen

Robbie was conscious, and the trauma doctors at the hospital thought he would be okay. They didn't suspect brain damage, although they thought he'd probably sustained a mild concussion. It was all those qualifying words that drove Chris crazy with fear, words like *thought*, *suspect*, *brain damage* and *concussion*.

Oh, yes—CAT scan, too. Robbie was having a CAT scan performed right now.

Wild with anxiety, Chris paced the hospital waiting room like a caged animal. If Stacy hadn't been with him, he didn't think he could have borne all of this. Even with her here, he was still having a hell of a time.

If anything happened to Robbie—

"It won't, Chris. He's going to be all right," Stacy said urgently, squeezing Chris's hand with her own small warm one, and that was the only way Chris knew he'd actually spoken his anguish out loud.

Stacy had kept Taylor and Ted corralled in an anteroom until Betty Thackery could come to fetch them. "Mom, I just left the little kids for a minute, to go to the bath-room,'' Taylor had explained.

"We knew we weren't supposed to dive," Ted had added. "Mr. Lorio said so, but Robbie climbed up in the tree and was showing off."

Although the other two boys were scared and upset, too, Chris was glad they were gone now. He just didn't have the energy to face their questions or address their fears. Stacy had done that, promising to phone regularly and keep them posted on developments.

She had also managed to get rid of the well-meaning but definitely intrusive Ellen Glover. Apparently Mrs. Glover did regular volunteer work here at the Langlois hospital. Dressed in her pink pinafore she had hurried straight down to Emergency as soon as she'd heard the news.

"Oh, my dears!" she'd exclaimed in anguish. "Oh, poor little Robbie! Is there *anything* I can do, anything at all?"

Chris had turned to look blankly at this woman who had always seemed a complete stranger to him and saw that Mrs. Glover was literally on the verge of tears. But all he could do was shake his head and turn back to stare at the swinging doors through which Robbie's doctor would eventually reappear.

Fortunately Stacy had been there to thank Mrs. Glover, promising to keep her informed as well.

Stacy... She was the lifeline that Chris clung to as the agonizing minutes passed and his fertile imagination spun terrifying fantasies. She went out for coffee and pressed it into his hands. She turned off the television set, which was broadcasting some damned game show with a laughing, braying idiot of a host. Finally she made Chris sit down and let her rub his back and shoulders to try and ease their tense stiffness.

"I'm getting a little worn out with water accidents," Chris said through clenched teeth while Stacy kneaded his knot ted muscles. "If we ever get through this one I may move us to your nice, dry desert. I'll buy a truck stop and fix tires for a living. You can run the bar and grill."

"Whatever you want," she said with perfect equanimity. "Just tell me what to do for you, Chris."

He turned to see the genuine appeal in her lovely green eyes and found himself clutching her hand once again.

"Just stay with me, Stacy," he whispered. "Don't leave me!"

"I won't, Chris," she promised.

"I need you, Stace."

Offhand he couldn't remember ever saying that to anyone in his life before, yet how quickly and easily the words came to him now. *I need you.*

Then a migraine headache started tormenting his skull as they continued to wait.

Probably it was inevitable, Chris thought glumly, considering the stress of the last several hours and all the anxiety he felt now. Anyway, what did a damned headache matter when his son might be dying? Chris just wished the migraine hadn't arrived full-blown in its intensity. Already fuzzy auras were appearing over the heads of people and the large wall clock was so blurred he couldn't read the time.

Then the swinging doors opened at last and Robbie's doctor stood there grinning. "I've got a little guy who's asking for his daddy!"

Chris was through the swinging doors before he remembered Stacy. "Go ahead," she urged him, her face wreathed in smiles when he turned back. "I'll start letting everyone know that Robbie's going to be all right."

Robbie said that his head hurt, a complaint with which Chris was in complete sympathy. And Robbie didn't like the hospital; he wanted to go home. And why wouldn't they let him have something to eat?

"I'm sorry, sport, but you're going to have to stay here a couple of days," Chris explained, gently stroking Robbie's foot, which protruded from between two starched white sheets.

"Two days?" said Robbie in horror.

"Well, all your tests look good, but the doc still wants to observe you to be sure your head is okay." Although Chris

spoke casually his feelings were far from nonchalant. The
relief and gratitude he felt at seeing his son thinking and
speaking normally was equalled only by the relief he'd felt
when he'd learned that Stacy had no intention of leaving
him. It had been quite a day for Chris Lorio, and he just
wished his own head wasn't aching quite so badly so he
could be more appreciative.

"Is there anything else you want, Robbie?" he asked his
son. "Is there anyone you want to see?"

"Is Stacy here, Daddy?"

Robbie's request didn't surprise Chris at all. Apparently
his son shared his fatal weakness for one special woman.
"She sure is! She's the one who pulled you out, you know.
My gosh, if it wasn't for Stacy we might still be looking for
you!"

"But I'd be dead by now," Robbie said so matter-of-
factly that Chris felt his heart chill.

He had to clear his throat to speak. "Yeah, you would be.
Thank God it didn't happen! I'll go get Stacy."

Chris went back out into the waiting room and found
that, in his absence, Stacy had asked Miriam to bring over
clean, dry clothes for both of them. "Change into something comfortable, Chris, while I go visit with Robbie," she
suggested. "You'll feel better."

He wondered how she could tell how really unwell he felt.
"All right," he agreed, exhaustion sweeping over him in
counterbalance to the adrenaline surges he'd had during the
past several hours. "Listen, Stace, keep Robbie entertained
for an extra five minutes. I need to make some phone calls."
He sighed and rubbed at his aching head, trying to remember where he was supposed to be tomorrow and just which
clients in his appointment book absolutely couldn't wait.

"Oh." Stacy glanced down at a piece of paper that she
held. "I called Knox Kinard and told him what had happened, and of course, he's volunteered his help. Then I
tracked down that secretary who's been working for you
temporarily and told her to phone Knox and go over everything on your desk and appointment book with him. I told
her you'd probably be out of your office tomorrow and

maybe the next day, too.'' She looked up at Chris in concern. ''I hope that was all right.''

Chris simply stared at her. ''What in the world made you think to do all that?''

''I was just trying to help you,'' Stacy said defensively. ''If it isn't all right—''

''It's perfect,'' he cut in, gathering up his clean clothes. ''Thank you very much.''

''You also need to eat something, Chris. I bought a couple of sandwiches and some milk for you in the hospital cafeteria,'' Stacy continued, handing him a small brown sack.

''Well, you seem to be thinking of everything,'' he mused with a half smile. That was all his pounding head could manage.

''Oh, I figured if I was going to be your partner and run the bar and grill I'd better get started.'' Stacy smiled back at him, then passed through the swinging doors.

A partner. While he changed clothes in the men's room, Chris reflected that he'd never had a partner in any of his close relationships before. Always they had been unequal ones. As a result, every single detail had always been his and his alone to handle. Even as a child he'd not only had to take care of himself but of Bonnie as well. Then there had been Lynn, whose physical frailties had always limited and restricted their relationship. Then Robbie...

What on earth would it be like to have a partner to share the burdens and divide the chores and make plans together? he wondered as he ate the sandwiches and drank the milk Stacy had thoughtfully provided. Certainly having someone to watch over him was proving a novel experience. Already he felt himself starting to worry less.

It was ten o'clock, Robbie's usual summer bedtime, but the child couldn't seem to settle down. He was still in a big, high hospital bed, rather than being in the children's wing, but the neurologist had wanted Robbie in this area for close monitoring overnight by nurses experienced in head injuries.

Now the little boy whimpered and tossed in the unfamiliar bed. He complained that his head hurt and he was hungry. Chris tried to console him but soon Robbie was crying, even as he tried manfully to conceal his tears.

"Are you sure he's all right?" Chris asked worriedly of the women seated at the nurses' station. Both of them nodded.

"What's the trouble?" Stacy said, coming up from behind Chris and laying her hand on his arm.

"Robbie," Chris said, turning to her with a frown. "I can't seem to get him settled down for the night."

"Sick children always feel worse at night," Stacy agreed. "Want me to try? I have a few tricks I used to use on Taylor."

"Please!" Chris said with relief.

She went back to Robbie's room and did the very things that Chris had been doing: smoothed the sheets that Robbie kept kicking at restlessly and turned the lights back down. She gave him a lump of ice to hold in his dry mouth and placed a cool damp cloth on his aching head.

From the doorway Chris watched them.

"Stacy, I sure wish I had my mom right now!" Robbie suddenly blurted, and then his body began to shake with sobs.

It was always when Robbie said something like that that Chris felt his most helpless. But Stacy didn't even hesitate. She simply kicked off her shoes, crawled right up on the hospital bed and curled her own body around Robbie's small back. She slipped an arm around him and hugged the child close. Even as Chris watched, Robbie's sobs slowly quieted. A few minutes later his eyes closed and his body began to relax at last.

It was the sort of thing only a woman would have thought to do, Chris reflected. Certainly providing simple body warmth and snuggling close to the child had not occurred to him. Not only would Chris have felt ridiculous crawling into bed with Robbie, but he was also much too large to do so.

Stacy understands Robbie even better than I do, Chris thought without a trace of resentment.

Around midnight, when it was obvious that Robbie was safely and deeply asleep, Chris sent Stacy home. He intended to stay all night, sleeping on a cot at the foot of his son's bed.

It wasn't until Chris had stretched out there that he realized his migraine had not only waned considerably during the past couple of hours, but to his astonishment, it was completely gone. Why, he'd never had a migraine simply disappear before.

But then he'd never had Stacy before, either.

Robbie didn't wake until morning. When he did, he was alert, his headache was gone and he was ravenously hungry, demanding something to eat *right now*.

Robbie was enjoying a hearty breakfast tray when Taylor, Ted and Preston came into his room. Then, with Robbie blessed by such an attentive audience to listen to his ordeal, Chris at last dared to go home to shower and shave, to see Stacy.

On the way out of the hospital he met Ellen Glover. She came over to him immediately, her eyes so filmed with worry that Chris took pity on her. He told her to drop by and visit Robbie, too, and he lied through his teeth when he added that he was sure Robbie would be pleased to see her.

Stacy kept waking up by degrees. She'd been so exhausted when she'd finally crawled into bed the previous night that although the sun had awakened her at eight, she had merely gotten up long enough to draw the blinds, then tumbled headlong into sleep again.

At nine she woke and went into the bathroom where she tossed water on her face and brushed her teeth and hair. But then the bed's irresistible allure called her back, and she crawled in for one last ten-minute nap.

Now it was ten, according to her bedside clock, and the low male voice she heard in the hall had the power to rouse her as nothing else had. Stacy sat up in bed, pushing pillows behind her back, but when the door opened it was Miriam who came in carrying a breakfast tray.

"Mr. Lorio thought you might be awake by now." She smiled, setting the tray across Stacy's lap.

"Where is he?" Stacy asked, her senses quickening at the thought of seeing Chris again.

"Gone to shave and dress. He says Master Robbie is doing just fine!" Miriam beamed.

That was certainly good news, Stacy thought, unfolding the napkin then reaching for the fragrant carafe of coffee.

She ate quickly. Finished, Stacy pushed the tray aside and dashed back into the bathroom to brush her teeth once again. When Chris's knock came on her door just a minute later Stacy was still padding around barefoot and wearing her nightgown. It was easier to pop back in bed and draw the sheet up over her than to hunt for a robe and slippers.

"Come in," she called.

He entered, wearing a pair of black shorts and a sleeveless shirt that hung mostly unbuttoned over his broad chest. If he'd bothered to comb the black hair on his head it had been only with his fingers. He walked over to Stacy's bed and reached down to remove the breakfast tray, and that allowed her a moment to compose her thoughts. Then he returned to sit on the edge of her bed. He smelled of soap and toothpaste, and he looked casual, rumpled and totally wonderful to Stacy's loving eyes.

"You seem to be having a lazy morning," he teased her gently.

"I am. I just couldn't seem to wake up. But tell me about Robbie?" Stacy said, looking up at Chris anxiously.

"He slept like a log all night, so *I* did, too. He woke up starving," Chris said lightly. "When I left he had a huge breakfast tray and a whole room full of company to keep him occupied."

"Oh, Chris, I'm so glad!" Stacy cried in relief.

"Me, too." He leaned over toward her, brushing her cheek with his knuckles, and when he spoke next his voice was soft. "Thank you for my son, Stacy. Thank you for *both* of my sons. I wouldn't have either one of them today if it hadn't been for you."

"Oh, Chris!" Tears suddenly threatened Stacy and she looked down, swallowing hard.

"So tell me, just what do I have in you?" One large brown hand gently swept back the sheet that covered Stacy's breasts. Slowly Chris bent down and kissed her cheek very, very gently. At almost the same moment his warm hand cupped her breast. The touch was so light as to be almost airy, yet it thrilled her, too, after the long empty days when they'd been apart.

"Tell me," Chris urged, his voice softer than Stacy had ever heard it.

"What do you mean?" Stacy asked over the heavy thudding of her heart.

His dark eyes riveted hers even as his hand moved to gently peel back the lacy fabric that covered her breast. It was more than a seductive gesture; he appeared irresistibly drawn to simply touch her skin. "Just who is this beautiful lady I married?" Chris asked caressingly yet curiously, too. "Both of my sons adore you and they seem like pretty smart boys. You've always seemed like a gift-wrapped package to me—I guess I saw the glitter and never bothered to open the gift. But right now, although I certainly do appreciate this lovely exterior—" Chris punctuated his words by letting his lips follow his hand to Stacy's breast.

"—Now," he breathed against her flesh, "I want to know about everything else. I want to know the substance and the heart of you. I wonder if one lifetime will be long enough, Stace, for all the time I want to spend with you and all the things I want to learn."

"Chris!" Stacy felt her hands being drawn equally irresistibly. She clutched his head and shivered when his lips moved slowly across her chest then roamed along one shoulder, before kissing an increasingly torrid path back up to her throat. The love and tenderness she felt for Chris got all mixed up with desire and need and suddenly Stacy couldn't get close enough to him.

As she felt his hands tighten on her flesh and heard the sound of his breathing deepen, Stacy pressed as close to

Chris as she could. Suddenly she was saying words she hadn't intended, indeed almost crying them.

"Love me, Chris! Oh please, just *love* me!"

It was more than a plea to be made one with him physically. The cry was her heart's own longing to be as special and unique to him as he was to her—to be his beloved, his treasured mate—and that drove her to say again, "*Love* me!"

She knew he had heard both her spoken and unspoken plea when Chris said in his very softest voice, "I always did. Oh, Stace, I *always* did!"

Her teal nightgown lay discarded on one side of the bed and Chris's black shorts lay atop it. Stacy could see both temporarily unnecessary garments as she lay in bed with him.

His body still half covered hers; his dark head rested on her breast. As she gently fingered the soft black strands she murmured regretfully, "We need to get up now."

"No," said Chris emphatically, tightening his grip on her.

"Yes, we do," she argued gently. "We need to go see about Robbie."

"Robbie is doing just fine. If he wanted us, there's a phone by his bed he can use to call. Anyway, Preston will stay in his room till we get back."

"I can't believe you're saying such things," Stacy exclaimed in frank surprise. "You've always been such a dutiful father. Why, yesterday you were—"

"Yesterday was Robbie's. This morning belongs to my wife."

"Thank you," said the startled Stacy.

"We'll go back to the hospital early this afternoon," Chris concluded, and Stacy smiled, knowing he could never be negligent or even overly complacent.

"That sounds good," she agreed.

Chris pressed more kisses on the twin mounds that pillowed his head, then he rolled over onto his back while his hand caressed Stacy lazily. "Robbie may be angry with me," he admitted. "I told Ellen Glover she could go see him, too

And, of course, Robbie doesn't like being drooled on by her.''

"Chris, what's with her, anyway?" Stacy asked, leaning up on her elbow to peer down into his face with its fascinating lines and planes.

She sensed Chris's sudden tenseness. "What do you mean?"

"Well, Mrs. Glover's reaction to Robbie's injury seemed a little . . . extreme. Didn't it to you?" Stacy probed.

He gave her hand a squeeze. "Maybe," he admitted. Then Stacy suddenly sensed his admission, even before he generously shared it. "Ellen Glover is overly attached to Robbie because he's her one and only grandchild."

"You mean she's— Startled as Stacy was, she was still surprised that the admission had come from Chris so easily.

"She's my biological mother, yes," Chris confided. "I found out on my fourteenth birthday. I knew someone always left gifts for me on birthdays and at Christmas. So I got up very early that morning and watched and waited. I saw her—I saw her face, the way she looked."

After a moment he shrugged. "I don't feel any connection to the woman, Stacy. I never did. And I certainly don't care to share any part of my life with her now," he said thoughtfully. "I don't think I'm being vindictive, but she didn't share any part of her life with me when I was a child."

"Did you ever talk to her?" Stacy said, curiosity at knowing the answer to the town's old riddle consuming her. "Did you ask her—"

"No. But she knows that I know. I guess she could read it in my face. Actually, we've never had any but the most casual and cursory of conversations."

"My grandmother thought it was Mrs. Glover's younger sister—"

"Kathryn Ann and Knox?" Chris asked with a smile. "Yes, those two took the rap for years. I bless Knox for not minding. He's got quite a sardonic sense of humor, you know. I guess anybody married to Lottie would have to. Every now and then he even calls me 'son' when he knows it's liable to rattle the cage of some pious hypocrite. No, Knox may have missed the chance of his life with pretty Kathryn Ann, but they weren't my parents. She wasn't the one who had an illegitimate baby on that fabricated Holy Land tour."

"How did you find all this out, Chris?" Stacy asked, surprised by the extent of his knowledge. "From Knox?"

"No, Knox always knew—but the person who confirmed it was my father," Chris replied matter-of-factly. He turned back to look at Stacy, studying her face as intently as she was studying his. "He was Hamilton Bainbridge, Stacy."

"The congressman?" she said, more surprised now than she'd ever been. She had only seen pictures of the man; possibly she'd watched him on TV a time or two. If memory served, he was dark but didn't look anything like Chris. And he hadn't been particularly tall, either, but then Ellen Glover's side of the family could have provided Chris's height.

"Yes, the congressman. You see, Bonnie always told me that the guy who'd dropped me off had a famous-sounding voice, though she couldn't explain what she'd meant by that. Finally, I began to hone in on him. Hamilton came back here every couple of years to run for reelection. Usually he wasn't even opposed, but he still had to go through the motions. Often he visited here at this house with Lynn's parents and, naturally, he and Ellen Glover met somewhere along the way."

"Did they fall in love?" Stacy asked.

Chris pulled her closer, settling her head on his shoulder. "I think they genuinely cared about each other," he said quietly. "But apparently neither of them ever considered divorcing their mates and marrying each other. Anyway, it would have been a royal mess. Hamilton had a wife and three legitimate kids in Washington."

"Then why—"

"Oh, I think it was as much mutual frustration as attraction," Chris went on after a minute. "Ellen was about thirty and finding the life of a parson's wife to be stifling. The congressman was forty-five and knew by then he'd never be president or even particularly famous."

"How did you find out that he was your father?" Stacy asked.

"He kept coming around the school yard, being a little too chummy toward me any time he visited Langlois. Then when I turned seventeen he offered to help me out with a 'scholarship' toward college and law school."

"So he admitted it?" Stacy asked.

"No, not really." Chris turned to look deeply into her eyes again. "Hamilton never really talked about it until much later. Knox phoned me out of the blue late one summer night. He said that Hamilton had recently been diagnosed with inoperable cancer. Since American doctors gave him no hope, he wanted to consult various European specialists. And wanted me to go with him. I knew it was probably my only chance to ever know my father. That's why I left you so suddenly that summer, Stace. Wild horses couldn't have dragged me off otherwise."

"Oh, Chris!" she exclaimed and then bent to cover his lips again with her own. At last she understood, and the old wound was finally healed.

"You really liked your father, didn't you?" she surmised.

Chris linked his hands behind his head and stared thoughtfully into the distance. "Yeah...I did. He had a lot more to lose, in my opinion, than Ellen Glover did if the truth came out. Yet he risked it all—a national reputation, important congressional committees, even a scandalous divorce—every time he came to see me." The warmth in Chris's voice chilled. "Mrs. Glover was here every day of my life and she risked damned little."

"It's hard to truly judge another person," Stacy said in a conciliatory tone. "I think she undoubtedly cares." Suddenly Stacy found herself smiling.

"What is it?" Chris asked, outlining Stacy's smile with a gentle finger.

"Oh, I should have guessed years ago that she was your mother, Chris."

"How could you have known?" he said, puzzled.

"Because when she offered to introduce us at that dance she said 'Chris Lorio is a very nice young man.' But you weren't—I'd been hearing all about your dreadful reputation, and you were glaring at all of us."

"Not at you," he said, tugging on a strand of Stacy's long auburn hair in tender reprimand. "I still remember staring at you. Hell, I couldn't look away!"

"Same here," she whispered, and suddenly they were tight in each other's arms and kissing hungrily.

Gradually Stacy slipped down in Chris's arms, dropping lighter kisses on his beautifully mobile mouth. "It's going to be wonderful for the four of us now," she added, dreaming aloud. "You and me and our boys—"

"Actually," he interrupted with a little smile, "I hope I can interest you in five of us."

"What?" Stacy gasped.

"I'd really like a daughter," Chris said, that same smile continuing to play around his lips. "Wouldn't you like one, too?"

"No! I mean I'd like the child, but I hated being pregnant. I was sick the whole time," Stacy blurted.

"You were unhappy," Chris said softly, letting his fingers glide tantalizingly over the softness of Stacy's stomach. "This time I'd be with you. And that was thirteen years ago—I'm sure doctors have better methods for dealing with morning sickness now."

"Oh, no you don't!" Stacy said, struggling to free herself from his embrace. "You're not talking me into having a baby, Chris Lorio!"

"Maybe not right away," he coaxed. "Not for a year or two. But you're such a good mother and we'd all enjoy a pretty little girl."

"Pretty, my eye," Stacy sniffed. "She'd probably be a hot-blooded little vixen—"

"No, she'll be sweet—and she'll grow up to be wonderful, and someday a man will adore her just the way I do you." Chris pressed against Stacy, his body unmistakably aroused again, and her heart gave an eager skip of antici- pation. Oh, how she loved making love with him!

Still, she pretended to grumble even as she sank deeper into the haven of his arms. "I am *not* agreeing to have a baby, Chris Lorio!" she teased.

"Okay," he said, swinging his body up and over hers. Then he looked deeply into Stacy's eyes, letting the antici- pation build between them until she reached for him hun- grily. She pressed her face into his chest and let her hands splay over his body until Chris gave a triumphant laugh.

He knows I'm going to wind up giving him that baby, Stacy thought with a whimsical smile, *just because I can't resist giving him anything he wants!* But as she looked up into the handsome face above her, its once hard lines soft- ened by his obvious love and tenderness for her, the accu- sation she voiced held a note of amusement, too.

"You always want it *all*, Chris Lorio."

"I sure do," he agreed. Then he bent to kiss her and claim her so powerfully that Stacy gasped with delight. "And I've always gotten it, too!"

* * * * *

Silhouette Special Edition

WHITE LIES*
by
Linda Howard

Bestselling author Linda Howard is back with a story that is exciting, enticing and—most of all—compellingly romantic.

Heroine Jay Granger's life was turned upside down when she was called to her ex-husband's side. Now, injured and unconscious, he needed her more than he ever had during their brief marriage. Finally he awoke, and Jay found him stronger and more fascinating than before. Was she asking too much, or could they have a chance to recapture the past and learn the value of love the second time around?

Find out the answer next month, only in SILHOUETTE SPECIAL EDITION.

*Previously advertised as MIRRORS.

COMING IN MAY

SSE452

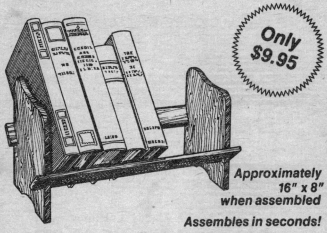

Silhouette Special Edition

NORA ROBERTS'S 50TH SILHOUETTE NOVEL

In May, SILHOUETTE SPECIAL EDITION celebrates Nora Roberts's "golden anniversary"— her 50th Silhouette novel!

The Last Honest Woman launches a three-book "family portrait" of entrancing triplet sisters. You'll fall in love with all THE O'HURLEYS!

The Last Honest Woman—May
Hardworking mother Abigail O'Hurley Rockwell finally meets a man she can trust...but she's forced to deceive him to protect her sons.

Dance to the Piper—July
Broadway hoofer Maddy O'Hurley easily lands a plum role, but it takes some fancy footwork to win the man of her dreams.

Skin Deep—September
Hollywood goddess Chantel O'Hurley remains deliberately icy...until she melts in the arms of the man she'd love to hate.

Look for THE O'HURLEYS! And join the excitement of Silhouette Special Edition!